PHANTOM ISLAND

2

WINDFALL

KRISSI DALLAS

Cover design by Kristen Verser
Interior design by April Marciszewski

Published in the United States of America

ISBN: 978-0-99973-111-6
Fiction / Fantasy / Contemporary
11.09.21

For Melody
You've been my real-life Morgan since middle school.
Nobody else could have lasted that long.

THE WHITE ISLAND

THE PILGRIM PROPHECY

"Excuse me, Whitnee! Whitnee?" Somebody was shaking me, and I groaned. It was certainly not morning yet. Between strange dreams and Amelia kicking me all night, I had not gotten nearly enough sleep. "I am terribly sorry to wake you, but you and your friends must get up."

My eyes slowly opened, and I squinted in the sunlight that filtered through the room. Hannah was standing over me with a flustered look on her face.

"What is it, Hannah? Did something happen? What's wrong?" I sat up, wide awake at the concern on the Aerodorian housegirl's face.

"Nothing is wrong." She flapped her hands nervously as she moved about the room. "There has just been an important change in plans. Ezekiel sent word that you and your friends are to get dressed for the day as soon as possible. He will send more instructions soon. Shall I create a bath for you?"

"Um, yeah, I guess." I watched her mannerisms curiously as she disappeared into the bathing room. Then I turned to Amelia, who was snuggled deep under the covers, not moving. "Amelia, you need to wake up!"

She groaned almost exactly as I had. I shook her until she sat up, looking confused about where she was.

"Morning, sunshine." I smiled. Her face was red and puffy from her emotional breakdown in the middle of the night.

"Are we still on a magical Island?" she yawned.

"Yep. And we're going to see the Wizard who will tell us how to get back home, to Camp Fusion."

Amelia rubbed her eyes, appearing more childlike and innocent than normal. "Did you really shoot tornadoes out of your hand? Or did I just dream that?"

"Definitely not a dream." I decided not to tell her about setting trees on Fire and then re-growing them—a few more troublesome talents I had discovered late last night.

Amelia grinned knowingly at me. "Which means Gabriel, the hottie tottie with a naughty body, probably wasn't a dream, either."

I smacked her with a pillow. "You're so bad!" I laughed.

Hannah came bustling back in. "Rachael has a bath ready for Amelia. Ezekiel had a fresh set of clothes delivered early this morning. I must insist that we hurry."

Amelia slowly got out of bed and stumbled her way back to her room. I got up also, preparing to get into my bath. I checked the adjoining door first to make sure it was closed.

"Is Gabriel awake yet, Hannah?" I questioned.

"Oh, yes. He is already gone," she said, busily straightening the room.

"Gone? Where did he go?"

"He was called out on important business this morning. I am sure he will return soon." She was acting very funny, like she knew something she was not supposed to tell me. And for some reason, the idea that Gabriel had gone somewhere without me made me nervous.

"Hannah, will you please tell me what is happening? I don't want to be unprepared."

She looked flustered at my question. "I am not allowed to speak of anything, and I really do not even know anything..." She would not meet my eyes.

I grabbed her arm and made her stop fidgeting. "Hannah, please tell me what you know."

She paused and looked like she had been cornered. "Oh, Whitnee...I should not say, but...the Guardian arrived here this morning!" She wrung her hands.

"Well, Hannah, this is good news! That means the Guardian can get us home faster, right?" I didn't really understand why the Guardian's presence would have her in such an upheaval.

"Yes, I suppose." She nodded. "I just feel very anxious around the people from the Palladium." And I briefly remembered how nervous she acted around Gabriel too. She turned back to making the bed, adding, "We had no warning that they were coming. And if I understand correctly, neither the Guardian nor Ezekiel is very happy about this visit. Now, please do not ask me any more questions. I was just instructed to get everyone up and ready to go. I am sure the Guardian will be meeting with you very soon. I must go check on the others."

That's when her words sank in, and I realized I would actually be meeting this mysterious Guardian. I would finally receive answers to all my questions. And yet I felt a tiny flutter of apprehension that I did not quite understand. It was very similar to the feeling I had yesterday before meeting Ezekiel— the feeling that everything I once knew to be true in the world was about to change.

But Ezekiel had not been at all what I was expecting. As the Wind tribe's leader, he had welcomed me into his village and made me feel a part of his family. Perhaps the Guardian would be the same way. Maybe he was not nearly as intimidating as people made him out to be. Even Gabriel had turned out to be much more *warm* than he let on in the beginning. Gabriel was loyal to the Guardian. And I trusted Gabriel, so there was no reason to be nervous now about meeting this ruler...no reason at all.

"Okay, you two are about to drive me nuts with the pacing! Take a break!" Morgan snapped at Caleb and me. We had been waiting in the Conclave foyer for what seemed like an hour while some great debate was going on. There was no way to hear what was being said, and we hadn't even seen anyone yet. Not Gabriel, not Ezekiel or Sarah, not the Guardian.

"This is so frustrating," I muttered. "What is taking so long? Don't we deserve to be in there hearing what's being said *about us?*"

"Exactly," Caleb agreed. "Are you sure that the Guardian is actually here, though?"

"That's what Hannah seemed to think." I shrugged.

"Man, I wish we could've gone back to the music center," Kevin remarked, his chin resting in his hands as he sat in one of the foyer chairs.

"I'm too tired to do anything," Amelia told Kevin.

"Not me. I slept great!" he said.

"Wish I could say the same," Caleb remarked, shooting Kevin a look. "Kevin's feet were in my face the whole night."

"It was your idea to sleep head to toe in separate blankets," Kevin defended himself.

"Yeah, I didn't want you cuddling up to me," Caleb teased him, but that didn't seem to bother Kevin.

"Well, my feet got cold, and your face was warm ..."

"What is this? Kevin slept in your room?" Morgan clarified.

Caleb rolled his eyes as he answered, "Mm-hmm. Apparently his room was too loud with the storm or it smelled funny or—"

"I got the worst room in the guesthouse!" Kevin stated.

"There's no such thing as a bad room in that guesthouse," Caleb corrected him. And he gave Morgan and me a look that told us *somebody* was scared to sleep alone last night. But Caleb wasn't about to rat Kevin out. Boys didn't do that to each other.

"It's okay, Kevin. Amelia slept in my room too," I said to make him feel better.

"Really? Was I the only one who had a room to myself last night?" Morgan asked.

"Guess so. And it's a good thing, because you talk way too much in your sleep, Morgie," I reminded her. I wandered back over to the doorway leading into the circular meeting room. "I wish I knew what was happening in there."

"The constant pacing really is making me more nervous, Whit," Morgan said again.

"I'm sorry. I just can't sit still. I'm ready to meet this Guardian person and find out the plan to get us back home."

"Do you not like having powers here?" Amelia asked me quietly.

"It's not that … I mean, it's weird. In fact, I haven't even told y'all everything that happened last night—" I started to tell them about using all the life forces when I remembered Levi and Tamir's quiet presence in the foyer. "I'll tell you later, though."

"Have you used *another* life force?" Caleb whispered, and I nodded slightly.

I loudly changed the subject, "Don't y'all just love the clothes here? How do they know my exact size? It's like these outfits were made specifically for me." I glanced down at the Capri pants and tunic with loose sleeves. I felt light as air in the soft material. Today I had been given a pale pink outfit and decided that it made my usually rosy cheeks appear calmer.

Morgan started to reply, but we were startled into silence when the big doors opened and Gabriel entered the foyer. I immediately approached him, surveying his expression and posture for some sign of what was to come.

"Gabriel, where have you been? You just left—"

"The Guardian arrived in the village early this morning," he interrupted, barely even looking at me. So that was how it was going to be, I noted with annoyance. He was playing the part of formal, authoritative Gabriel now.

"Did you know he was coming?" I asked, prepared to be mad at him if he had kept that piece of information from me. Again, still hardly noticing me, he spoke to the whole group.

"Your presence at this Council meeting is now requested. Because you are Travelers and unfamiliar with our customs, allow me to advise you on a few topics. First, you are to show respect to the Guardian and the four Tetrarch Council members at all times, as they are the ones who govern and lead the Dorian people. Second, you would be wise to answer every question honestly and speak only when you are spoken to—"

"You know what? I have already answered all of your questions, *Gabriel*," I spat, frustrated by the fact that he wouldn't look at me. "I am here because your people owe *us* some answers now."

"Oh, don't worry, we will get our answers, Whit," Caleb said behind me.

"Let's calm down," Morgan jumped in. "If this Guardian is the only person who can help us, we don't want to go marching in with a bunch of demands, right?"

"You are wise to note that, Morgan," Gabriel said. "The last thing I would caution you about is to not make enemies in this room." He finally met my angry eyes, as if warning me specifically.

"I'm not interested in making enemies, Gabriel. Surely you know that. I just…I expect that certain things you promised will be explained today, right?" I searched his face, silently pleading for some sign of softness toward me.

He gave a stiff nod, and then with a cautious flick of a glance toward Levi and Tamir, he said to us, "It would be wise to remember what we have previously discussed *before*. We would not want to make Whitnee appear as anything *more* or less than she actually is…" I furrowed my eyebrows at his comment. Was he talking about the ability to use more than one life force? He was staring at me intensely. "Do you each understand my meaning?"

Slowly, we nodded as we caught on. He didn't think we should tell the Council about my extra abilities. *How interesting...*

Morgan whispered to Kevin and Amelia, explaining Gabriel's meaning.

"We understand. Let's go," I told him, taking a deep breath. With a final glance at me, he opened both doors and led us into the circular room. This time the room did not hold Ezekiel's advisors. There were only five people waiting for us—well, sort of five people. The first thing I noticed was two holographic images of people sitting in holographic chairs. There were two large objects resembling bigger versions of zephyras that projected the moving images. Ezekiel sat to the right of the big desk. He had a solemn set to his face today, unlike the joyful man I had met yesterday. To the left of the large desk stood another man; he was quite powerful in stature with thick, wiry muscles and a completely bald head. His lack of hair made him appear sharp and dangerous. He appraised me with such narrowed, intimidating eyes that I could not make out his eye color. Was this the Guardian?

And then standing majestically in the center of the group was a very beautiful woman whose age was hard to guess at first glance. She was wearing a gorgeous, silver-colored dress with tiny, sparkly pieces stitched in the fabric, reflecting the light that poured in softly from the clear dome above. I was struck by her quietly astounding presence. She was watching me carefully with glittering gray eyes, and her thick, shiny black hair fell around her shoulders in loose curls. One streak of silver ran through her hair, giving her a very exotic and artistic look. She seemed very... well preserved and strikingly attractive. Only the silver streak, the wrinkles at the corners of her eyes, and her slightly aging hands gave any sign of being older than her thirties.

We approached our chairs, and I instinctively felt like this graceful woman was the person I should greet first. So I bowed to her, and my friends followed suit. Then I ignored Gabriel's advice about waiting to be spoken to.

"Good morning, Ezekiel." I greeted him with a bow. He bowed back, and a genial smile broke out on his face.

"Good morning, Whitnee, Caleb, Morgan … and, of course, our little ones, Amelia and Kevin. I hope you all found some sleep in the middle of the storm last night."

We all nodded graciously.

"I apologize for the abrupt start to your day, but we had a slight change in our plans. Please allow me to introduce to you the Guardian of our Dorian Island, Abrianna." Ezekiel gestured formally to the woman standing in front of the desk. I know my mouth dropped open, as did the others.

"The Guardian is a *girl?*" Kevin blurted, and Amelia elbowed him with a shush. Ezekiel's face showed the hint of a smile. Even the Guardian herself allowed a gracious smile in Kevin's direction.

"You mean Gabriel did not tell you?" Her voice was silky smooth with a deep musical quality. I glanced at Gabriel, who did not show any sign of emotion in his face as he quietly took his place at the Guardian's right-hand side. I had grown accustomed to him by my side. It was suddenly very clear then that he was not one of us. The Guardian moved closer until she was standing directly in front of Kevin, examining him carefully. "You must be Kevin. Your eyes are very blue, and your hair is fair. How old are you?" I found her comments on his appearance interesting. Did these Dorians not understand that eye color is not an indication of anything special in our world?

"Twelve years old, sir. I mean, ma'am, or, uh, mistress?" he replied nervously.

"You seem to be a very energetic boy. Do you like to play games, Kevin?" she asked him. She sounded friendly enough, but her words lacked warmth.

"Yes, mistress," he gulped.

"Well, you remind me very much of our fun-loving Hydrodorians," she stated and then her eyes moved to Morgan.

"You, too, would probably have much in common with the Hydros. You are Morgan, yes?"

"Yes, mistress. I actually met a Hydrodorian last night, and he was very entertaining," Morgan told her amiably.

"Ah, really? Who was that?" the Guardian questioned her.

"A man named Thomas, a Water Purifier," Morgan replied.

"Yes, we know Thomas, right, Simeon?" the Guardian said, turning to one of the holographic images, the one on the far right next to Ezekiel.

"Thomas, of course!" Simeon answered in a jolly tone. His hair had surpassed Ezekiel's silver color and gone completely white. He had a long beard to match his white hair and sparkling blue eyes. Though he was just an image of the real man, I thought I saw something pure and true in his eyes. "He travels quite a bit between villages! How did you find him here?" the image named Simeon questioned Morgan.

"We went dancing last night…" she answered a bit shyly.

"At the Nightingale?" the Guardian interrupted.

"Yes, mistress," Morgan said.

"Well, Ezekiel, you wasted no time in entertaining our guests," she remarked in what should have sounded like a cordial tone, but almost came across as sharp. "And I assume they were well-*protected* in their endeavors?" She looked from Gabriel to Ezekiel.

"Well, of course, Abrianna!" Ezekiel replied in a falsely cheerful tone. "Levi and Tamir have been on constant guard duty, as well as your very own Gabriel, who has not left their side until you arrived."

"I am at least glad to hear that," she replied with an approving nod at Gabriel. She then moved to stand in front of Caleb. "You must be Caleb. Did you know your name means 'faithful and loyal'? And your eyes are green just like our faithful and *loyal* Geodorians." Caleb stared back at her, and I could tell from his unflinching manner that he was not as taken in by her beauty as the rest of us were. I couldn't stop staring at her in utter fascination, yet he seemed to match her coolly indifferent attitude.

"Yes, I am Caleb. And I am loyal to my friends only. Your Island is very beautiful, but I'm sure you understand how important it is for us to get back to our own home." The man appearing in the other holographic image laughed heartily at Caleb's words, causing all of us to turn and look at him expectantly. He was a large man, but not in the same muscled way that the silent man with dark eyes appeared. This man was just plain fat, and his very large smile caused his green eyes to disappear into half moons. His hair was cut shorter than the others and his beard was not long like Simeon's or Ezekiel's, more like mud caking the lower half of his face.

"I like this Caleb!" The man laughed his approval. "He must come visit the Geodora village before he leaves. I can tell he has natural ability already!"

"Yes, Joseph, he does sound very much like you. However, we will see about abilities very soon." The Guardian took control again of her inspection and just when I thought she would move toward me, she paused. Slowly, she approached Amelia, who stared back at her curiously. "Amelia, you are a very pretty girl. And I adore your eyes, rich with many different colors. I assume they change colors as you ... *feel* different emotions?"

Amelia raised her eyebrows and nodded. "When I'm angry, they look more golden than brown," she told her.

"Well, now you must not let yourself give in to those emotions too much." The Guardian spoke softly. "I can tell you are a very special girl and would probably like to experience more of the Island than you have so far. Am I right?" She spoke so smoothly, and something inside me felt a bit uneasy as I watched Amelia's curious eyes begin to gaze at this woman adoringly.

"Oh, yes! I'm ready to try anything!" Amelia gushed. The Guardian smiled and patted Amelia's dark head.

"There are many amazing things I could show you, if you are willing. I have a feeling, though, that you are a keeper of

Fire, of power. Like Gabriel." The Guardian spoke intensely as she gestured to Gabriel. I pulled my gaze away from the Guardian to watch Gabriel. He was still standing there stoically, but his eyebrows were turned down slightly. He did not return my gaze, and I could feel my annoyance rising.

"I would love to learn how to use Fire. But I don't have any special powers here on the Island," Amelia told her and I stiffened a bit at this. I hoped she would remember to be careful with what she said.

"You do not have powers *yet*." The Guardian held up her hand. "But you can be gifted by another. Perhaps we can arrange that later ..." she said, flicking a glance at the silent bald man. Amelia's eyes lit up with anticipation at the thought.

I couldn't help clearing my throat loudly. Nobody on this Island had any right to make that kind of decision for Amelia except one of us.

"I beg your pardon, mistress, but before we get to any of that, there are some questions that we have. Gabriel has refused to explain some things to us until we were in your presence," I told her, trying my best to show no fear even though I was greatly intimidated by her. Gabriel threw a disapproving glance at my interruption.

"Well, Gabriel was wise to wait. You will find he is very loyal to me and to the position of Guardian," she said as she left Amelia to stroll toward me. Her gray eyes appeared cautious as she finally gave me her full attention.

"Oh, believe me, I have discovered that to be very true. You should be very *proud* of him," I replied, glancing coldly at Gabriel.

The Guardian glided right up to me and gazed at my full appearance before responding. Something unreadable flickered in her eyes as she looked into my face, making me wonder what exactly she was thinking.

"Whitnee," she sighed and reached out to touch my hair. I did not flinch as she ran an elegant hand through my long, straight blonde locks, although I wanted to recoil with annoyance. "Your hair is so light and your eyes are gray—like mine. You really are an Aerodorian," she finished. Her intensity was getting to me. "You may call me Abrianna. I am also a Daughter of the Wind, and there is much you and I have to discuss."

I couldn't look away from her eyes, which seemed so much deeper and darker than my own, reminding me of the stormy ocean last night. She confused me. She seemed so in control, so cautiously impassive, but I could swear there was some other emotion lingering somewhere in the uncharted depths of her soul. In that moment, I truly could not decide if she was a force for good or evil. Before I could settle my thoughts, she spun sharply away and moved back to the desk, instructing us to sit. Once she was perched in the ornate seat, Gabriel moved to stand at the back, between her and the bald man.

"I know you have many questions, and Ezekiel has already informed me of how you arrived here. However, the details of what brought you here are not nearly as important as discovering *why* you are here." She lightly fingered the old book lying on the desk in front of her. "It is for this reason that the Tetrarch Council has been called here today. I would like to note that this is not standard procedure. Under normal circumstances, we would have met at the Palladium. However, *Ezekiel* took matters into his own hands by bringing you here instead of to me." She gave a harsh look at Ezekiel, who spoke in a clipped tone.

"Once again, Abrianna, I felt that they would be safe here, as we are much closer to the Southern Beach than the Palladium, especially given the harsh weather that was approaching. We had every intention of moving her once the—"

"—storm was over," she finished for him. "Yes, yes. I am sure you would have, but you can imagine how alarmed I was when I mysteriously lost contact with Gabriel. You had to know I would come the moment I could travel." She waved her hands as if to dismiss his reasoning. "Before we proceed, I shall introduce the Council members to our Travelers. Of course, you already know Ezekiel. And the man in the zephyra next to him is Simeon, Council member for the Hydrodora tribe." She gestured to the white-haired man with sparkling blue eyes. He bowed slightly to us.

"To my right is Eli, Council member for the Pyradora tribe. He traveled with me this morning." She gestured to the menacing man whose eyes must have been a very dark brown. He barely nodded in our direction, and I was struck by the contrast between him and Simeon.

"And then to Eli's right is Joseph, our Council member for the Geodora tribe," she continued. The fat man smiled at us in greeting. "Thank you again, gentlemen, for being here on such short notice. Now, as I understand, Whitnee is the only one who has been able to draw from a life force since she arrived?" We all nodded. Abrianna stared at me intensely again.

"Which life force have you used, Whitnee?"

My eyes flickered ever so briefly to Gabriel, who was actually watching me very closely now.

"Wind," I answered her.

"How about the others? Earth? Water? Fire?" I was holding my breath because I didn't want to lie. But Gabriel had been adamant that I remain silent about this, and I remembered what he said about not knowing who could be trusted. Maybe even someone in this very room could be the powerful one protecting the rebel Islanders.

So I replied, "Wind is the only life force that has come naturally to me." That was mostly true—I could access the Wind and use it more easily than I could the others.

"Hmm." Abrianna didn't look too convinced. "Is this true, Gabriel?" She turned to her right.

"Yes," he said without hesitation, and he refused to look directly at me.

"Well, that is interesting. I would have expected..." She paused, and I took that moment to jump in with my own question.

"Speaking of expectations, *Abrianna* ... I had the impression that you were expecting me to arrive here. How would you have known that?" Gabriel's face broke into a haughty frown. Eli shifted slightly in his chair, but the others looked expectantly at Abrianna, who showed no emotion.

Ezekiel spoke. "I am quite curious about that myself, Abrianna."

"Well, it was only a matter of time before the Pilgrim would come. The wall that separates us from the Mainland has been growing thin recently. That is why I sent Gabriel to be on the lookout. And now that we have seen her, is there any doubt that she belongs here? She is the right age and associates herself as an Aero," she explained. None of this made any sense to me.

"The Pilgrim? What wall? What do you know about me?" I asked impatiently.

"Perhaps we should start from the beginning, Abrianna?" Simeon asked. "It is obvious she came with no prior knowledge of the Island." Ezekiel and Joseph nodded in agreement. Eli just continued to watch silently.

"Very well. This book contains the history of the Dorian Island." She placed a hand on the open book. "Recorded here are laws of the Island, mysteries of the life forces, and prophecies of old ... some of which have yet to come true. Our knowledge of the Mainland Beyond is very sparse, and we have gleaned what information we can from those few who have traveled here before you. We know enough to believe that the Dorian Island is in the same world as the Mainland, because we have compared our sun, moon, stars, and atmosphere with yours. We also have the same language. And our history alludes to the theory that the tribes were begun by Travelers on a voyage from a distant land, who happened upon what they referred to as the White Island."

"If that is true, then how come I have never heard of the White Island from the Mainland?" I asked her, trying to make sense of where exactly we were.

"That is a complicated question." Simeon spoke up. "We Hydros have sought to understand the mystery of this water-bound land mass for centuries. There have been those who have sailed away from here, never to return. We do know that the ocean takes away our connection with the life forces. The ability to conjure a life force only seems to work as long as you are in close proximity to the land itself. Once you reach a certain point in the ocean, your abilities no longer work."

Abrianna took over his explanation. "We have come to believe that those who have tried to leave the Island by ocean were either lost forever at sea or did, in fact, arrive at the Mainland with no memory of the Island whatsoever," she said softly, looking past us as if seeing something beyond the present. "We have no way to know for sure, but as far as we can tell, people on the Mainland know nothing of us and have never been able to track the Island."

I exchanged glances with my friends. I'd heard of phantom islands that explorers had charted in their travels, only to come back and find the islands had disappeared. Strange things always happened in the ocean, right? Hadn't the Bermuda Triangle been a source of mystery for years? The Mainland may not know of this strange White Island, but there have always been phenomena in the world that seemingly could not be explained by science and reason. And with a majority of our planet being covered in water, how could we adequately know everything that was out there? Could it be that we really were somewhere still on Earth?

"So, what does this have to do with any of us?" Caleb asked, folding his arms over his chest.

"It has very little to do with you and everything to do with Whitnee. In fact, we did not expect the Pilgrim to bring others on the journey," Abrianna said tensely.

"Who is the Pilgrim?" Morgan asked.

Ezekiel spoke up in a quiet voice now. "Abrianna, may I explain?"

She gave him a hesitant stare before replying, "Very well. Only give her the *facts*, though."

Ezekiel rose slowly to his feet and using his typically dramatic voice, he began: "There was a prophecy made years and years ago in a time when all the tribes had fallen into chaos. There was an abundance of violence, and horrible acts were committed. In the middle of such depravity, an old wise man from the Aerodora tribe was given a vision of a Pilgrim who would come one day and bring order and peace to the tribes. The prophecy was recorded, along with the signs ordained to identify the Pilgrim. The tribes have always believed in the ancient prophecies, and so the people met and decided to set up the position of Guardian—a position intended to be a *temporary* guide over the tribes until the Pilgrim would come and set things right. The first Guardian was ordained by a vision given to a wise man from the Pyradora tribe. It would become custom later for the wise man in the Pyra village to receive the vision for the next successor. On the night of the baby's birth, the wise man would set a sign in the stars—the sign of the tribe to which the baby was born.

"In this pivotal time period, the Tetrarch Council was also formed to give the individual tribes a voice in the matters of the Island. These members were not ordained, but elected by their own tribe to assist the Guardian. After a period of tumult in adapting to the changes, the Dorians fell into peace of their own making. Everyone was united in preparing for the Pilgrim. A beautiful Watch Tower was constructed on the Southern Beach, and guards from each tribe were posted at all hours of the days and nights, searching the landscape for signs of the Pilgrim.

"You see, though the first Aerodorian wise man had prophesied about what the Pilgrim would accomplish, he never knew *how* it would be accomplished—and neither did anyone else. Most everyone believed that the Pilgrim would come as a Traveler across the sea. Some said he would be a strong and mighty warrior who could rule in power! Some believed he would have abilities in all the life forces and would create a new land for the people. Some even said that the Pilgrim would take them to the Mainland to rejoin the rest of the world they had been cut off from. You can imagine the full range of theories constructed as time went by. The White Island experienced the most prosperity and growth in these years, and the tribes got along with each other like they never had before."

He paused in his story to take a deep breath, and I found that I had been completely immersed in his retelling of the Island's history. I still could not see where I fit into all of it, so I desperately wanted him to continue.

"After a time, though, the people grew arrogant in their own ability to govern and create peace. They soon began to believe that they did not need a Pilgrim to bring them order, since they had apparently created it for themselves. They decided they did not need a Traveler unaccustomed to their own land to rule. And so, eventually, one by one, the tribes stopped placing a guard at the Watch Tower, and the building itself fell into disrepair. The people forgot the old prophecies or reasoned them away. They turned instead to their current Guardian as a ruler and peacemaker, though the position was never set up to be that way. Centuries passed with different Guardians coming and going. New Tetrarch Council members were chosen and then eventually replaced, and nobody spoke any more of a Pilgrim." He stopped short then and glanced at Abrianna, forcing me to tear my own eyes away from him to observe her. She was perched in her seat, her back perfectly straight and her body frozen like a beautifully carved statue of a goddess. Gabriel had a perturbed look on his face as he stared off into nothingness.

Caleb broke the silence. "Once again, what does this have to do with Whitnee? You act as if you believe she is the Pilgrim..." His words startled Abrianna and Gabriel both from their reverie. She stood up and peered down at the great book on the desk.

"Perhaps you would like to read the prophecy about the Pilgrim for yourself, Whitnee. Come." She motioned for me to join her. I sent back one uncertain look at my friends before standing and walking slowly to the desk. All eyes in the room were fixed on me. She turned the book so that it faced me, and with one delicate finger, she pointed to a spot for me to read. The page was very old, and the writing was very ornate, unlike any handwriting in English I'd ever seen. I read out loud, and my voice seemed to echo across the large domed space.

"*This is the gift you shall receive: A Pilgrim resembling a native, yet of a pale color and missing birthmark, will appear in the midst of dark times. From this all-gifted Pilgrim, the tribes will learn the way to true peace, and the White Island will prosper.*" I shook my head, once again not seeing what this had to do with me.

"What does it mean, 'a pale color' and 'missing birthmark'...? That description could fit anybody..." I stated, taking a step away from the book. Abrianna watched me closely.

"Have you not noticed how different you look from us? You have pale golden hair, and your skin is much lighter than ours," Abrianna said.

"But Kevin is blond too... he has a fair complexion. And Morgan's hair is actually the same color as mine—we can change our hair color on the Mainland. How can you be sure it's not one of them?" I argued, still not buying it.

"Kevin and Morgan cannot access the life forces on their own. And the 'all-gifted' part seems to refer to a natural ability in all the life forces," Ezekiel said intensely, his eyes wide as he spoke. "This Island *knows* you, Whitnee. Your name means 'White Island.' You are a Dorian deep down inside. How else could you have transported yourself here? Do you not *feel* the connection?"

I got the impression he was trying to convey something deeper than what his words were saying, but it was lost on me.

"I don't know … I had nothing to do with transporting us here … The wind just came and the light …" I shook my head helplessly.

"Then how did you get here? Nobody has ever transported without the help of a Dorian," Abrianna insisted, gesturing to the group. "You brought yourself here with your ability, and you brought them as well."

FEEL THE WINDS OF CHANGE BLOW

My friends glanced at me incredulously. Could *I* have been the one to transport us here? How was that possible?

"Look..." I tried again. "This doesn't make any sense. For all I know, someone could have gifted me with abilities once I got here." I shrugged, trying to ignore the fact that I had already used all four life forces. Imagine if I told them that ... that would certainly give credibility to their theory, wouldn't it?

"You can only be gifted by a physical touch and transfer of life force by someone in that tribe." Gabriel spoke for the first time. "You were not gifted, Whitnee. I promise."

"Maybe. What about the birthmark part?" I questioned, trying to remember if I had any birthmarks on me somewhere.

"Every person on this Island is born with a birthmark, a sign of the tribe they are born into," Abrianna said.

Gabriel spoke sharply. "I already explained this to her. And she has no birthmark on her back."

I turned to him in shock.

"And how would *you* know what's on her back, Gabriel?" Caleb stood to his feet suddenly, his eyes ablaze.

"Drop it, Caleb. He saw her in a towel," Morgan said quietly, trying to pull Caleb back down to his seat.

"What! You let him see—" Caleb exploded.

Way to go, Morgan.

I turned around. "I did not *let him* see anything. *Geez*, Caleb! Is that really important to discuss right now? Gabriel's right either way. I don't have some sign on my back, but neither does anyone else who traveled here. They're trying to convince me I'm some prophecy come true, sent to bring peace and prosperity! Maybe you could worry about *that* instead," I told him, throwing up my hands in frustration.

Caleb swallowed and clenched his hands. "Fine." He turned to Abrianna. "But Whitnee has a point. There is nothing besides her ability and hair color that necessarily identifies her as the Pilgrim. And even if she was, what exactly do you want from her?"

That was a very good question, and it made me spin back around to face the Tetrarch Council.

"Well, if you are the Pilgrim, Whitnee, you offer hope to our Island," Simeon said through his zephyra. "Surely that is not something you would take lightly. It would also mean that you are not here by accident but by some greater ordainment."

"Look, I am so sorry to disappoint you, but I am nothing special," I confessed, backing away to stand beside Caleb. "I came here by choosing to break a rule on the Mainland, not by some magical plan of your Island's. My friends and I need to get home. We have families and friends and responsibilities where we came from, and they have nothing to do with your prophecy."

Strangely enough, Abrianna and Ezekiel exchanged a meaningful glance that caught my attention. Ezekiel spoke first. "We understand your hesitance in believing what we say, Whitnee, but you have to believe that there are other factors—years of history—that we are taking into account, and we do believe that you could be the Pilgrim our ancient prophecies spoke of."

"I agree with Ezekiel," Joseph said, his large face appearing serious now. "But if the girl does not believe she is the Pilgrim, then what good does that do for us?"

Simeon nodded voraciously. "Exactly. She must believe it for herself if there is to be any change, and how can she know until she has had time to think it through? Perhaps she may exhibit abilities in the other life forces if given enough time." I gave Simeon a nervous look. He did not know that I had already used all the elements, but I couldn't tell them that for fear it would finalize everything. And I had a feeling I didn't like where this conversation was heading. The silent and solemn Pyradorian Councilman, Eli, cleared his throat all of a sudden and stood to his feet. Everyone in the room turned to give him attention.

In a very deep and throaty voice, he said, "I must insist that Whitnee not be allowed to leave the Island until this matter is settled. Perhaps we can arrange for her friends to return, but my recommendation to the Council is that she stays until we determine for sure if she is the Pilgrim."

"*What*?" I cried.

"Absolutely not!" Caleb stated.

Even Morgan jumped to her feet, exclaiming, "If we go, she goes with us!"

Amelia and Kevin also stood, and the five of us faced the Tetrarch Council fiercely. I was so thankful in that moment that my friends were by my side, because I was completely overwhelmed with what I was hearing. Everything seemed to be spinning out of my control.

"We will not be separated," Caleb repeated forcefully, earning an approving nod from Joseph.

Abrianna faced the five of us squarely and stated, "Very well. You *all* will stay on the Island until this matter is settled."

"But—" I interrupted.

"They either go without you or stay with you. What shall it be?"

I turned to my friends, a full range of emotions flitting across my face.

"Oh, please," Morgan reprimanded me. "Don't even look at us like we have to think about it. There's no way we're leaving you. If you stay, we all stay." Caleb grunted his agreement, and Amelia and Kevin nodded anxiously.

"If that is settled, then I recommend we move them immediately to the Palladium where they will be under the best protection, and Advisors can work with Whitnee on her abilities—"

"Excuse me, Abrianna, but I do not agree that they should go straight to the Palladium if they are going to stay," Joseph interrupted her. "Would it not be better for her to visit the different tribes and see if she can develop her abilities there?" Abrianna was clearly displeased with this suggestion.

"I hardly see how visiting the villages will help with that, Joseph. I had hoped to avoid her going into any villages in the first place, but Ezekiel ruined that plan. I do not find it prudent to stir up the Dorians over this matter until we know the truth. Remember what happened last time, gentlemen..." She sent a pointed look in Ezekiel's direction. He seemed to seethe with anger. "It took a long time to gain control again. Surely her presence in the villages will only make things worse."

What did she mean, *last time*?

Eli sided with her. "Abrianna is right. We do not want to give false hope to the tribes. If she just ends up leaving us like what happened before, there will be major upheaval. We cannot afford to go through that again. My tribe is still bitter over what happened."

"Well, that is not surprising," Ezekiel muttered.

"What does that mean?" Eli flashed his eyes at Ezekiel, who immediately responded.

"You know exactly what it means. And Whitnee is obviously the direct result of last time... look at her! None of you can sit here in my Conclave and ignore the past. Especially you, Eli! Let us not forget that in this matter, as in almost all matters, your relationship with the Guardian tends to... dictate your motives."

"Enough!" Abrianna shouted before Eli could respond. I jumped at the harshness in her voice. Joseph grinned humorlessly, and Simeon's hand pressed to his forehead as if the topic gave him a headache. Ezekiel hushed but did not appear scared by Abrianna or the intimidating Eli, who looked ready to throw a punch (or a Fireball). "Eli is a free thinker and *if* he did disagree with me, I am sure he would not hesitate to let me know. And do not forget, gentlemen, there are *sacred topics* that we are all forbidden to speak of..." Abrianna spoke in a dangerously quiet voice, almost reminding me of the tone Gabriel took when some dark emotion was brewing beneath the surface.

"I still stand by my statement." Eli spoke through gritted teeth. "The Travelers should go immediately to the Palladium before this gets out of control again."

"Well, I disagree," Joseph said. "I would very much like for them to visit Geodora and learn more about the Island. I am curious if she can learn the language of the Earth."

"And the wonderful properties of Water!" Simeon threw in. "My tribe would welcome her with open arms. Now that she has been around the Aeros, I am sure it is only a matter of time before word of her arrival spreads anyway. When Thomas returns, he is bound to tell others in my tribe."

"If we agree to this, I fear for their safety," Abrianna told them. "We cannot forget that travel is dangerous in this time. Gabriel has been assigned to track down this group of rebels, and what he is discovering does not bode well. They are still untraceable. The last thing we would want is for Whitnee to fall into the wrong hands."

"I would not allow harm to come to her," Gabriel suddenly declared, and that seemed to take everyone by surprise, especially me.

Abrianna glanced suspiciously at him. "What are you saying, Gabriel?" she questioned.

Before he could respond, Ezekiel, who was staring at Gabriel contemplatively, remarked, "If I may say so, Gabriel really should have a say in this matter too. He has spent the most time with the Travelers, and I believe that his motive in protecting Whitnee is genuine."

Gabriel registered a brief amount of surprise on his face before recovering.

"Gabriel, do you think it a wise decision to allow them to visit the other villages?" Ezekiel asked him. The Council anticipated his answer in silence.

Gabriel hesitated, glancing at Abrianna and then at Eli. Both looked at him with no emotion, but I could tell they expected him to agree with them. I was positive Gabriel would not be in favor of me traveling. Hadn't he been the one to worry about making any stops on the way to the Palladium? Hadn't he been overly obsessive about keeping me away from others and what they might say to me? There was no way he would agree with Joseph and Simeon.

Yet he appeared to be torn as he made eye contact with the Guardian herself. Finally, he allowed his gaze to fall on me, and I thought I detected the softer side of him radiating in his captivating eyes.

"I will obviously do whatever the Council ultimately decides," he stated, his eyes remaining on my face. I could only stare back at him, waiting breathlessly to hear what else he would say. "However, I do not see the harm in allowing Whitnee to experience the rest of the Island. She seems to have enjoyed Aerodora, and it is only fair to allow her the same privilege in the other villages. If the Council sees fit for her to travel, and Abrianna agrees, I will accompany the group for protection and guidance." I gave him a confused look, and Abrianna narrowed her eyes as she watched her Attendant say all of this. Then she cast her eyes on the subject of his attention—me.

"Ezekiel? What do you say?" she asked in that quietly intense voice while she stared me down.

"I say that I would prefer to send Levi and Tamir along also. That is not because I do not trust Gabriel. I just think that *if* anything were to happen, he would need help. The more companions there are, the safer it is for them."

"I agree," Simeon said. "I can send word for Thomas to accompany the group. This will give aid from the Hydros."

"And my daughter, Eden, is also well-rehearsed in defensive techniques and would be an excellent travel companion. She is a Scent Artist and is actually making deliveries in your village this week. I will contact her as soon as we finish here and let you know," Joseph spoke enthusiastically.

"Whoa, whoa, whoa," I finally jumped in. "You have already decided that I am staying, but I don't think you realize how desperately I need to get home. The longer I am here, the more time passes there! Do I not have a say in this at all?" I looked to Ezekiel and Gabriel for help.

"I can assure you that you will be well cared for while on the Island, Whitnee," Abrianna addressed me. "As for the problem of time, it is not even clear how much time actually passes on the Mainland in relation to us. For all we know, *weeks* could have already passed on the Mainland. What would a few more days matter?"

"Are you *serious*?" I gasped, all sense of hope draining from me.

"Weeks!" Caleb cried. "How can that be? You said you are on the same planet as us and even share the same sun. If we are rotating around the same sun, then the rules of time should also apply."

"Yes, but it seems that anytime transport takes place through a portal, it is not just space that is manipulated. Time is interrupted as well. It is a very fragile experience to use a portal. You could arrive back mere minutes after you left, by the same logic. We just do not know enough about it. But we will not discuss that any further," she said authoritatively. "It has been ruled by the majority in the Council for you to remain on the Island until further notice, and in that time you will visit each tribe. This is against my better judgment, but only you can really know if you are the Pilgrim, Whitnee. With that in mind, I implore you to put thoughts of returning home aside and focus on your purpose. The sooner you figure that out, the sooner you can go home." I could only gape at her and at the powerlessness I felt at her words. Morgan and Caleb grew very still and quiet, and I felt guilty once again that I was the one keeping them here. It just wasn't fair.

Abrianna turned to Gabriel then: "I will expect frequent and detailed updates from you, Gabriel, regarding her progress. Ezekiel, see to it that his zephyra does not *accidentally* quit working again."

Ezekiel ignored her, walked over to me, and placed his cool, wrinkled hands on my shoulders. Looking into my eyes, he said comfortingly, "Please do not think of yourself as a prisoner here. You are a Daughter of the Wind and of utmost importance to me. We will not keep you here any longer than is necessary. I will do everything in my power to see to that. Do you believe me?" He seemed so kind and genuine that I just nodded.

With one arm around me, he addressed the Council. "I believe this has been quite an overwhelming experience for Whitnee. Surely we can discuss the details and route of travel without her here. Does everyone agree to release her and her friends from the meeting?" The Council members gave their consent, and Simeon said, "We look forward to meeting you in person, Whitnee." Joseph made a hum of agreement.

I could hardly respond, I was so taken aback at the turn of events. Ezekiel's hand was still on my shoulder as he called Tamir over to him. "Tamir, please take them back to the guest-house, and make sure Hannah has food prepared for them. Keep your zephyra on you if you take them anywhere else. We will contact you when arrangements have been made." Tamir nodded and then bowed to the Guardian before turning to exit. "Levi, I would like you to stay, as we will need your aid in planning the journey. Now, Whitnee," Ezekiel said kindly, "Go with your friends and Tamir."

I just stared at him in a bit of a fog until Caleb firmly took my hand and led me from the room. I guess everyone must have formally given their farewells, but I could not focus on anything but putting one foot in front of the other. I glanced back behind me—Abrianna watched me leave, her eyes unreadable.

When Ezekiel said I was overwhelmed, that did not even scratch the surface.

LEGAL GUARDIAN

I stared out at the clear waves rolling peacefully toward the shore while the wind whipped my hair around and pushed right through my thin clothing. The sunlight cast a warm glow over me, and yet I could feel nothing. I wasn't even sure how to form complete thoughts as I stood there alone, digging my toes into the moist, cool sand.

Off in the distance, Aerodorians were cleaning up storm damage along the shore and near the thunderfly port—the warehouse-structure where the thunderflies were housed and trained. Morgan and Caleb had taken Amelia and Kevin to the port for a tour. I had no desire to go, especially after my initial encounter with a thunderfly. They didn't seem happy about that, but they allowed me to stay out here under Tamir's watchful eye. Perhaps they could sense my need to be alone and think about what had just happened in that meeting.

These people believed that I was the prophesied Pilgrim, but I had never heard anything about this Island in the seventeen years I had been on this Earth. I shouldn't have any special connection to this place. Yet, if what Gabriel said was true, and nobody before had ever accessed more than one element, didn't it mean something that I could? And then what was I supposed to do with that ability? These people spent years learning how to perfect the art of using their life force. I couldn't stay here long enough to ever accomplish anything significant with my abilities. I had to get home—I had to get my friends home too.

Briefly I wondered what would happen if I told Abrianna I could use all four life forces already. That might confirm her suspicions, but then it might free me to choose not to be their Pilgrim and say bye-bye, time to go home. But if they knew of my abilities, would they ever let me go home? How did I get out of this situation? There were still things the Council was not telling me—who could I really trust on this Island? I felt completely at their mercy.

I was pondering all of this when I became aware of a presence behind me. I spun around to find Gabriel standing there, his face an emotionless mask. I turned back around to face the endless ocean. Neither one of us spoke for a moment.

"Why didn't you tell them I could use all four life forces?" I finally asked evenly.

He heaved a sigh before answering, "I was not sure everyone in that room could be trusted."

"Like whom?" I asked, thinking involuntarily of Eli.

"I am still not sure. But I know that something is not right, and it is coming from one of them."

"Will you tell the Guardian the truth?"

"Eventually. I do not know how important it is for her to know yet," he said—this surprised me. I turned to face him.

"Interesting. Since when did you start keeping secrets from your beloved Guardian?" I asked him suspiciously.

"This would be a first," he admitted.

"But you're so ... loyal to her."

"Yes, I am ... for many reasons. But that does not mean I always agree with her."

"What did Ezekiel mean when he said something about the relationship between Eli and Abrianna?"

Gabriel's face clouded over then as he answered, "They are married to each other."

"Abrianna and Eli? I thought it was frowned upon for two people from different—"

"It is. But when Abrianna wants something, nothing stops her. Their relationship was secret for many years and did not come out into the open until after he had been chosen as an Elder and Councilman for the Pyradora tribe."

"Wow," I breathed. "That sounds complicated and a bit shady... By the way, you let me just assume that the Guardian was a man. Is it always a woman or what?"

"It can be either. She is not the first woman to be chosen Guardian, but it is still rare."

"And how old is she?"

"Forty-nine."

"She looks great..." I commented, wondering at how young she appeared. And then I remembered what Gabriel had explained to us by the campfire. The Guardian took over the position at twenty years of age and ruled for thirty years. Abrianna's time was almost up. That meant that another Guardian had already been chosen and would take over soon.

And all the pieces fell into place. Gabriel's apparent authority suddenly made sense. And he was nineteen years old... one more year before he would turn twenty. I gasped and turned my full attention on him.

"You're the next Guardian, aren't you?"

He matched my gaze. "Yes," he answered simply.

I raised my voice. "Why didn't you tell me that?"

"What difference would it make in this situation? I am not the Guardian ... yet."

"But you must know everything ... you can help me get home!"

"I do not know everything. Abrianna has her secrets, and one of those is the portals and the connection between the Island and the Mainland. She guards that secret very closely."

"Doesn't that bother you? If you're going to be the next Guardian, shouldn't you know about that?"

"Yes, but there has not been a Traveler in my lifetime—until now. I had not given much thought about her dabblings in that area because it did not seem a real issue. Besides, she has always had me out working among the tribes. Now, everything has changed…" I could only stare at him as I thought about all of this. What a complicated mess I had fallen into.

"Gabriel, why did you agree for me to stay and visit all the tribes? Why wouldn't you just help me get home sooner?" I asked. He paused, peering out over the ocean. My eyes followed his every movement, watching his face closely for some sign of emotion.

"It is not time for you to go home yet, Whitnee," he told me, and I felt the annoyance bubble up inside of me again.

"Who are you to decide that?"

"And who are you to reject all that is ancient and sacred to our culture?" he spat back. "You think you just stumbled onto some other place and you can leave as you please. But we are real people with a real history. We have waited for generations for a prophecy to come true, and you act as if it is nothing!"

"So are you saying that you believe I am the Pilgrim? You really think that I, Whitnee Skye Terradora, am the one to make everything on this Island all perfect and peaceful? Look at me! I'm just a teenager!"

His face had changed dramatically at my words—he was staring at me like I had just grown a second nose. "What did you just say about your name?" He grabbed my arms and gave me a little shake.

"Huh?"

"Your name!"

"Whitnee Skye Terradora?"

"Terradora—who gave you that name?" he breathed.

"It was my father's last name—" I failed to see the importance of that.

"It is a Dorian name! It means land-gifted. Did you not know that?"

"Well... I guess I hadn't thought about it. What are you saying...?"

"There is much you still do not understand about your situation. Do you really not sense a connection between you and this Island?" He watched me closely before he dropped his hands and gazed out at the ocean again, lost in deep thought. I did not know what to make of his words.

"*What* connection? Does this have anything to do with what the Council said about 'last time'?"

He seemed genuinely puzzled and more than a little tired. "Whatever they are referring to happened before I was born. I only know of rumors... nothing more."

"Do you think it has anything to do with me? Or my father?" I pressed.

"I do not know how that would be possible." He shook his head, which only frustrated me further.

"Gabriel, I want to understand how I'm connected to this place, but it seems like nobody is telling me the whole truth! You won't even answer my question!"

"You tend to ask a *multitude* of questions." He grimaced. "Which one are you referring to this time?"

I ignored his sarcasm. "Do you think I am the Pilgrim? Is that what you meant when you said I was here for a purpose?" I was hugging my arms to myself as I watched him for an answer.

"I already told you that only you can know what your purpose here is," he said without looking at me. "What do you believe?"

"I don't know," I told him truthfully.

"Then you need more time."

"You know I don't need to visit the other tribes to figure out how to access the other life forces. Why didn't you just agree with Abrianna for me to go to the Palladium? You could have been rid of me finally." I spoke softly. Could it be that he wasn't ready *personally* for me to leave?

He turned sharply then to stare at me. "You are right. Visiting the other tribes is not necessary, but I believe it could be beneficial at the same time," he stated. Then his voice softened as he said, "But, if you go to the Palladium, it is just a matter of time before you leave. And I do agree with Eli that we cannot let you leave until you know for sure who you are."

Of course, he was only thinking of his people. He wanted me to stay so he could know my purpose here. It had nothing whatsoever to do with spending more time with me ... what was wrong with me that knowing that hurt just a little bit? I had just seen Gabriel as some sort of bodyguard to the Guardian of this Island. But he was actually the future ruler and would be taking Abrianna's place. I needed to start looking at him through that lens, because I was starting to sense that when it came down to it, his devotion would fall to his own people and not me.

"What are you thinking about?" he asked. I realized he was still watching me closely.

"Huh? Nothing," I said and tried to wipe off whatever expression was showing on my face.

"Did you know you can be quite entertaining to watch? I have never known someone whose face changes so often ... Even Ezekiel in all his dramatics cannot rival you." Gabriel had a bit of a grin turning up the corners of his mouth.

"Whatever. I'm not trying to entertain you. I'm just trying to figure all of this out," I told him fiercely, trying to hide the blush that was threatening to color my cheeks.

"I imagine this is all very confusing. I promise I will try to help you discover the truth."

"And how do you propose I handle all this life force business while we travel? Am I supposed to pretend like I can't use anything but the Wind? And what happens when I accidentally use one? People will know ..."

"That is something to consider—" He was interrupted by a commanding voice from behind us.

"Gabriel!"

We both spun around to find Abrianna somehow gracefully walking toward us in the sand with Tamir trailing behind. Gabriel and I started toward her. I noticed Eli standing under the shade of a tree watching from afar.

"Gabriel, Eli would like to speak with you. Whitnee, will you take a walk with me?" Gabriel and I hesitated, stealing a quick glance at each other. She seemed ever the kind and diplomatic speaker, and we could find no reason not to do as she asked. With a short nod, Gabriel took off toward Eli, throwing one last cautionary look behind him on his way.

I turned to Abrianna and followed her as she strolled casually along the shore. I waited until she spoke first.

"Whitnee, you have a very strong spirit within you. One that seems to have captured the attention of my Attendant in the short time that you have been here."

Okay, so this was not what I was expecting ... I didn't even know how to respond.

"You should know that men from the Pyradora tribe are very ... passionate in their endeavors. I know this, having spent much time with Eli and Gabriel. When something—or someone, for that matter—catches their interest, it is difficult to tame their pursuit of it." She continued to walk as she spoke. I was really not sure where this conversation was heading. "My point is that Gabriel is obviously very fascinated by you." She paused to take in my reaction, and I felt like she was expecting me to say something.

"Well, Abrianna, it seems like many people here are fascinated by me for no apparent reason. I know what the prophecy says, but I am nothing special—"

"Ah, well, you may not know it yet, but you are *very* special. However, that is not what I am talking about. Surely you know by now that Gabriel is next in line for the position of Guardian?"

"Yes, I do." It hardly seemed necessary for her to know I had just learned this five minutes ago.

"To be Guardian of this Island is to be in a position of much power. I speak freely with you on this topic because you are not from here, but it is a position that can be abused if not handled properly. I am concerned about Gabriel's apparent vested interest in you, and I caution you to be careful with him." She stopped then and faced me. I could only stare back at her. What exactly was she saying?

"I'm not sure I know what you mean," I told her.

"Speaking confidentially, Whitnee, there are things I have never taught Gabriel because I worried that, given his personality, he might be tempted to misuse the knowledge I have. It is so rare for a Pyra to be chosen as Guardian. Usually the Guardian comes from the Aerodora or Geodora tribe."

"Why? What about the Hydros?"

"Hydrodorians try too hard to please everyone—sometimes a good leader has to make difficult choices that may not be popular. And Pyradorians are too volatile—real decisions cannot be made on emotional whims. Geos are logical, and Aeros are natural-born communicators. The strongest Guardians in history have been Aeros. It is proven by time and experience. But Gabriel is another matter … he is thirsty for knowledge and authority, and I have only given him what I believe he is capable of handling."

"I don't understand."

"Of course you do not understand. I will only say this … there are those out there who might be tempted to *use* you and your abilities for personal gain. And if you are the Pilgrim, you can imagine how much more tempting that becomes."

I was silent for a moment as I allowed her words to sink in.

"You think that Gabriel wants to use me for his own power?"

"Not necessarily. However, imagine if he has the Pilgrim by his side while he rules ... it would certainly place him in a position of great power and prestige. I just encourage you to exercise caution. As another Daughter of the Wind, you should be warned how easy it is to be caught up in *emotions* that may not be real. There have been torrid love affairs between Aeros and Pyras because both are given to emotion and passion in similar ways. I would like to believe that Gabriel is sincere in his motivations, but he is very serious about his calling to the position of Guardian. I just want you to be careful. If he starts asking you to keep certain secrets or you find that he is not telling you the truth in all matters, then you must contact me immediately." She looked completely solemn as she said this, and my mind started turning over all the conversations I'd already had with Gabriel. But I still wasn't sure I completely trusted her, either.

She continued, "We have mapped out a travel schedule that I am sure Gabriel will review with you later. I have given you a zephyra that will allow you to contact me at any time for any reason. I am deeply concerned about your safety as you travel, especially the safety of the little ones you brought with you. I suggested that Amelia and Kevin come with me while you and the others—"

"No!" I interrupted her vehemently. "Amelia and Kevin stay with me. We will not be separated."

"Gabriel assured me you would feel that way," she soothed, and I found myself warmed by the fact that Gabriel had known what my reaction would be. "However, should you change your mind at any time, you will be able to contact me, and I will gladly arrange for their safe transport to the Palladium. You must believe that your safety, as well as your friends' safety, is our priority." I nodded slowly at that. I really did believe her. Too much was at stake for her if something happened to the supposed Pilgrim or her friends.

"Abrianna, I must know something..." I hesitated before continuing. She watched me carefully. "What happened 'last time'? The Council referred to something … Ezekiel said something about me being the direct result."

"Ah, yes. Last time …" She let out a deep sigh and avoided my eyes then. "There was a time many years ago, long before you were born, when we thought we had found the Pilgrim and we were wrong …" She trailed off, and that emotion entered her eyes again—the emotion I couldn't read. The one that almost made her appear vulnerable. She glanced out at the endless ocean, as if clearing her head, and then spoke again. "Naturally, it stirred the tribes up with hope. And then it ended up not working out the way we expected, and everything on the Island became chaotic again. It has taken us a long time to clean up that mess, and it left many people … scarred. But that is neither here nor there, Whitnee. We do not speak of it anymore, and we have forbidden the tribes to speak on the topic of the Pilgrim any further. Therefore, it is best for you not to ask questions."

"Well, surely people will begin talking again once I visit the villages?"

"Yes, that is what I am afraid of … but the Council will handle that as it comes. If you start to exhibit abilities in any more life forces while you travel, you must contact me immediately. Do you understand?" I opened my mouth to say something … perhaps to just tell her I could already use the four elements? But then I shut it at the last minute and nodded obediently.

"And be careful with Gabriel. He is a good person, but his fascination over you as the Pilgrim may confuse *other* emotions he has … it would be unwise for you to get caught up in such affairs while you are here. And believe me, the affections of a Pyradorian can be very difficult to ignore. Please bear that in mind on your journey." She raised her eyebrows at me.

Again I just nodded, unsure what to believe anymore. I thought I could trust Gabriel, but now even that seemed uncertain. Who was really on my side here? Abrianna? Gabriel? What about Ezekiel? The only people I knew I could trust were the friends I brought with me. And yet, I was beginning to feel distant from them too. I hated being the reason they couldn't go home. And on that note ... what was the point of me wasting time to travel around this Island? Was I really a part of some pre-ordained plan? Or just a pawn in somebody's own selfish ambition? Either way, I suddenly felt that more was at stake here than just getting back to the Mainland.

MEET BOOMER

Hours later, we were each given leather bags with clothing and supplies for our journey. I discovered my Camp Fusion t-shirt, khaki shorts, and flip-flops inside my bag, kindly cleaned and looking newer than when I got them. I tucked my Swiss Army knife into a little pocket as I glanced one last time at the lavender guest room. We said our good-byes to Hannah and Rachael on the way out.

We were taken down to the thunderfly port where Thomas was already waiting with his own bag. He greeted us warmly, but I still felt that he was a little reserved when he addressed me directly. Levi and Tamir were accompanying us, and we were just waiting on Joseph's daughter, the Scent Artist. I was nervously watching the thunderfly we would be traveling on when Ezekiel and Sarah came over to me.

"We wish you a safe journey, Whitnee," Ezekiel said as he hugged me, and Sarah did the same. His face looked clouded with worry. "You should find all of your personal belongings in your satchel. I am sure there will come a point where you will want your old clothes. Until then, we have also included clothing and other necessities for your comfort." He paused and then said what I felt was probably his most pressing concern. "I cannot stress to you enough to be careful and watchful at all times. You can contact us at any time for any reason."

"I know. I'm sure everything will be fine. Will I get to see you again before I leave ... for good?" I asked hopefully.

He nodded. "We shall figure something out. There is still much to be determined. We are in the midst of dark times, and not everyone can be trusted. Remember that," Ezekiel warned me, which did little to put my fears at ease. "However, try to enjoy yourself too. There are many wonders contained on this Island, and you may find yourself falling in love with it before you leave!" He smiled broadly. "Now, I must go attend to a few details." He grabbed Sarah's hand and wandered away. She gave me one last forced smile, and then I was standing there alone, trying to put my anxious thoughts to rest. There was nothing I could do about this situation so I guess I had to make the most of it, even though I felt like curling into a ball and crying. I looked around to see what everyone else was doing.

Amelia and Kevin were talking to the thunderfly attendant and petting the large insect. Morgan was conversing animatedly with Thomas. Levi and Tamir were off to the side, deep in discussion with Gabriel. Abrianna and Eli had departed earlier for the Palladium.

"I know that expression ..." Caleb spoke with a smile as he approached me.

"Oh yeah?" I challenged. "Which one is it?"

"It's the one you get when you are completely overwhelmed and trying to decide whether to run or cry. Am I right?"

I nodded without saying anything. He had nailed it. I held my bag and rocked back and forth on my heels as I stood there.

"Who are we waiting on again?" I asked him, changing the subject.

"Some Geo girl named Eden? A Scent Artist ... sounds like a nice title for 'ditsy perfume salesgirl' ..." He laughed. I could hardly produce much of a real smile in response.

"*Whit*," Caleb said and bent down to meet my eyes.

"Hmm?"

"It's all going to be okay, you know. We'll get home before you know it. And according to Abrianna, we could end up back only minutes after we left. Wouldn't that be great?"

"She also said it could be weeks and weeks later, Caleb."

"Yes, but let's think positively while we're here."

"I'm finding that harder and harder to do."

"Why? Because of the whole Pilgrim thing?" he scoffed. "Who cares what they think? You are Whitnee Terradora from San Antonio, Texas, and we're going to get you back there as soon as possible, okay?" Caleb always had to think logically, and I was reminded of Gabriel's words earlier ... how their history was real and we were acting like it didn't matter. I couldn't shake that off.

"Caleb, would you think differently if I told you I had already used all four life forces? That they came as naturally to me as learning a new song or the lines to a play? Did you know my last name means 'land-gifted'?" Though I was speaking quietly, I was starting to feel a bit hysterical. "What if I told you that I found something familiar in the faces of these people who I know I've never met before? Would any of that change your mind?"

He stared at me as if unsure he believed what I was saying.

"You know what? Never mind." I shook my head and started to walk away.

"Hey, hey, hey," he called and planted himself right in front of me. "Don't be like that, okay? I'm just trying to think about what you're telling me. Are you saying—I mean, do you believe that you ... are the Pilgrim?" He looked skeptical.

"I'm saying that I don't know! I'm confused and I'm scared and there are too many secrets on this Island ..." I trailed off as hot tears formed in my eyes. Without thinking, I leaned into his chest and hid my face there. I couldn't cry right now. This was not the place or the time ... I just wanted the support of someone I knew who wouldn't and couldn't lie to me right now. He didn't even hesitate to drop his bag and hold me close.

There was such a sense of security with Caleb. I felt one hand stroke my hair and the other pat my back as he comforted me.

"Hey, whatever happens here, we're in it together, okay? You know Morgan and I would never leave you here. And I don't care if you are the Pilgrim or not…you're still our Whitnee. They're not taking you away from us," he whispered. I nodded thankfully and pulled back to look up into his face.

"Thank you," I whispered back. I guess that was what I needed to hear. I just wanted to be reminded of my normal life. The longer I was here, the more I felt out of touch with my real self. It was so easy to buy into everything the Islanders were telling me. Even my feelings for Gabriel were confusing.

Hey, Pilgrim! Remember me? a high-pitched, raspy voice said.

I abruptly pulled away from Caleb and looked around for the person who spoke. There was nobody in close enough proximity to us.

"What is it?" Caleb asked.

"Did you just say something?" I asked him.

"I asked you, 'What is it'?"

"No. Before that."

"Um…"

I am right over here! the voice called again, and I started spinning around madly trying to figure out who it was. It had to be the strangest voice I'd ever heard, almost inhuman.

"Did you hear that?" I asked Caleb.

"Hear what? There's a lot going on in here."

He cannot hear me, Pilgrim. Only you can.

"Okay, you don't hear that voice? That horribly scratchy voice?"

Ouch. That hurts my feelings, the voice replied. What was the deal about this place? Was I not already enough of a freak? Now I was hearing voices? I started walking, peering into the faces of every person in the port, trying to determine who was talking to me. Caleb followed me with a puzzled look on his face. I edged closer to Amelia and Kevin, who were still petting the thunderfly we would soon board.

Ahh. You found me. You know, we really should discuss that whirlwind business from the other day. You could have killed me.

I froze in terror. Was the thunderfly the one talking to me? I peered into its huge bulbous eyes, which were directed at me. But there was no mouth moving that I could see. And Kevin and Amelia didn't appear to react to his words. They continued to pet the overgrown insect and ask the attendant questions.

"Whitnee, what is the deal?" Caleb piped up from behind me, causing me to jump with a startled cry.

"Ummm...I think the thunderfly is...talking to me."

There you go! You figured it out, Pilgrim, the thunderfly said with a slight shuffle my direction. I continued to stare at the large bug in fear. Was I supposed to talk back? Could it read my mind? Nobody else appeared to hear the thunderfly speak, so what was I supposed to do now?

I closed my eyes and thought, *How do I communicate with you?* No response.

"What is it saying?" Caleb questioned me, and I opened my eyes in confusion.

"Nothing now. I don't think it can hear me."

Yes, I can. I can hear what you say out loud.

"Oh," I replied. "Can you hear me now?" I asked him, realizing I sounded like a cell phone commercial from back home.

Yes.

"How come I can hear you and nobody else can?" I asked aloud, moving closer to the bug. The conversation between the attendant and Kevin and Amelia started to die down. Caleb watched curiously.

I can only talk to Aeros. I speak through your mind.

"So...can you hear my thoughts?"

No. I can only cast my words into your thoughts. So, you still have some explaining to do about that whirlwind action. I have never seen an Aero do that!

"Oh. Yeah, I didn't mean to … it just kind of came out of me, you know? Uh … I'm sorry?" I was apologizing to a large bug that I had previously thought was going to eat me.

You need to learn to control the Wind better. Somebody could have been seriously hurt. My wings are still sore.

"Yeah … I'll remember that next time," I trailed off, not sure how normal it was to be lectured on safety by a thunder-fly. I became aware that my one-sided conversation must sound strange to those who were listening in. "Do you have a name?" I asked, trying to sound kind.

They call me Boomer.

I laughed out loud. "Seriously?"

You think my name is funny?

"What's so funny?" Amelia wanted to know.

"No," I quickly corrected myself. "It's a perfect name. Just not what I was expecting …"

"Huh?" Amelia questioned.

Before I could explain the conversation, Ezekiel clapped his hands. "Eden is here! Time to board the thunderflies!"

We appraised the girl who had arrived and was currently standing beside Ezekiel. She was actually quite beautiful in an understated way, with startling green eyes that reminded me of Caleb's. Her dark hair was curly and swept back into a low, loose ponytail. Her only adornment was a bright fuchsia flower tucked into her curls. She was simply dressed in white and wore a very natural smile as her eyes surveyed the Travelers.

"I apologize for being so late! It took me longer to make my scent deliveries than I expected!" she announced, and there was something immediately likeable about her. Gabriel left Tamir and Levi to head our direction.

"Hello, Gabriel. It has been quite a while since I have seen you," Eden remarked coolly when she saw him.

"Hello, Eden." He bowed slightly and a bit stiffly. So they already knew each other … interesting. There had to be a background story here, because there appeared to be some kind of animosity between them. An ex-girlfriend of his, maybe? I immediately squelched any feelings of jealousy that threatened to surface. Quickly, Gabriel introduced everybody since we had all moved in closer at Eden's arrival. Eden's eyes lingered a bit longer on me, but she smiled politely and acted as if nothing was out of the ordinary about this gathering.

"We must load the carriers now. Each carrier can hold a maximum of six people. Whitnee, you are with me over here." He gestured to my new thunderfly friend, Boomer.

"I think I'll ride over there with you then," Caleb jumped in, stepping up protectively by my side.

"Me too," Eden added and, though I detected Gabriel's annoyance at the arrangement, he did not protest.

"I shall use the other carrier. Morgan, would you care to join me?" Thomas suggested.

Morgan agreed and asked, "Kevin and Amelia, how about you ride with me too?" Amelia looked longingly at me for a moment before agreeing to go. Gabriel immediately settled the rest.

"Then Levi and Tamir should split up. Levi, come with us and we shall take the lead. Tamir can ride with the others."

I hugged Ezekiel and Sarah one last time and boarded the cramped carrier that was like a cage strapped to the thunderfly's back. It was open, allowing Wind to move freely through the space, but it did have a roof. In the back was an area for our belongings, and in the main part were two rows of three seats facing each other. Caleb stepped in first and I followed, taking the seat in the middle next to him. Eden moved in across from him, bringing the pleasant smell of fresh flowers with her, and Gabriel took the seat on the other side of me. Levi sat across from Gabriel. So there I was, packed tightly in between Caleb and Gabriel. Every time Gabriel's skin brushed against mine, it was like an electric shock to my heart, and I felt ridiculous for reacting in such a way. I prayed Caleb would not be able to read my emotion this time.

Hold on. I am about to start my wings. It may get windy, Boomer called from ahead.

"Thanks for the warning!" I called back and everyone in the carrier looked at me quizzically. "It was Boomer... the thunderfly. He said we're about to take off," I explained, once again feeling like a freak.

"So you really can hear him?" Gabriel clarified.

"Apparently," I sighed and rested my head back into the seat.

"She is a true Aero," Levi commented. Gabriel looked away then, thinking about something. Caleb still looked skeptical.

"Now," Eden said, looking to Gabriel and Levi, "I understand that we are heading to Geodora first. My father told me he would meet the thunderflies outside the village and escort us to the banquet hall. And from what I hear, there is going to be a spectacular feast in the Travelers' honor tonight!" Her eyes lit up at this and so did Levi's.

"That is something to look forward to!" Levi smiled.

"We Geos will use any occasion as an excuse to cook and experiment!" she agreed. Then she turned to me and, as if she were asking about nothing more than the weather, said conversationally, "Are you really the Pilgrim, Whitnee?" I know my mouth must have dropped open at her candidness.

"Eden!" Gabriel warned.

"I am asking a simple question, Gabriel." And she waved her hand at him as if to dismiss his emotion. Her eyes were genuinely curious as she waited for my response.

"I don't know yet..." I answered honestly.

Gabriel cut in. "We are not discussing that topic any further, Eden. Do not push it—"

"Oh, please, Gabriel! You are not *my* Guardian. I do not need you ordering me around." She rolled her eyes. "He has done this since we were children," she added as an aside to me. So, I was really liking her now... not just because she was clearly comfortable with putting Gabriel in his place, but because it didn't appear that they had any kind of romantic history. I could feel Gabriel's body temperature rising next to me at her apparent lack of concern for his authority, and I wanted to laugh.

"How long have you known each other?" Caleb asked.

"Pretty much our whole lives," she answered at the same time Gabriel replied curtly, "Too long."

She glared at him before continuing. "The Attendant to the Guardian has to be trained in all the villages from a young age so he can adequately understand the culture of each tribe. On those rare occasions, I was so very privileged to take classes alongside Gabriel and work beside him in the fields when we were children." There was a slight twinkle to her eyes that made me think she was just trying to goad Gabriel.

"Oh, yes," he responded, "Such wonderful memories of you messing up crops and creating the foulest scents a person could imagine."

She didn't let him bother her. "I am obviously much better at it now. At least I was not the one to set an entire crop aflame ..." She looked at him with raised eyebrows.

"What?" I asked, looking up at him. "You mean you set plants on Fire?" I was remembering the night before when I had done the same thing. He had been appalled.

He returned my knowing gaze. "Do you remember how I told you life forces can often be released in moments of intense emotion? Well, *somebody* vexed me beyond the point of control that summer, and it just happened ..." he replied, not looking at her. Caleb and I exchanged glances with a smile. They almost sounded like us when we picked at each other.

I had been so immersed in the exchange between Gabriel and Eden that I hardly noticed we had taken off and were flying above the treetops of the Island. I leaned forward to look out the side of the carrier just in time to see the treetop village fade from view. The last thing visible was the purple flag waving the symbol of the thunderfly in a silent good-bye. I wondered if I would ever make it back there again.

The shores of the Island disappeared as we headed inland. I remembered that, on Gabriel's map, Geodora had been almost central to the Island. The dormant volcano still loomed in the distance ahead. It appeared much larger and farther away than I realized the first time I landed on the Island. I found myself very curious about the village there...the village that Gabriel came from.

"Will we visit Pyradora?" I asked him over the Wind inside the carrier. He frowned slightly.

"We will start with the Geos, then travel to the Hydros, and the Pyras will be the last stop. Eli is not happy about this, but he will change his mind..." Gabriel explained.

"Eli is never happy about anything," Eden remarked loudly. Gabriel just ignored her.

"So, we hear that you're really good at defensive techniques with your life force?" Caleb prompted Eden. "How does that work?"

She smiled as she explained, "The Earth life force is very different from the others when it comes to fighting techniques. Although there are certain ways you can use it to fight offensively, the Earth does not like to be a weapon. The land beneath us desires to be in harmony with all living things. It is more likely to become a defense to a negative force than it is to fight against it. Does that make sense?"

Caleb and I nodded hesitantly. She continued, "For example, we can create shields from the Earth pretty much wherever we go. This is an excellent defense technique when in a fight, but it is also used for practical reasons. I am sure when it stormed so hard last night, the Geos were casting shields over some of the more delicate crops. Certain weather, animals, or *elements*"—she cast a dirty look at Gabriel—"can be guarded against with the shield technique. I have learned to do the defensive work well, but unlike many other Geos, I took extra training to also learn offensive techniques."

"Like what?" Caleb wanted to know.

Pilgrim! Look below! Do you see the smoke? Boomer called out, and I realized that I really needed to tell him to call me Whitnee. I looked out past Gabriel and, sure enough, there were smoke plumes rising up through some of the trees.

"What's happening down there?" I pointed, interrupting Eden. Everybody turned to look.

"I do not know. There should be nothing there," Gabriel replied and stared down in confusion. "Thunderfly, circle around so we can have a closer look."

"His name's Boomer," I corrected him, but he was too occupied with the scene below. Boomer obeyed, and the other thunderfly followed behind us.

"I cannot see anything," Gabriel complained as we moved closer. Some kind of devastation had occurred.

"Do you think there is anyone down there?" I asked. "We should land somewhere close just to make sure!"

Gabriel looked torn. I could tell that stopping to investigate was what he would normally do, but there was some other concern in his face. I questioned, "What? Do you think it's that group ... ?"

"I do not know, but I cannot risk anything happening to you. We will have to continue on, and I will contact Abrianna to send guards out here—"

"Gabriel, no! What if somebody is hurt? And that fire could easily get out of control and spread, couldn't it?" I cried. "We need to check it out now before it gets worse." He hesitated, so I called out, "Boomer! Do you see a place where we could land and check out the damage?"

Ahhh ... I believe there is a clearing ahead.

"Land there, please. Are you able to contact the other thunderfly to let them know what we're doing?"

Sure.

"Whitnee ..." Gabriel growled.

"We will be very careful, and we won't take any unnecessary risks, okay? But you need to figure out what's happening and somehow put out that fire," I told him, remembering the pain my spark had caused the tree branch on the balcony. Eden watched the destruction with disgusted eyes. Gabriel just shook his head but did not argue as Boomer lowered himself to the ground several yards away from the fire.

Before we alighted from the carrier, Gabriel placed a hot hand on my arm. "You agree to stay in my sight and do exactly as I say, or we take off again."

Eden rolled her eyes but said nothing as she watched for my reaction.

"I promise I will not put myself in danger. Now let's go!" I replied and brushed past him to leave the carrier. The smoke was blowing all around us the closer we got to the heart of the fire. Thomas had flown out of his carrier with a bottle of pure Water in his hands. I couldn't help thinking that his little bottle would not put out such a massive fire. I was surprised when he poured the Water into his hand. Setting the bottle down, he used his other hand to cast circles over the Water so that it appeared to grow in quantity. Then with sharp flicks of his wrists, he started casting sprays toward the flames, his eyes glowing an intense blue while he concentrated.

Without being asked, Levi held out his hands and moved alongside Thomas, blowing the smoke away from their path so Thomas could move closer. Levi's eyes, too, were alight with a silver glow. We stood back and watched in awe as they worked. While the two were making some progress, it became clear pretty quickly that one person with Water was not enough for the job. The fire was spreading at about the same rate that he was putting it out.

"I am going to need more Water!" Thomas shouted.

"I'll get it!" I responded, thinking I could help with dousing the fire. I would just have to figure out exactly how Thomas made the Water multiply ... Rushing back to Boomer's carrier, I reached into the baggage area, and my hand made contact with a bottle. But before I could pull it out, Gabriel's hand shot out from behind me and stayed my progress.

"No," he stated firmly. "I know what you are thinking, and we cannot let them know what you can do."

With his hand holding my wrist tightly, I stared up at him in shock. "Are you serious? Gabriel, now is not a time to worry about that!"

"I am trying to protect you, and I do not think that—"

"Well, what if I disagree with you? How would you stop me, huh?" Was he really protecting me or just himself?

"Do not put me in that position. I can stop you if I must. Now, give me the bottle and I will take it to Thomas. Perhaps he can gift Morgan to help." Gabriel released his hold on me.

"What?!" I was appalled. "There's no time for that! If I have the ability to help already, why wouldn't you just let—"

"Is something wrong?" A voice rang out behind us. Eden was standing there staring suspiciously at both of us. Gabriel was the first to recover since I could only stare at him in anger.

"We are just looking for more Water. Perhaps Thomas can gift Morgan to help?"

Eden gave him a funny look. "Without prior experience? I am not sure that would work very well. What about you, Whitnee? Have you tried using the element of Water yet? Surely if you are the Pilgrim—"

"Eden, you were warned already. Do not finish that sentence, or you will be off this journey immediately," Gabriel snapped at her, and she raised her hands in surrender.

"Just trying to help. Here, give me the Water, and I will let you two get back to whatever it is you were arguing about." She held her hands out.

Instead of handing her both bottles, I gave her one, saying, "You know what? I can help. Let's go!" And before anyone could argue, I took off, uncorking the bottle. In my head, I barely heard Boomer's words of disapproval, as he must have been listening in to our conversation.

"Whitnee, do not do this—" Gabriel called as he followed after me.

"Too late!" I called over my shoulder and ran past my friends who were still unsure of exactly what to do.

"Tamir! Take care of the smoke for me!" I called out while mimicking Thomas's procedures. Tamir hesitated to follow me, appearing confused by my command. I was having difficulty getting the Water to multiply in my hand the way Thomas had done. I tried focusing really hard on it, and I was getting nothing but a puddle of lifeless Water in my palm.

"Thomas! How do I make more Water?" I yelled out.

He barely turned to acknowledge me. "What?" He was too busy concentrating, and his face was getting red with the heat. Tamir was watching me closely instead of blowing the smoke away from my face, and I started coughing. There had to be a way to put all of this out more efficiently! Thomas was having a hard time making his Water spurts reach the top of the trees.

"Whitnee! Just leave it for Thomas!" I heard Gabriel yell, and then there was an ominous cracking sound above us. My eyes were starting to tear up from the smoke and I couldn't see exactly what was going on.

"Look out! The branch is falling!" Amelia screamed. I thrust my palms out, Water puddling in both of them, and concentrated on pushing the Water out and upward with the strongest gust I could conjure. About the same time I closed my eyes to do this, several things happened at once. All time seemed to pause once again, and my body felt light, but not exactly the weightless sensation I had felt before...more like the kind of lightness I felt when I was floating in water. A sound like a thunderclap boomed around me, and the world caught back up in time. I felt a pair of strong arms pulling me out of the smoky darkness, but it was not necessary, because some kind of force sent both of us hurtling backwards. My entire body weight fell on top of my rescuer, who I realized was Tamir the moment I opened my eyes again. However, I did not miss the evidence of the force that sent us flying backward. The same force that caused Morgan and Amelia to shriek and Thomas and Levi to fall flat on their faces was what appeared to be a powerful cyclone comprised of dangerous Wind and sharp droplets of Water. In a matter of seconds, the forceful combination of Wind and Water suffocated most of the flames, sucked up the smoke, and carried tree limbs and debris a significant distance away before it died out. It literally looked like a small tornado had just blown through.

TRAVEL DELAYS

I sat there, half-sprawled over Tamir, staring in shock at the aftermath of the cyclone. Thomas and Levi slowly pulled themselves up from the ground in puzzlement, trying to figure out what had just happened. Everyone was silent for a moment, taking in the fact that only a few small patches of fire still remained. However, an entire section of plant life had been wiped out.

"I do not believe it..." Eden gasped as she glanced at me with renewed curiosity. At the same time, Gabriel was shooting me angry looks and muttering something under his breath. I wasn't sure how Dorians cussed, but I had a feeling that was close to what he might be doing.

"You did it again, Whitnee!" Kevin yelled, as if congratulating me, while Amelia stood there gaping. Caleb and Morgan seemed to recover the fastest and came immediately to help Tamir and me to our feet.

"What? What did she do?" Thomas questioned, breathing with difficulty. "I missed it because something knocked me over."

"It was Whitnee's whirlwind!" Kevin told him.

"Your eyes are different," Caleb commented quietly, his hand still on my shoulder. "They're blue with a silver ring around them … what exactly did you just do?" I shook my head in confusion.

Somebody could have been hurt again, Pilgrim … Boomer chided.

"Thomas, you are never going to believe this …" Eden started, and before Gabriel could interrupt her, she proclaimed, "I believe Whitnee just used two life forces at the same time!"

"Huh?" I said, simultaneously as Gabriel snapped, "No!"

"You are correct, Eden. I do not believe it." Thomas frowned and rubbed his sternum in pain. He and Levi were spotted with Water, like they had just run through a sprinkler.

"That's impossible, isn't it?" I said timidly, looking to Gabriel. Even as I spoke, I could feel the life force dying down inside of me, and a sudden shakiness began to start in my arms and legs. It wasn't the complete and utter weakness I had felt last night, but it was difficult to control my movements. "I mean, Tamir—he pulled me away before the branch fell and—"

"The branch never fell because your little storm picked it up and tossed it all the way out there!" Eden said excitedly, pointing down the alley of destruction.

"Morgan and Caleb, will you take Whitnee back to the thunderfly? Thomas, I need you to finish extinguishing the flames that are left. Eden,"—Gabriel turned to her with a flash of annoyance—"perhaps you can salvage some of the plants and fix the damage? Levi, Tamir, please clear out the debris and search the area for signs of who or what started this. I will join you in a moment." Each person who received instruction hopped into action at Gabriel's command. I could only stand there shaking. My body felt like it had turned into wobbly Jell-O. Caleb placed his hand at the small of my back and gave me a gentle push forward in Boomer's direction. I took one step and stumbled.

"I'm sorry," I whispered, embarrassed when he pulled me back up. Concern registered on his face. "I can't walk very well. I just feel kind of weak."

"Morgan, get her other side," Caleb instructed, but before Morgan could do anything, Gabriel stepped in and roughly picked me up like I was a small, annoying child. I was completely embarrassed again by his action even though my stomach flipped at the sensation of full body contact with him. I briefly registered the annoyance that flashed across Caleb's face at Gabriel's apparent comfort level with me, but there was nothing I could do. And, truthfully, I had no problem with Gabriel feeling comfortable with this kind of physical closeness. The downside was that Gabriel's face only showed anger as he marched me back to the thunderfly and plopped me down inside the carrier in a not-so-gentle manner.

"I told you *not* to get involved—" he growled at me, completely ignoring my friends, who had followed us.

"Hey, man, you need to cool down. She just put out almost the entire mess! Maybe you should be thanking her." Caleb spoke fiercely.

Gabriel surprised us both when he turned on Caleb. "I appreciate your feelings for her, Caleb, but you need to stay out of this for a moment! She is stubborn and made a poor choice! Do you want something terrible to happen to her? All it takes is one time for her to push her limitations too far, and that could be the end!"

This quieted Caleb, but not happily. I stared at Gabriel, trying to sort out his words. I raised a shaky hand.

"So you're mad at me for using too much energy? Not for revealing my abilities to the others?" I tried to clarify. Even my voice quavered a bit.

"I am angry about both! Obviously, after your little stunt, the greater concern is what you are doing to yourself. Drink more Water." He thrust the half-empty bottle into my hands and I dutifully sipped as much as I could, protesting, "I didn't mean to do that! I had no idea I was capable of producing something like that again—"

"Exactly. And that is where my concern lies. I want you to listen to me, and I am going to say this in front of your friends in the hopes that they will help reinforce this..." He took a deep breath, and those beautiful hazel eyes gazed intensely into mine. "Nobody can argue that you are clearly capable of doing great things with your abilities, but right now you have no control over them! You could end up hurting yourself or others if you do not master each life force."

He makes a good point, Pilgrim, Boomer piped up, and I made a face, though nobody understood why.

"How am I supposed to do that?" I wondered aloud.

Gabriel gave a regretful sigh. "Well, I do not see how we can keep your abilities a complete secret anymore. And, if that is the case, then I believe you will need to start training immediately in each life force. You cannot be trusted to learn on your own, and you need someone within each tribe to show you the safe way to use your gifts."

"Really? All the life forces?"

"Yes."

"If I do that, I want my friends to be gifted in their own element so they can train with me," I demanded. He looked reluctant, but Amelia jumped in with, "Yeah! That sounds fair, Gabe!" My four companions looked at him expectantly.

"Fine, but I do believe all training should be kept confidential," he eventually gave in. "Are you really ready for this, Whitnee? You do realize what this means and how the tribes are going to respond if this gets out..." His face looked almost sad for a moment.

"They'll believe she really is the Pilgrim?" Morgan spoke quietly. Gabriel nodded slowly.

"Well, isn't that the whole point of this journey? I mean, I am not agreeing that I am the Pilgrim. I'm just saying that if we're going to figure this out, we need to be *truthful*." And I gave Gabriel a pointed look. "It was a matter of time before people found out what I could do, Gabriel. I would rather go into each village prepared for that."

He sighed and shifted his gaze to the ground, as if collecting himself. "This makes my job much harder," he stated. "Especially now that you have surprised me once again. The storm ... how did you do that, Whitnee?"

I peered up at him quizzically. "Did I really use Wind and Water at the same time?"

"It appeared that way. It was like the whirlwind you produced before, but it was made of Water ... I have never seen anything like that before that was not a natural phenomenon." He focused on me again with intensity. "No more combining life forces, either, until you understand how each one individually works. I imagine that is why you are trembling like this. It must be an aftereffect of using too much energy ..." He trailed off, and his face softened a little. "You really need to be careful."

"I'm sorry. I just wanted to help," I told him honestly. I felt kind of bad now that I knew he was more concerned with my safety than the fact that I had given away the secret ... Just when I was starting to doubt his intentions, he threw me again. It was probably best if I just cut off all emotional connection to these people. How else could I keep a clear head and get back home?

"I agree with Gabriel," Morgan said, and I looked at her. Her big blue eyes were filled with fear. "I don't want anything to happen to you, Whit. And imagine if you ever created something so big, it could hurt somebody else ..." She paused. "I know you would never mean to do that, but it's something to think about. This whole power of yours is bigger than any of us knew." This made me feel bad, especially as I knew she was right.

"Are you going to tell the Guardian about this, Gabe?" Caleb asked him.

Gabriel shook his head and shrugged. "I do not see that I have a choice now."

"I don't like that idea," Caleb growled.

"Nor do I," Gabriel replied, surprising all of us.

At that moment, Levi and Tamir rushed into view and Levi called for Gabriel. He left us then, and the three of them formed a private circle away from us. I watched their faces for signs of what they might have discovered. Levi was talking and gesturing back to the destruction. Gabriel's face became darker and darker the more Levi spoke.

"This doesn't look good," I whispered, finishing off the rest of the Water in the bottle.

I was right. They had found the remains of a campsite near the fire and evidence that pointed to a group of people having been here. Gabriel immediately used his zephyra to communicate this information to Abrianna. I noticed in his conversation that he left out my involvement in dousing the fire. Abrianna attempted to persuade Gabriel to send the rest of us on ahead so he could track down the perpetrators, but Gabriel would not hear of being separated from us. So they agreed that Tamir would follow the tracks until her Palladium guards could take over the work. He would then meet up with us later.

Gabriel seemed to be in a thoughtful mood afterward. Before we were about to board the thunderflies again, Gabriel gathered all of us together. Tamir had already left to hunt for more tracks, so he was the only one missing.

"I know that everyone is confused by what just happened," Gabriel started, looking sharply into each person's eyes, "and the truth is that Whitnee is able to use all four life forces without being gifted."

"I knew it!" Eden cried, and Thomas looked skeptical. Levi remained silent.

"Obviously, if this knowledge begins to spread, it could create quite a disturbance among the tribes and quite possibly even place her in danger. I am asking for your help with this. I will be letting the Council and the Guardian know as soon as necessary about this development, but I must have your sworn secrecy on this matter before we arrive in Geodora. Do I have your word?"

"Of course! This is huge!" Eden exclaimed.

"I will hold this secret, as long as I have *your* word that you will be informing Ezekiel as soon as possible," Levi answered carefully.

"You have my word, Levi." Gabriel looked him straight in the eye and bowed slightly. Levi returned the bow, which I took as his agreement. "Thomas?" Gabriel turned to him. Thomas again glanced furtively at me and then addressed Gabriel.

"Forgive me, friend, but I just cannot believe she is the Pilgrim, the one we have been waiting on for so many years! She is small and weak and has no prior knowledge of our land. She does not even seem to care if she is the one or not." His words were spoken logically, but I couldn't help feeling the harshness in his meaning. "Out of loyalty to you and the good of my own tribe, I will hold your secret, but I feel very strongly that the sooner we can get the Travelers back to their Mainland Beyond, the better for all of us," he finished honestly.

On one hand he was right, and I should want to agree with him about me not being the Pilgrim. But on the other hand, I felt like he was wrong, and I deserved a chance ... *You can't have it both ways, Whitnee,* I thought to myself. *Either you want no part of this, or you decide that you are some sort of pre-ordained help for these people.*

"I respect your thoughts, my friend. I believe only time will tell in this matter. And I ask one other favor of each of you." Gabriel hesitated, while we all waited to hear what else he would say. "Whitnee must learn how to use each life force in a safe way. While she has the ability to access them, she has no knowledge or understanding of how they work. I would like Levi to train her with the Wind, Eden with the Earth, Thomas with Water, and I will teach her Fire. She cannot do this without our help."

Again, Eden was the first to agree. "I would love to teach her the language of the Earth!"

"What kind of training do you mean?" Thomas questioned.

"She needs to know what each life force is capable of doing as well as how to use it practically and defensively. I fear that danger will have a way of finding her here, and she should not be unprepared..." Gabriel said and glanced apprehensively in my direction.

"Don't forget what else we discussed," I reminded Gabriel.

"Ah, yes. Each of the Travelers should be gifted and taught how to access their own life force. It is only right while they are here that they experience the White Island as we do. Do you all agree?" Everybody nodded, even Levi. Thomas was the only one who seemed reluctant to agree, although when Morgan smiled at him, he seemed to give in.

"How do we keep her abilities a secret and train her at the same time?" Thomas asked.

Gabriel replied, "That is where I need your help."

CAMP GEODORA

Though I was learning not to place too much value on my preconceived ideas about each tribe on this Island, I found that Geodora initially looked more like what I expected a tribal village to look like. We had flown past the dense jungle, and soon the land evened out into more frequent patches of open territory. The landscape varied between large fields of organized crops and structures that I would liken to cabins and huts. Tall trees and dense patches of forest still provided shade in certain concentrated areas, but the whole village appeared more rural and spread out. If the Aerodorians preferred to be as close to the sky as possible, the Geodorians were the exact opposite, choosing to be as close to the land as possible.

The second thing I noticed as we drew closer was the plethora of different scents that wafted even as high as the sky. Some areas seemed concentrated with more floral smells, some with very sharp spice smells, and then once we landed, the scent of flavorful food came floating our direction. Our stomachs all growled in one accord.

Once Boomer had landed in a nondescript grassy area, we were greeted warmly by Joseph and a few other green-eyed people whose names I knew I would not remember the first time.

Now that I had met Joseph in person, I could see a sure resemblance between him and Eden. Eden was certainly not large (like her father), but she was more curvy than the thin, wispy girls of the Aerodora Tribe. Not only that, but both of them had infectious laughs and big smiles.

"Welcome to Geodora!" Each person greeted us with hefty hugs, not with formal bows. The Geos helped us unload our belongings, and a few took charge of caring for the thunderflies. Fortunately, my shakiness had passed by the time we landed, and I felt somewhat normal again, if a bit emotionally tired.

Until we meet again, Pilgrim! Work hard in your training, Boomer said in farewell, and I turned back to wave, hoping he could see me. I never really was sure where exactly those insect eyes were looking.

Joseph and another man led us across the field to a wide dirt road, where a long wooden wagon stood hitched to the backs of two enormous animals. Initially I thought they were abnormally huge horses, but when one turned its face toward us, it had two ivory unicorn-like horns protruding from its forehead. Its body was deep brown in color, but its tail and mane were white. I tore my gaze away from the disorienting creatures to focus on what Joseph was telling us.

"You landed on the outskirts of our village, so we shall give you a tour through the fields on our way to the feast. We have a cabin reserved for you near the banquet hall. Please, climb on." He gestured to the wagon, and we all settled ourselves in the back. I was reminded of our hayrides back home, except those were typically pulled by a tractor or pickup truck instead of freaky, horned horses.

Joseph settled in the back with us and asked conversationally, "Did you have delays in leaving? We were expecting you quite a while ago."

We all exchanged glances before Gabriel explained what had happened, again leaving out the part where I wiped out the vegetation with a cyclone of Wind and Water. When he had finished, Joseph looked slightly suspicious.

"We have received word of strange occurrences like that all around our area. Perhaps since we are located so centrally we hear more of these stories, but it troubles me to know how close it was to our village this time. Have you made any progress in tracking down the group responsible?" He directed this question at Gabriel.

"Not since the Travelers arrived. Whoever is causing these problems is able to escape with almost no traceable evidence. We left Tamir to follow what traces were left until Palladium guards could arrive. I felt it best to get the Travelers here as soon as possible," Gabriel told him.

Joseph still looked suspicious. "Tamir, you say? He is the tall guard of Ezekiel's, correct?"

"Yes," Gabriel answered, and Joseph appeared to think that over for a moment before replying, "Did anything else happen? I sense that there is more to this story than what I am hearing." Joseph looked at me in particular, and I could feel my cheeks begin to color. Gabriel said that Geos could tell when you were keeping a secret ... I opened my mouth to speak, but Eden jumped in suddenly.

"Oh, look! We are at the floral fields where I work!" And she pointed to one of the most gorgeous sites I had ever seen. I had been to botanical gardens and seen greenhouses full of flowers, but none of that compared to the explosion of color and beauty that lay before us.

"That is amazing ..." I breathed, gazing at the endless sea of blossoms. Some flowers grew up straight from the ground, others on trees or bushes, but the entire field was a masterpiece of color and texture. The fresh scent of blooming flowers was strong in the air, and Kevin began sneezing. A small path veered off toward a large hut with an open roof.

"That is where I mix my different scents and create perfumes and oils." She pointed to the building. "You cannot see it from here, but on the other side of this field are the fruit fields—we often mix in fruit scents, too, although the flowers are my favorite!"

"I love the flower in your hair," I commented to Eden. It was a star-shaped flower with thick, leathery petals, and it carried a very pleasant aroma, like a mixture of jasmine with citrus and other smells I couldn't identify.

"This flower is my signature creation, and I have worked several years on growing it. I call it Pinkberry," she explained proudly.

"Well you can't get any more girly than that, can you?" Caleb teased from across the wagon, and I kicked him.

"It's beautiful!" I told her sincerely, and Morgan and Amelia echoed my sentiments.

"What do you mean, you've worked on growing it? Can you control how a plant grows?" Morgan asked her.

"Not exactly. Being a Geo means that you can communicate with the Earth; we just tell the Earth what we need or what we are looking for, and it provides it," she told us.

Joseph added, "Likewise, we have the responsibility of making sure we meet the Earth's needs. We have to properly feed and water it, as well as protect it. It is a partnership."

"It has taken me years to learn the language of scents and how to find the right fusion of scent and color to grow the results I am looking for," Eden said. "You never know what might come up from the ground."

"Yes, and we remember some of your more … pungent experiments. Do we not, Gabriel?" Joseph teased her.

With a small smile, Gabriel agreed, "Yes, to this day, I cannot forget …" Eden ignored him.

The wagon continued its passage down the dirt road, and Joseph and Eden continued to point out different sections of the land used to grow different crops. There was a crop like cotton that they referred to as "weave." This area they called Weaver's Field. From there, they produced all the material needed to make clothes and fabric for the tribes. We were amazed to discover that their cotton (I mean, *weave*) grew in colors, though!

"In our world, we have to dye it to change the color," Caleb explained, and Joseph and Eden laughed at this concept.

We passed the spice fields next, and Kevin began sneezing again at the array of sharp smells that pervaded the air. They explained that these plants could be used for cooking or medicinal purposes.

Before long the road curved and led into a more concentrated area of huts and cabins, and more Geodorians came into view. Many stopped to stare at us, and several children ran behind the wagon.

"Go to the banquet hall! We will be there shortly!" Joseph commanded them, and they immediately obeyed. I was desperately reminded of Camp Fusion in this village. The dirt paths, the cabins, and the random scattering of people walking and talking as they moved from place to place felt familiar to me. Joseph turned to us and said, "This feast is being given in your honor, so you will probably receive many questions and stares throughout the night. My best advice is to avoid discussion on the prophecy but be yourself. You will find Geos naturally curious and direct about their thoughts. You will not have to guess what they are thinking," he told us, and I thought of how direct Eden had already been with me in her questions. "Ah, and speaking of direct personalities, here is my family now!" He gestured proudly to a group of people varying in age and size standing outside a large log cabin.

"You have a very big family," Caleb remarked.

"You have no idea." Eden rolled her eyes as the wagon rolled to a stop. As soon as we jumped down, Eden greeted her mother, a chubby woman with flushed cheeks, sparkly eyes, and a loud voice.

"We are so glad to meet you! Welcome, welcome!" She greeted us loudly with a huge smile, hugging each one of us to her ample bosom.

"This is my wife, Joanna," Joseph introduced her and then pointed to each child. "Eden is our oldest, of course, and then we have the twins, John and Jacob." He gestured to two stocky teenage boys who seemed to be close to our own age. "The next oldest is Elizabeth, and then Elon." These two girls couldn't have looked more opposite. Elizabeth was very tall and athletic-looking, and Elon was probably the smallest in the family as far as weight and stature went. She had flowers in her hair and on her tunic, and she smiled up at us in adoration. "And here is our youngest one, Esther." Joseph picked up a toddler hiding behind Elizabeth, and she hid her face in her father's shoulder.

"What a charming family!" I smiled.

"So many girls ..." I heard Kevin mutter behind me.

"I am sure you are hungry, so John and Jacob will take you quickly to your cabin," Joanna offered. "You may leave your belongings there and freshen up before the feast begins. Practically the entire village has gathered in the banquet hall for this occasion, so we will start as soon as you get there!" She clapped her hands then and said to her daughters, "Girls, come with me!"

The twin boys showed us our cabin; if I hadn't already been missing Camp Fusion, this would have done it. The cabin featured a general sitting area at the front with a door that led back to the sleeping quarters. I almost expected bunk beds as we moved to the back, but we were all surprised instead to find the room full of thick hammocks that hung from the ceiling.

"This is where we sleep?" Amelia asked, looking confused.

"Yes. There are ten bed-swings in here. There is another room on the other side that houses two larger bed-swings. That is usually where the parents sleep when we have guests, but ... I do not know how you want to separate yourselves," one of the twins told us (I wasn't sure which one he was yet).

"Can we please all be together this time?" Kevin asked, and Amelia looked up expectantly. I exchanged looks with Morgan and Caleb and then looked to Gabriel, as I was sure he would have an opinion.

"Are there separate bathing rooms?" I asked hesitantly.

"Yes. There are four separate bathing rooms at the back. You will also find an armoire for each bed-swing," the other twin answered us.

"Let's all stay in here! Please? I don't want to be separated again," Amelia pleaded. I didn't blame her for feeling that way. Being in such a foreign place had me wanting my friends nearby as well.

"That's fine. It's only for one night, right?" I gave in.

"Two nights," Gabriel corrected. *Two nights?* Were we spending that much time in each village? I was never going to get back home …

"I must insist that I stay in the same room with you, Whitnee," Gabriel announced, and I didn't even argue. I had already guessed as much. "But Levi and Thomas are free to take the other room, if they would like."

"I will stay in here, too, if the Travelers do not mind," Thomas said. "Levi can have the other room, and when Tamir finally joins the group again, he can be in there with him."

"Awesome!" Kevin shouted and ran to a bed-swing. He threw himself on it with such enthusiasm that it flipped completely upside down and dumped him on the floor. This sent all of us into fits of laughter.

A little while later, we arrived at the banquet hall to find something we hadn't quite expected. First of all, the banquet hall was more like a building with huge kitchens where the food was prepared and set out for self-service. The "hall" part where the tables were set up was outside under an extensive covered patio. Beautiful trees and flower gardens lined the area. Where the Aerodorians used a lot of custom design and color in their architecture, the Geodorians' furniture and buildings were simple. The rich colors in the backdrop of nature were their only decoration. The Geos also dressed plainly and only embellished their appearances with flowers in their hair or around their necks. In fact, the only décor I noticed in the village was a set of green flags, similar to the Aeros' purple ones, except the symbol was not of a thunderfly. Rather, the Geos' symbol seemed to resemble a plant or tree. There was one vertical line with four triangles growing out of the top like the palm fronds on a tree. I was starting to notice a pattern. The Aerodorian symbol had four wings. The Pyradorian symbol I had seen on Gabriel's back had four rays coming out of its top. Now the Geodorians had four triangles … I wondered what the Hydrodorian symbol looked like.

Eden greeted us with sets of Pinkberry flowers. She threw long necklaces around the boys' necks. For Morgan, Amelia, and me, she and Elon had made wreaths of Pinkberries that they placed on top of our heads like crowns. I had never been to the Hawaiian Islands, but wasn't this kind of like the tradition of giving leis to visitors?

For the first time, I really felt like I was on some tropical Island about to attend a luau. And speaking of luaus … the rich smells that were coming out of the kitchen area were so intoxicating that we were all salivating. I could not believe how many people were there—how much food had been prepared? There were Geos even sitting out in the grassy areas, since all of the tables were taken. Everywhere I looked, tan faces with green eyes watched us curiously in the midst of their own conversations. We took our places at a table with Joseph and his family, and Joseph blew on a large conch shell to get everyone's attention.

Once the crowd had quieted, Joseph gave a formal speech about the "Travelers," including where we had come from and our names. I was grateful that he did not single me out in his

speech. He kept things simple. He thanked those who had prepared the meal for this festive occasion (to which everyone loudly
clapped and hollered in appreciation) and then announced that
after dinner, we would play "coconut launch."

This news, too, was greeted by many cheers. And with that,
he excused us as "the first Travelers on the Island in decades"
to go through the food line first. We were too hungry to argue,
so Eden led the way while the crowd filled in close behind. We
piled our plates high with meats, fruits, and desserts. I understood why the Geos, as a rule, seemed to be more overweight
than the lofty Aeros. If I had access to this kind of food all the
time, I would blow up like a balloon. I didn't recognize much
on my plate, but my sense of smell did not disagree with my
selections. So instead of asking questions, I just decided to go
for it—avoiding anything that remotely resembled a pickle or
mustard, of course.

Dinner was a happy and noisy occasion for the tribe. People
continuously greeted us as they moved past our table, and I
could not recall being asked so many questions about my home
since being on this Island. It seemed that in Aerodora we had
been isolated from talking too much with the people, and even
when we had gone out into the village, the Aeros' formality
kept them from questioning us too much. Geos did not seem to
care if their questions were too many or too personal; they asked
them anyway. I liked them for their straightforward nature and
simplicity.

Once people started noticing Caleb's green eyes, they
became obsessed with him. He was sitting across from me next
to Eden, and it had become obvious that they were two of a
kind. They laughed at the same jokes, and there never seemed
to be a lull in their conversation. She continued to introduce
him to new people, and he appeared to love the attention. Caleb
always had been a social butterfly in his own right.

As I listened to Caleb and Eden, I realized that back at home
I might have been jealous of the obvious connection between

them. For some reason, though, I was more amused with it and glad that he had someone on which to focus his attention other than me. Granted, he had been much better since Morgan had reprimanded both of us, but I hadn't forgotten his words of affection. I was just choosing not to think about them, and if Eden distracted him from those emotions, it was better off for me in the end. Besides, I could not see how anyone could ever hate Eden. She was unlike most girls my age in the sense that she wasn't putting on an act to impress anyone. She was independent, down-to-earth, and refreshing to be around.

Morgan, who had always loved babies, was holding little Esther and carrying on a vibrant conversation with Joanna on one side of her and Thomas on the other. Thomas did seem quite taken with Morgan, and it kind of bothered me that he so readily accepted her but not me. I wanted to like him and trust him, but I had my doubts. Morgan could get along with just about anybody, which was a wonderful trait; but the downside was that she could be too trusting, even when a person didn't deserve it. I vowed to keep an eye on Thomas when he was with my best friend. If there was one thing I was learning, it was that everybody on this Island had their own set of motivations, and it was not clear yet who was on our side.

Down the table, Amelia and Kevin had found friendship with Elizabeth, Jacob, and John, who apparently could not soak up enough information about the Mainland. They were particularly interested in the concept of video games, and I laughed inwardly as both sides tried to explain and understand the differences in their worlds.

On one side of me was the silent Gabriel, who spoke only when spoken to. He seemed to have much on his mind, and I could almost relate to him on that. Though there was much activity and merrymaking happening around me, I still felt like a distant observer. On the other side of me was little Elon, who had been trailing after me the whole evening, quiet and curious. Eden told me Elon was eight years old, but her delicacy made her appear younger. Her big green eyes just stole my heart, and she seemed mesmerized by my hair. Once I had finished eating, I let her play with braiding it. She wore a little dress that tied at her neck, leaving her frail, tan shoulders open. I could see the little birthmark on her right shoulder that matched the Geodorian symbol, a stick with four triangles sprouting out of the top. She removed a single white flower from her own hair and tucked it into my crown. It was the same shape as the Pinkberry.

"What is that flower called?" I asked her.

"Eden calls it Pureberry because it is pure white. It is my *favorite*," she smiled.

"You must really love flowers," I commented, returning her smile.

"Oh, yes. I want to create new flowers someday, but Eden says I still have much to learn," she told me seriously. "Your hair is so pretty... I wish I could grow a flower that color. It is not white. But it is not quite yellow, either." She scrunched her eyebrows as if concentrating on exactly how she could accomplish that.

"Perhaps someday you'll figure it out. I would love to see it, if you do!" I told her.

"Are you going to stay on the Island forever?" she questioned innocently, and I felt my very full stomach tense up a bit.

"Not forever, no. But for a while."

Then she threw her arms around my neck and gave me a hug. "I will work really hard then," she whispered and then excused herself to go play with her friends. I felt a twinge of guilt as I watched her skip away.

"It will be nearing twilight soon. They are beginning to set up for coconut launch," Joseph remarked, leaning back in his chair and patting his large belly in satisfaction. The tables were starting to clear out, and people were heading to a large field beyond the patio.

"Father, you know how to gift someone with the Earth life force, right?" Eden asked Joseph. "I think we should try gifting Caleb so he can learn how to play coconut launch with us!"

"I have never actually gifted someone. After all, it has been years and years since we have seen a Traveler, but I am aware of how it is done. What do you say, Caleb?" Joseph offered.

"Uh … I guess we could try. I mean, I would love to try, but what if I hurt somebody or damage something?" And he sent one involuntary glance my direction.

Joseph laughed. "That is difficult to do with the Earth force. Come here, young man. I will gift you, and Eden can instruct you on how to play." Joseph and Caleb stood to their feet; Gabriel and I were suddenly at attention. I was more than curious to see how gifting occurred. Even Morgan paused in her conversation to observe.

"From what I have read and heard, the actual transfer varies a little bit between each tribe. You place your hands like this." And he had Caleb hold his hands up, palms outward, while he placed his own palms against Caleb's as if they were about to play pattycake. "Keep your eyes open, and I will transfer life force to you. When your eyes light up, we shall know it worked." Joseph took a deep breath, and his lips moved as if he were speaking, only no sound came out. His eyes began to glow a bright green, reminding me of glow sticks. Then his palms lit up against Caleb's. Caleb's face registered shock, and he inhaled sharply as if in pain. His eyes became expressionless, giving the appearance that his mind was a million miles away.

"Caleb!" I cried and jumped up from my seat, scared that something was not right. He didn't seem to hear me, and I would have jumped over the table to him if Gabriel hadn't pulled me back.

"Just wait," he whispered as we both watched intensely. I could've sworn Caleb was not breathing, and if he didn't take a breath soon, I was going to put an end to this experiment. Nobody but Morgan and I seemed concerned. After a few more moments, Caleb's eyes began to illuminate, and his lips, too, began to move, forming silent words. That was when Joseph broke contact, and Caleb suddenly staggered backward and drew in deep breaths, his eyes returning to normal. I found that I had also been holding my breath, because I exhaled quickly, thankful that it was over.

"Wow!" he gasped.

"Are you okay?" I said, my voice coming out more choked than I had intended.

"I feel great! That was like nothing I've ever experienced before. This is going to sound so corny, but it feels like my body is in perfect harmony with everything around me," he told us.

"You're right. It does sound corny," I replied, allowing myself to smile. I don't know why that had scared me so badly. It wasn't like Joseph would have hurt him ...

"So, let us see if it worked!" Eden exclaimed. "The simplest task is to see if this plant will respond to you. Hold your hand out and imagine that you are communicating with the plant. If you truly have the life force within you, the language will come to you without words." She gestured to a plant growing in the grass near our table.

"Okay ..." Caleb held out his hand and closed his eyes to concentrate. We watched the plant carefully, and in a moment, it started waving its long leaves in Caleb's direction. It was the most unnatural way I'd ever seen a plant act. When Caleb opened his eyes, they were glowing again.

"You did it!" we all cried out, and Eden gave him a quick hug. Naturally, he hugged her back, but when his eyes fell on me, he pulled away quickly. I averted my gaze and found Gabriel studying my face quietly. I raised my eyebrows at him as if to say, *What?*

"Now we must teach you the rules of the game ..." Eden began. And then, without thinking, she turned to me and said, "Oh, Whitnee, you will want to listen to this, too, in case you want to play. Basically you start out on two teams ..." But when she saw the panicked look on my face at her slip, she trailed off. Fortunately, there was nobody but Joseph and his family left at our table. Everyone else had gone to the field to match up for the game. In fact, I was suddenly aware that Amelia and Kevin were no longer at the table, and that gave me an uneasy feeling. They must have left with the twins and Elizabeth. Joseph did not miss Eden's slip and so gazed at me expectantly.

"Is there something I am missing here about Whitnee?" he asked pointedly. We were all frozen for a moment, knowing we had just been busted. Gabriel glared at Eden, but instead of letting him get mad at her, I spoke.

"We fully intended to tell you, Joseph, when there was an opportune time…" I started, and then decided that instead of telling him, I would just show him. I walked over to the plant and placed a hand on the ground near the stem. I allowed the language of the Earth to speak within me and coaxed the plant to lengthen its long, green leaves. It agreed with me and did so. When I released my hand, everyone gasped at the now larger plant.

"That is advanced usage, Whitnee! How did you…?" Joseph looked completely taken aback.

"I don't know, sir," I answered as I automatically reached toward a half-empty glass of Water on the table. Bending over, I dumped the contents near the root of the plant.

"What are you doing?" Morgan asked.

"It's thirsty now," I explained in a matter-of-fact tone.

Joseph's eyes widened even more.

"The language just came to me last night. I'm just as surprised as you are." I looked around the group who had surrounded me. Each one seemed to be in awe, except for Gabriel.

"Last night? Why did you not say so in our meeting?" Joseph was still looking shell-shocked.

"Nobody knew except Gabriel," I told him meekly. "We felt it better to wait until… well, we just weren't sure what to do about it. I did not completely lie, though. The Wind does come most naturally to me." I peered carefully into his face, waiting for his response. That was when he let out a hearty laugh and threw a heavy arm around me.

"Well, you are not only a Daughter of the Wind, but a Child of the Earth too! Oh, wait until Ezekiel hears this…" He chuckled as if this thought gave him great joy.

"Joseph, if you would please allow me to inform the others—" Gabriel started.

"You know, I knew you children were keeping a secret from me. Eden, you should know better…" He gave her a warning look, but his smile was still in place. "Gabriel, I trust that you will let the rest of the Council know of this change before she leaves the village. Let us speak no more of it and go play coconut launch! This is truly a night to remember!" And he took off, one arm around Joanna, who had kindly taken Esther from Morgan's arms.

I noticed nobody informed him that I could use more than just the Wind and Earth, but I guessed that would come later… Before we followed, I grabbed Caleb and Morgan by the arm.

"Where are Kevin and Amelia?" Judging by their reactions, they hadn't noticed them missing. "Now that we are surrounded by villagers, we have *got* to keep an eye on them. And they need to know not to wander away from us, no matter how comfortable they feel!"

"I'm sure they're with Elizabeth and the boys," Morgan said. And with that thought, we followed quickly after the departing group.

COCONUT LAUNCH

Imagine a game of dodgeball, only played with airborne coconuts instead of balls and individual force fields instead of actual dodging. That would sum up coconut launch in a nutshell. (Or should I say "coconut shell"?) The villagers divided into two teams, and huge piles of coconuts still in their husks rested ominously at the center of the field. The grass had been coaxed into growing higher along the center of the field, creating a natural line for the teams not to cross. The goal was to get people out of the game by smacking them with a coconut. Sounds brutal, right? But the Geos are able to conjure translucent green shields around their own bodies to protect from getting hit. The difficulty was that in order to launch a coconut, your shield had to be down. Shields caused you to become stationary, and you couldn't help your team in that position.

"Can't people get hurt in a game like this?" I asked Thomas, who stood on the sidelines with Morgan and me.

"Oh, yes!" he exclaimed excitedly like a typical guy at a violent sporting event.

I watched Caleb move hesitantly out on the field with Eden. His team cheered for him and slapped him on the back. He had conjured something of a shield a little while ago when Eden was trying to give him very quick lessons, but it hadn't stayed up for very long. I was a little worried about him and hoped the villagers would know to go easy on him.

"I guess it can't be any worse than paintball," Morgan commented.

"Uh, I'm pretty sure a coconut to the head could knock you out, Morgie," I replied nervously.

"Well, a paintball to the head isn't a good thing, either," she pointed out. "Don't worry. I'm sure Eden won't let him get hurt," she assured me and then whispered near my ear, "What is wrong with you? You are really on edge tonight."

"I know ... I'm sorry. I guess I'm just missing home," I confessed, even though it wasn't the complete truth. She tucked her arm in mine and leaned in toward me comfortingly. How could I explain to her all the thoughts running through my mind? I hadn't told anyone about my conversation with Abrianna that morning and, once again, I was struck by just how long the days felt here. My mind felt like it needed rest more than my body did.

Amelia and Kevin waved to us from the other side of the large field, and I forced a smile and waved back. I desperately wished they would stay by my side, especially with that dark wall of trees behind that side of the field. But they seemed to be having fun. We had found them earlier, and Morgan and Caleb informed me that I had been a bit harsh with them about running off without telling us where they were going. My friends didn't know half of what I did about the potential dangers on this Island, and I didn't want to worry them with it. But just because they were becoming more and more acquainted with the people here didn't mean they should relax on their watchfulness. Even Caleb and Morgan were acting as if it was totally natural that we were here in this village, away from all that was normal in our world. They had been the ones to react the least to my cyclone earlier today, and now they were telling me that I was too uptight ...

Perhaps Gabriel's paranoia was rubbing off on me. This thought had me scanning the sidelines unsuccessfully for him. Come to think of it, it had been a while since I had seen Levi too. I wondered if Tamir had returned by now.

Before I could give it another thought, the conch shell blew and the game began. The players ran to the center, grabbed coconuts, and began launching at the other side. Shield after shield appeared, and coconuts glanced off the Geos' hazy green force fields. Every once in a while, someone on the sideline would throw out a shield to protect the onlookers from rogue coconuts.

The first time a coconut was launched so forcefully at a shield that it exploded, spraying everyone around it with coconut juice, the crowd went nuts. I learned that if a coconut actually broke apart on your shield, you could rescue one team member who was already out. Caleb happened to be near the explosive coconut and looked stunned at the sticky sweetness dripping off him.

"Caleb, look out!" Morgan and I screamed at the same time. One of the twins had thrown a coconut his direction. Thanks to our warning, he deflected it with his shield just in time. We cheered loudly and jumped up and down in excitement. It was impossible to not become immersed in this game. Eden was knocking people out like crazy. It was obvious she was very good at this game, mostly because she could launch and protect back and forth very quickly. It took her no time to recover, and she was constantly moving and dodging coconuts. Caleb was a little slow at first, but his natural athleticism seemed to kick in eventually. His shield became increasingly more powerful and steady as the game went on.

Finally, the conch shell was blown, signaling a time out for both teams. During the time out, several torches along the field were lit to provide more light in the gathering dusk. Water was brought out for the remaining players to drink while they strategized.

"Do you remember how intense dodgeball could be in elementary school?" I asked Morgan.

"Oh my gosh, yes! I don't think dodgeball's even allowed anymore at my old school. It got too dangerous ... this is kind of like that, huh?" Morgan laughed.

"Oh, look! Caleb's waving at us!" I gave him a thumbs-up, and Morgan waved back. I loved the way he ran his hands through his hair when he was "in the zone" like that. Such a Caleb-ism. Having been a spectator at many of his sports games, I knew this was a sign of his concentration and love for a good game.

"Yeah, he's sweating bullets out there," Morgan mumbled.

"*Mmmhmm*," I nodded with a laugh. "Wonder how long his life force will last? Hopefully until the game is over ..."

"Please tell me about this dodgeball that you are talking about ..." Thomas joined our conversation. Morgan directed her attention to him and explained dodgeball and paintball. I took a few steps away from her, still scanning for Gabriel. Caleb broke away from his team huddle suddenly and ran toward me.

"Hey there, coconut boy!" I greeted him. He wiped one sticky hand on my arm. "Gross, Caleb!"

"Listen, I really think you should screw this whole secrecy thing and come play ... it's so much fun, and I could really use some help out there." He winked at me.

"Um, I don't know ..." I hesitated, wondering where the heck Gabriel had gone. What would he think of that idea?

"Come on, Whit ..." Caleb pleaded, attempting to pull me out onto the field.

"Go, Whitnee!" Morgan cheered. "You can do it!"

"I don't know how to do the shield thing," I protested. "It might not be a good idea—"

"I'll teach you," Caleb promised, and soon more people around us noticed what was happening and started chanting for me to join the game.

"Great, Caleb ... look what you started." I gave him an exasperated look.

"Get in the game, Whitnee!" Eden shouted above the growing cheers from the sidelines. *Oh, geez.* I was stuck now. How could I explain to the Islanders that I was not very athletic and terrified of experiencing pain ... especially in the form of a coconut detonating in my face? With an unsure sigh, I gave in and stopped pulling away. With a loud whoop, Caleb picked me up off my feet and spun me around in front of everybody. He smelled like coconut juice and fresh sweat, and in the excitement of the moment with the crowd chanting around us, he planted a quick, rough kiss on my cheek before setting me down.

"She's in! Let's go!" he yelled like nothing out of the ordinary had just happened. Utterly stunned, I allowed him to lead me to the huddle. The cheering had become an uproar. I may have appeared blank on the outside, but I was certainly screaming on the inside. Caleb's lips had just been on my face ... my friend, Caleb Austin! And he did it in front of all these people! What the *heck*! I didn't know how to react and, fortunately, the game was about to start up again, so I didn't have much time to think about what had just happened.

Briefly, Caleb explained the shield to me, and before I knew it, I was thrust out onto a field of flying coconuts. I ran around dodging the coconuts at first like I had unsuccessfully dodged balls in elementary school. I narrowly dodged a few that had glanced off the shields of team members.

"Watch it, Whitnee!" Eden called, and I moved to the side as one particularly angry coconut came at me. Unfortunately, though, it had cost Eden to look out for me. She got nailed in the side with a coconut and was ruled as an out. The crowd booed, but the launching didn't stop. I finally noticed the twins across the field were the ones aiming at me. I was so worried about attempting a shield that I sidestepped and moved behind other players to keep away from the offensive fruit.

Is coconut even a fruit?

Quickly, I picked up a coconut from the ground and threw it as far as I could ... which didn't turn out to be very far. I could hear Morgan cheering me on from the sidelines. Even Amelia and Kevin's voices rang out over the crowd. I was in total survival mode.

Caleb was actually doing pretty well, and we wove in and around each other. Finally, I saw one of the twins launch a large coconut at me, and there was no way I could dodge this one. I held out one hand to protect my face, praying in vain for the shield to come up around me ...

BANG! The coconut splattered across the glowing, transparent, green block that had appeared an inch in front of my face. The crowd screamed and yelled. Whether they were excited about my shield or the violence of a coconut obliterating itself that close to my face, I didn't know. I was just happy I had done it! And on top of that, the coconut had split into several pieces, spraying the crowd with juice, and allowing me to get someone back in the game.

"Eden!" I yelled, and kept playing while she skipped happily back onto the field.

"That was amazing, Whitnee!" she called.

"Well, it's nothing like what you can do ... !" I called back, and then we scattered to avoid a squadron of flying coconuts. I ended up deflecting a few more before one finally hit me in the arm with quite a bit of force. Again, the crowd booed, but I was actually happy to be done with the game. It was too intense out there, like being on a battlefield. I ran off the field to where Morgan and Thomas were, and that's when I finally spotted Gabriel. He was standing in the back watching the scene, a sour look on his face. Morgan ran to me, jumping up and down enthusiastically.

"So cool, Whit! Your shield was perfect and ... ouch! Doesn't that hurt?" She examined my arm. A huge red splotch was forming, and I knew it would quickly turn black and blue.

"It's not great, but I can go take care of it pretty quickly back at the cabin," I told her quietly with a cautious glance at Thomas.

"Oh, okay ... do you want me to come with you?" she asked.

"No ... stay here and cheer Caleb on. Gabriel's right back there. I'll make him go with me and be back before the game's even over!" I told her, moving away from the crowd to Gabriel's isolated watching place. He was glaring at me with so much anger that I almost decided to change my plan and go alone.

"You are hurt," he growled, stating the obvious.

"It's really not as bad as it looks, but I should probably go fix it," I told him, trying to make light of the throbbing pain beginning to shoot up my arm. But his face only darkened, so I said somewhat tartly, "I was going to ask you to come with me to the cabin, but maybe you should stay here and calm down instead ..." And I turned away from him to head toward the banquet hall and, ultimately, the cabin right beyond. Though he didn't say anything, he fell into silent step with me, and I was very aware of his body heat radiating my direction. I was learning to read the signs when he was upset. Higher body temperature was an indication that something had really gotten him worked up. I waited for him to say something more as we trekked in silence, the rowdy villagers' chants and cheers fading out the further away we moved. Finally I could stand it no more. I launched into a defensive tirade.

"I'm sorry if you don't like the choice I made to go play in the game. I just don't see the point in hiding all of this, especially since Joseph was already aware ... and where were *you*? I didn't see you trying to stop me or give me any advice about what to do! Besides, it wasn't like anyone started chanting 'pilgrim' just because I could use the Earth life force in a game of coconut launch. And it was actually kind of fun, except the part where that stupid coconut hit me. But *come on*, I was bound to get hurt in the game, just like everyone who gets out! You don't see Eden crying about the pain on her way off the field.

It's part of the game—*big freaking deal.* I can heal it on my own. It's not life threatening! So, whatever it is that you're mad at me about ... you can just *get over it*! I'm sick of playing by your rules." I finished with a huff and didn't realize that my pace had picked up speed as I spoke. We were passing the empty banquet hall, and I grabbed a Water bottle as I stormed my way through the building and outside again to the cabin.

"Fine." Gabriel spoke in that dangerously calm voice.

"Fine? That's all you can say to that? *Fine?*" I screeched. I didn't even wait to be in the privacy of the cabin before I uncorked the bottle and guzzled the Water down in a very unladylike fashion. The frustrations of the day were taking their toll on me. I allowed the cold Water to trickle through my system and do its work on my bruise. Most of the icy sensation centered near my upper arm where the coconut had hit me.

He shrugged at my outburst as he took long strides beside me. "If you do not want to play by my rules, as you so eloquently put it, then *fine!*" He spat his words at me. "If you really are the *Pilgrim*, then what is stopping you from just telling *me* what to do?" He raised his voice at me for the first time, and I stopped my marching and took several steps away from him. "Is that why you came here, Whitnee? For power? There is nothing you cannot do on your own, right? So take it! It is all yours to control, is it not?"

I was taken aback. "What are you *saying*?" I cried out in anger. "You think *I* am after power and control? Take a good look at yourself, Gabriel! How do I know you're not just using me? After all, you're the one who's keeping secrets from the Council and the Guardian and ... how could you say that about *me*? Do you think I like what's happening to me here?" I pointed viciously at my eyes which I was sure were glowing a fierce blue right now. "I am a complete freak of nature, and I don't understand why *I* would have these abilities. Why would the Island choose me? What exactly am I supposed to do here?"

"Well, I am sure once you and your friends leave here, it will no longer matter to you. This is all still just a dream to you, is it not? You care nothing for this Island or for the people or … for me!" he yelled, and I could feel nothing but that whirlwind of fury welling up in me at his words.

With a shout of frustration, I released a powerful gust of the coldest Wind I could muster in his direction, but the Fire within him must have been just as close to the surface, because he counteracted it with a ball of flame. The two forces were evenly matched and briefly met in an explosion of flame and steam before disappearing. I took a step toward him and released another furious gust. He buffered it again, taking a step closer to me.

"You obviously don't know me!" I yelled at him. The crown of flowers blew off my head in the frigid Wind tunnel I had created around myself. Actual flames were issuing from his hands as we faced each other in an apparent standoff.

"I could say the same about you, Whitnee! You know nothing about me or the way I feel about you!" he shouted over the whistling Wind.

"Oh, that's rich!" I mocked with a bitter laugh. "Is this your master plan? Make me think I'm something special to you and then manipulate me into helping you gain ultimate control over the Island? I won't be a part of that, Gabriel! So don't even try!" I could feel tears starting to form in my eyes, and my vortex of Wind was losing some of its power. It hurt to know I was just being used.

"Where are you getting these ridiculous ideas?" He looked frustrated, but all I could feel was a cracking wall of ice in my heart. After all, Abrianna had warned me about him … "From Caleb? I know he does not trust me, even though I have done everything I can to keep you safe here. You could have at least been honest with me about your relationship with *him!*" Gabriel's eyes were still glowing gold and, with anger slashing across his face, he appeared more intimidating than I had ever found him before.

"Wait... *what*?" I shook my head, trying to make sense of his words. What did Caleb have to do with it? I relaxed my guard for just a moment. That was all it took—Gabriel was upon me in a flash. He captured my wrists roughly in his heated hands.

"You and Caleb!" he roared. "I had picked up on his feelings for you from the start, but I did not realize... you feel the same way for him! Like a fool, I had started to believe that perhaps you felt something for me!" His words cut right through me, and his close presence was overwhelming. I swallowed and tried mirroring his hateful expression.

"Caleb is just my friend—" I started.

"Do not lie to me!" He shook me slightly. "I saw him kiss you on the field! I see how comfortable you are with him... how you feel more at ease when he is near. I see how protective you are—"

"That's called friendship, you jerk! If you had any real friends, you would know that!" I knew I was being hateful, but he had struck a sensitive spot. I didn't want to think about Caleb right then.

"What exactly is required of me to be *your* friend, Whitnee? I am the one sent to guide you, and I have done everything I can to help you. Yet it is only *him* whom you trust!"

Did he really not know what I was feeling for *him*? I was torn between angry mistrust and desperate longing for him.

"I *want* to trust you. But how can I when there is so much I don't understand?" I cried out hoarsely. "What exactly do you *want* from me, Gabriel? If you want me to be your stupid Pilgrim, fine! I'll be the answer to your prophecy! If you want me to go home, then send me home! I'm tired of the games we're playing. Just tell me what you want!"

He glared at me fiercely, and without another word, his mouth came crashing down on mine in a forceful kiss. It took only a breathtaking moment to realize what was happening before all the anger and confusion between us melted into one lake of passion. In that moment, it was more than just a kiss; the two elements within us physically collided. It was Fire against Wind, which only seemed to build into a hot windstorm of emotion that could set aflame the entire forest surrounding us. I lost all sense of reason as his lips crushed against mine.

FIERY FEELINGS

Somehow I became aware that one of his hands had moved to my back, pressing me closer to him. The other had tangled itself in my windblown hair, locking me in place. There was no escape, even if I had wanted one. My hands finally felt free to run through his beautiful dark curls while his lips felt feverish against my own. It occurred to me somewhere in the back of my mind that this was wrong ... I couldn't get any more involved or attached to this guy. But when his kiss was so demanding and insistent ... I temporarily lost my willpower to fight him off. I could almost taste the Fire within him, and the contrast of temperature between us only heightened my awareness of him.

And speaking of temperature, I was becoming aware of the Fire that was starting to spread throughout me. As the heat grew to dangerously high temperatures, I felt like I couldn't breathe. This *definitely* needed to stop ...

"Gabriel," I sighed, but taking that as encouragement, he only kissed me harder. I wanted to push him away so I could think clearly, but *dang*, he was a good kisser. My body temperature began to match his, and I could no longer feel any sort of Wind within me. The blood coursing through my veins became like lava, seeking a way out of its prison. "Gabriel ..."

I murmured and tried to pull away, removing my glowing hands from his hair and fisting them into the front of his tunic.

I could just shove him off... if only I could make my reluctant body cooperate with my mind. Either he wasn't hearing me or he didn't care. My eyes suddenly fluttered wide open, and the explosion of Fire left my hands before I could stop it.

Bright blue flames emanated out of my palms, which had previously been pushing against his chest. I heard myself scream and felt his body vanish as he was propelled several feet away from me by the force of what I had conjured. A bright flash of orange engulfed his entire body—as soon as I realized that it was *me* throwing flames at *him*, I dropped my hands in a silent scream. The blue flames died, but the orange wall up in front of him remained a moment longer. What had I done? Had I just set him on Fire? I stared in horror. *Oh my gosh, oh my gosh, oh my—*

The orange wall disappeared as if turned off by a switch, and there he was, standing there in the darkness. His chest was heaving, but he didn't appear to be burned or hurt in any way. I began to gasp for breath then, too, and leaned over, hands on my knees. We stared at each other, both panting for air, unable to speak. Only the golden flames illuminating our eyes cast light in the darkness separating us.

In an effort to calm down, I ran my burning hands across my face and hid my expression there for a moment. My lips felt bruised and swollen. When I peered out again, Gabriel took one step toward me.

"Don't!" I held out a hand, not to threaten him with any more fighting, but as a warning. "Don't come near me... I can't believe... what just happened! I mean, you just—" I took in another deep breath and stared at him wide-eyed. "I could have just killed you!" I wasn't sure what scared me more—the fact that I had lost control of a life force or of my own hormones. His face broke into a tentative smile then, and I frowned in confusion at his reaction.

"I promise it will take more than a kiss to kill me," he said in a low voice. I desperately wished he would not sound so sexy and confident. He took another step, and my stomach flipped.

"You are so not allowed to do that again..." I told him breathlessly at the same time I mentally told myself to *shut up*. That was the most amazing kiss ever.

He came another step closer. *Move back, Whitnee. Don't let him come near you until you can process all of this*, the smart girl inside me said. It wasn't working. My body refused to obey me, which allowed him another step closer to me.

"Please," I begged softly. "I'm really confused right now." His eyes never left my face as their glow started to extinguish like the embers of a dying campfire. Likewise, I could feel my own body releasing the Fire life force and returning to normal. And that's when the fatigue hit me again. Only this time it almost knocked me over, and I think Gabriel could visibly see the moment my strength gave out.

Shoot! I had used all four life forces again. It was too much, and I knew it this time. I had to lie down before I passed out here on the dirt road. I spun around and stumbled in the direction of the cabin, but my body was shutting down on me. I was vaguely aware that I wouldn't make it.

Without a word, Gabriel scooped me into his arms before I could fall. I wanted to kick and scream at him to let me go. I could walk on my own. I didn't need his help.

But I did need him then, and we both knew it. Ever so carefully, he carried me inside the cabin and back to the room with all the bed-swings. As gently as if I were a breakable doll, he laid me down in one of the swings, cradling my head and smoothing back my hair. I could feel my eyes closing and wondered if this was the moment I had finally overdone it with these powers. It wasn't that I was experiencing any pain. In fact, the absence of pain or feeling was what concerned me. There was only the darkness of sleep that threatened to take over.

"Try to stay awake," he commanded me, and I saw concern and a little bit of fear distorting his beautiful features. He left me there for a moment and then the next thing I knew, he was holding a bottle of Water to my lips. I tried to take a sip, but ended up choking on it. "Come on, Whitnee. You must drink! It is the only element that will replenish your body!" I could sense his urgency, but I couldn't even pull myself up. I didn't want to drink anything, do anything ... I just wanted to fade into the abyss of nothingness. With a grunt, he pulled my upper body off the hanging mattress and sat behind me where I could lean against his chest. His arms came around me from behind, one holding the bottle to my mouth and the other cradling my head in an upright position. "Drink, Little One. Please!" he whispered.

I tried again and flinched as the icy liquid poured into my mouth. I swallowed the Water in small doses, groaning as the cold traced its path through my system once again. This was all we focused on for a while ... him patiently helping me take small sips, and me fighting back the drowsiness that I so desperately wanted to give in to.

Slowly, I could feel my arms and legs again. And while the heavy sleepiness had lifted a bit, I grew very cold and began shaking uncontrollably. It felt like the Water had poured awareness back into my body but left ice patches everywhere. Gabriel seemed satisfied with my progress and placed the almost-empty bottle down on the floor.

"It's so c-cold ..." My teeth chattered. I expected him to get up and get me a blanket, but instead he drew me into the natural warmth of his own body. His large arms wrapped around me, creating a cocoon of heat around my shivers. I leaned my head to the side, where it rested comfortably in the pocket of his solid upper arm and chest. I could feel his heart beating with every breath he took, and I focused on that as the chilly tremors rocked my body. It was another while before they subsided and the warmth crept back in. The sweetness of him holding me like that in comfortable silence was such a contrast to the dynamic explosion of desire we had experienced outside. I wasn't even sure which I enjoyed more…

Finally, he spoke.

"I never expected to feel these emotions toward you," he confessed, his voice coming out above my ear. I could not see his face, but he sounded tormented in some way.

"What emotions?" I prompted him in a timid voice.

He was quiet for a little bit as he seemed to think about what to say. I could hear his heartbeat pick up. "I know that Pyras are given to emotion, but I was raised away from my home village. I was taught to approach all situations with logic and reason, instead of giving in to fleeting emotion. A good leader does not lose control." He stated this in a very matter-of-fact tone. "But with you … I feel more out of control than ever before. It makes me angry when you question my authority and when you actually have the courage to use your life force against me."

I could hear a faint smile touch his words then, but he grew solemn again. "I hate losing so much sleep at night, just fearing that you will disappear. I do not trust anyone else to protect you, and I get angry at the thought of someone hurting you while you are here. I feel frustrated when I do not understand your world—especially when Caleb knows you in ways that I cannot, because you are both from the same place. I have to watch every expression on your face just to figure out what you are really thinking." He stopped, and I couldn't decide if this was jealousy in him talking or if my presence just really bothered him.

"It sounds like all I do is make you angry…" I observed.

"Anger is the only *explainable* emotion, I suppose. There is something about you that I cannot resist, Whitnee. You were supposed to be nothing more than an assignment for me. One more situation to handle in my long list of lifelong duties for the Guardian … but then there you were in the water that day, looking completely lost and confused. I did not expect that." I could hear a smile in his voice then as he remembered. "I also did not expect you to be so young and so …"

"So what?" I prompted quietly, curious to hear more.

"So feisty," he finished, and I smiled to myself as I felt him chuckle.

"You're not the first to accuse me of that," I said weakly. "What exactly were you expecting that day?" I questioned, and he became serious again.

"I suppose if I want you to trust me, I should explain some of this to you."

"It would help," I admitted with a weak sigh.

He sighed, too, and began, "Abrianna only told me that an important Traveler, one who could be the Pilgrim, would be arriving soon, and I was to camp out on the Southern Beach and wait for you. How she knew this was never made very clear. I knew you would be a girl, and that was about it. She told me I was the only one she could trust to deliver you safely and promptly to her. You were never supposed to go to any of the villages. No one was ever supposed to know you were here."

"So ... how did all of that get so messed up?"

"I asked myself that over and over that first day. It began when you told me you had friends that might have transported with you. I could not just whisk you away to the Palladium until we had located all the Travelers. It was a complication I had not prepared for and even Abrianna had not expected. And then you grew sick, and I knew you had ingested too much ocean water. But your reaction was so severe, so life-threatening. It scared me." He took a deep breath before continuing. "I pulled you into the shade, but instead of taking the time to carry you to the tent, I left you there while I ran to get Water. I only had enough time to send Abrianna a brief message through the zephyra saying that I had found you, but there were potential complications and I would contact her later. Then the rest of the story you know already."

"You came back for me and found Caleb there ... then the thunderfly incident ... and somewhere in there, Ezekiel must have sent that message to you. But wait—" I paused thoughtfully. "How did Ezekiel know about me if Abrianna had kept it a secret?"

"I believe Ezekiel has been sensing for quite some time that Abrianna was hiding something important. I found out later that he had been monitoring my zephyra, and that is how he learned about our plans."

"Like a phone tap? Is that allowed here?"

"I do not know what a phone tap is."

"It's where someone listens in on your conversations without you knowing about it."

"Then, yes. That is what he was doing."

"Why would my arrival have anything to do with him, though?"

"I am still trying to discover the real answer to that. Abrianna believes he just wants his hand in every important matter."

"But what do you believe?" I asked, sensing his doubt.

"I do not know yet." He paused, and I desperately wished I could see his face. "There is something going on that I fear even I do not know about."

"And you think Ezekiel has something to do with that?"

"Perhaps. Abrianna warned me at the start of all this that he might try to sabotage your purpose here—just another reason why I was to take you straight to her. Now I simply do not know what to think."

That caused both of us to fall silent, absorbed with our own separate thoughts. I really believed Gabriel was telling me the truth, and I felt a deeper connection with him. I'm sure the physical closeness we had experienced had something to do with that, but that also seemed to have opened up some vulnerability within him that I hadn't been able to reach up to this point. I traced the contours of his forearm absently with my fingers and wondered where all of this left us.

"Gabriel," I started and then stopped, not sure how to phrase what was in my heart. "My feelings for Caleb … they're not like … I mean, what happened outside with you and me—"

He didn't say anything, but his body had become very still. "Look, no matter what I think I might be feeling for you, I *can't* give in to that."

"I know," he whispered.

"We come from two totally different worlds."

"I know."

"There's nothing ahead of us but a good-bye," I finished sadly, because I knew it was the truth. I had finally found the proverbial knight in shining armor, and he wasn't even from my own world! He heaved a great sigh and tightened his arms around me.

"Good-bye is not here yet. And I will not give up until that day comes," he stated firmly. I found myself wanting to believe him. I clasped my hands over his and leaned to the side, so I could tilt my face up to look at him behind me.

"I am sorry for losing my temper," I whispered, meeting his eyes, which looked surprisingly darker at that moment. His response was to dip his face down to mine and brush his lips tantalizingly across mine, leaving a delicate kiss at the corner of my mouth.

"I am sorry for my ridiculous accusations," he said tenderly. "We start afresh from this point forward. How are you feeling now?"

"*Mmmm* ... not really sure when you kiss me like that," I replied fuzzily. "I think I feel able to walk, though."

"The Water seems to work faster on you than on the rest of us. We will need to keep plenty around if you are to continue mastering the life forces," he commented thoughtfully, then said, "I imagine the game should be over soon, if it has not ended already." That caused me to sit up straight. *The game!* I had completely forgotten about everything and everyone else around me! Oh my gosh, what if someone had walked in on us like this? What if *Caleb* had seen us? It didn't exactly look good for me to be sharing a bed-swing with Gabriel ... What was I doing? As much as I absolutely loathed leaving the warmth of his embrace and the physical and emotional closeness we were sharing, I knew I had to get up.

"We need to go!" I exclaimed. I believe he realized, too, that our time had ended. We both had responsibilities and appearances to maintain. Speaking of appearances... "I need to go to the bathing room first," I told him as I slowly stood up on wobbly legs. He stood up also, stretching his long body out, and I tried not to look at him differently. Tried not to remember the way that body felt pressed in close to mine. Tried to resist the now comfortable urge to reach out and touch his muscular stomach ... *yeah, okay. Enough of that.* I fumbled around for my leather satchel on my way to the bathing room and prayed I didn't look as bad as I felt.

The small mirror in the bathroom confirmed my fears. I truly looked like I had walked through a violent storm and barely lived to tell about it. My hair was tangled and my face pallid. With trembling hands, I combed through my long hair until it felt smooth and soft again. I splashed Water on my face and used the powerful mouthwash to freshen up. I wasn't exactly a work of art, but it was somewhat of an improvement. I think I was starting to understand that using a life force drained my body in the same way extreme physical exertion did. And that made me believe that in the same way I could train my body to handle more physical activity, I could build mental and physical power over each element if I kept at it. It was just so hard to know how to control the amount of energy I used.

My thoughts were interrupted by a loud commotion at the front of the cabin. Weakly, I gathered my stuff and padded back into the room. Gabriel wasn't there, but the door leading out to the sitting area was wide open and I could hear shouts and scuffling. Something was wrong. I could sense the tension in the air before I even entered the room.

I observed several things at once in the scene unfolding before me. Gabriel was shouting instructions, Morgan was crying, Eden was trying to reassure her, Thomas and Joseph were carrying a limp body—and that's when everyone else faded in my peripheral vision. It was Caleb. They were carrying Caleb's lifeless body. It was his bloodied face that filled my vision.

"Whitnee!" Morgan cried. "Caleb's been hurt!"

HEALING THE HARD-HEADED

Caleb was unresponsive as they laid him down on a bed-swing. I pushed through the group without thinking and knelt by his side. There was a gash across his right temple, and blood continued to creep down his face and neck into his tunic. I reached out and tried to wipe the blood on his cheek away. I could only register snatches of the chaos going on around me as I surveyed the damage.

"...We need the HydroHealer for this one..."

"His shield didn't work..."

"If I had seen that coconut coming I would have stopped it. It happened so fast—"

"Is he breathing?"

"Get some Water!"

"Whitnee, I need you to move!" This was Gabriel—he practically picked me up off the floor and moved me aside. "Thomas, what can you do for him?"

"I am a Purifier, not a Healer, Gabriel..." He sighed, and I turned my attention on him. He looked anxious, shaken. But couldn't all Hydros heal? Surely he could do something here! "I could try to seal the wound and stop the flow of blood, but that is not something that I have ever been very accomplished at. And even if the cut is sealed, it will take someone with more experience to heal the internal wound. A cut on the head does not make you lose consciousness. There is some kind of damage beneath—"

"Like a concussion?" I interjected and received only confused looks from the Dorians in the room. "It's like a bump or bruise to your brain … it's totally treatable. Right?" I looked for confirmation from Morgan who only came to my side and tucked her arm into mine. I could feel her shaking as she cried softly. I refused to break down about this. I lived in the modern world where medicine could fix anything. These kinds of injuries happened all the time in sports—in my world, this was fixable. Surely, with all these life force powers, these people could handle such an injury just as well.

"Father just stepped out to contact a HydroHealer …" Eden told us. "We usually have one who lives here locally, but she has gone back to Hydrodora to visit family. It could be several hours before someone can get here …"

"Thomas? Can you do this?" Gabriel prompted.

Thomas looked unsure of himself, but said, "I will try my best. I will need Water—"

"Let Whitnee do it!" Morgan cried out suddenly. Everyone in the room paused, and my eyes met Gabriel's.

He was shaking his head. "She is exhausted. She has done too much already today. It will have to be Thomas."

"Gabriel, I'm sorry, but I think Whitnee should do it," Morgan insisted, and she turned to me with tears in her eyes. "You can heal, Whit. And remember when Caleb got a mild concussion playing football in ninth grade? You remember how it was … we were so scared, we researched everything on the Internet … you remember, don't you?" Her voice was quavering, and I nodded to show her I remembered. "Can't you use that knowledge to heal him?"

I protested, "Morgie, I think Thomas would do a better job. And once the HydroHealer gets here—"

"No!" she practically shouted through her sobs. "He's *our* Caleb ... you wouldn't let anything happen to him. I know you wouldn't!" I glanced again at Gabriel, who watched our exchange with uncertainty. Morgan was so upset, and it was unlike her to be so adamant about something like this. "Whitnee, look at me." I flicked my eyes back to her distraught face. "I believe in you. I absolutely believe you are the Pilgrim, and you can help him ... *you* have to do this ... please."

My best friend believed I was the Pilgrim. I felt tears spring to my eyes.

"Morgie, I can't—" I started.

"Yes, you can. Do it for Caleb." She pulled me to the side of the bed-swing, pushing Thomas aside. "Somebody give her some Water!" she called, and Gabriel moved across from us on the other side of the bed-swing. We peered at each other while Eden ran for Water. There was hesitation in his face, but he gave me a short nod.

"Gabriel, are you serious about letting her try this?" Thomas asked. It was clear he did not like this idea any more than he liked the idea of attempting it himself.

"Thomas, you just stand there and watch what she can do," Morgan snapped at him. "Have some faith."

"Morgan ..." I tried again to protest.

"She is right, Whitnee," Gabriel declared softly. I jerked my head to stare at him in surprise. There was a quiet reserve and confidence in his face and a sense of peace stole over me. "Only use a necessary amount of energy. You do not need to heal him all the way if you start feeling ..." He paused and then finished, "Take your time and only go as far as you can."

Eden came running back in with the Water, Joseph and Joanna right behind her. She handed the bottle to me and the room grew quiet. I stared at Caleb for a moment before I did anything. His face was so pale against the dark red blood. He still hadn't moved, and I ignored the terror that threatened to choke me. I could not break down. The emotion could not control me. I had to stay focused.

Gabriel carefully shifted Caleb's head so that I could more easily reach him. One of my hands was already coated in his blood. With the other hand, I gently ran my fingers along his hairline, and his face felt cooler than I was expecting. Unnaturally cool. Quickly, I poured out some Water, which immediately became murky red as it mixed with his blood in my hands. I could hear Morgan suck in her breath as I moved my dripping hands toward Caleb's head. This time I did not close my eyes, but kept them open as I focused on the sensation of iciness pouring itself out into Caleb's wound. I was aware of the liquid sensation coursing through my own body as the element came to life within me. In my mind, I envisioned the Water's purities soaking down deep through Caleb's skin and the hard exterior of his skull. I knew that the tender matter that made up Caleb's brain was just below that, swimming in some kind of fluid. I imagined the healing properties of the Water flooding into that fluid as it cushioned his brain. And that's when something happened that I did not expect... I felt pain there.

His brain was throbbing painfully, and somehow another kind of connection forged between my body and Caleb's. There was another element at work here. I felt his pain as if it were inside my own body. It was talking to me, crying out in agony, asking for help. I started speaking back... but not aloud and not with human words. It was just a language I knew. Could it be that the language of the Earth was at work here also? It was unexplainable and yet understandable to me all at the same time. I tried to comfort and coax the pain into releasing itself of Caleb's body, just as I had spoken to the plants.

It was quite a longer conversation than I had experienced with the tree branch. The pain was stubborn, and the Water unobtrusively moved and cleansed while we spoke. I pressed on patiently to my goal, and the suffering eventually began to subside with the ebb and flow of Water in his system. All that remained was a slight tenderness in the brain from being jarred so abruptly. I slowly began removing the healing properties as carefully as I could, imagining the pain leaving Caleb's body and the gash sealing itself up in perfect precision. The now lukewarm Water moved back through my body, drying up as it moved closer to the deepest part of my soul. Then it evaporated.

Carefully, I pulled my damp, bloodstained hands away from Caleb's head and peered closely at his face. Was it just me, or had some of his color returned?

"Did it work?" Morgan barely whispered beside me. Gabriel leaned in closer, as did Thomas and Eden and everyone else in that room.

"The cut is sealed ..." Gabriel confirmed quietly, and his eyes roved over my face in concern, "Explain what you did ... your eyes are all wrong."

"What do you mean?" We were all speaking in hushed tones.

"They are blue and green ..."

"I don't know," I told him and turned my attention back to Caleb's still form. He was breathing evenly.

"Why won't he move?" Morgan wanted to know.

"I think ... he's better," I said slowly. "But ... he's sleeping. He might still be a bit sore." I couldn't adequately explain to them *how* I knew this, I just did.

"How did you ... ?" Thomas began, but stopped as Caleb stirred. Morgan and I leaned in closely. I ignored the random throbbing sensation that had begun in my head.

"Caleb? Can you hear me?" Morgan called. He moved a little bit, and then his eyes fluttered open, resting first on Morgan and then me.

"Yeah ..." he mumbled. And that was all it took for both of us to launch ourselves on top of his chest, crushing him with hugs at the same time. I didn't care that I smeared his own blood all over him. I just didn't want to let go.

"Unbelievable ..." Thomas gaped from behind us.

"Caleb ..." I breathed, a wave of emotion washing over me.

He focused very closely on me then and said, "It was you ... I could sense you there in my head." I nodded and squeezed my eyes shut, forbidding the tears of relief to release themselves. He rested a weak hand on the back of my head as I lay against his chest, half on the floor, and half on the bed-swing. The other arm he placed around Morgan and the three of us hugged. Vaguely I was aware of whispering as the room cleared out to give us some privacy. Even Gabriel left and shut the door quietly behind him.

"Caleb, you scared us to death." I shuddered and clung to my friends.

"Don't ever do that to me again, Caleb," Morgan sobbed. "If it hadn't been for Whitnee—"

"Thank you, Whit," Caleb whispered with a slight pat on my head, and that was my breaking point—I spilled a fountain of tears onto his stained tunic. I hadn't realized just how scared I had been. What if the injury had been worse, or even fatal? Now that Caleb was okay, I gave in to the thought of my life without him, and it was too much. For the first time, I could really picture the heartache Morgan had already been through when she lost Carrie. I did not ever want to experience that. I felt Caleb gently stroking my hair as I cried, and then I looked at him through glassy, wet eyes. The tenderness in his expression sent waves of guilt crashing over me, because I knew what I had been doing while he was out there getting injured.

Just like Caleb kissing Claire, I would never be able to take back that kiss with Gabriel. And I knew then that I didn't *want* to take back that kiss. So what the heck *did* I want? Suddenly, my feelings for Caleb and Gabriel seemed so complicated. I knew he was trying to read my expression because he said with a weak smile, "It's okay. You can't get rid of me that easily." And I froze for the briefest of moments, considering what I had just been thinking about. But, of course, he meant the injury ...

I reached out and grabbed Morgan's hand, wiping my eyes with the other. "Thanks for believing in me, Morgie," I cried.

"I was so afraid I would screw up. Just like when I started with Kevin's leg..." I stopped and realized that something was wrong with this picture. "Where *is* Kevin? And Amelia?"

Morgan's eyes became alarmed. "I'm sure they're with the twins," she mumbled, not sounding so certain this time.

"Wouldn't they come here when Caleb...?" I thought aloud. Something was not right.

"Don't panic. They're probably right outside," Caleb said and we all began to move apart from each other. Caleb tried to stand up but became dizzy and had to sit back down.

"Caleb... are you okay?" Morgan asked.

"Just dizzy."

"Stay here while I go figure out where the kids are, okay? Morgan can help you clean up," I instructed them on my way out the door. I wiped at my eyes with the cleaner backs of my hands, trying to clear out my tears.

"How is he?" Thomas asked at the same time Gabriel moved to me and asked, "How are you?"

"Fine, I think." And that really did answer both questions. I wasn't sure if I was more emotionally or physically tired at this point. And my head hurt. It was like I had taken on some form of Caleb's infirmities. However, it didn't matter because my mind was totally focused on my missing campers. "Where are Kevin and Amelia?" Everyone's faces mirrored my uncertainty. "The last time I saw them was out on the field... we need to find them immediately."

"I am sure they are somewhere with Jacob and John... or Elizabeth?" Eden spoke up. "I will go find out. Do not worry..." She and Joanna immediately left the cabin at the same time that a tiny wrinkled woman entered with a satchel.

"Ah, Maya, thank you for coming," Joseph greeted her. "Whitnee, this is Maya, one of our wisest Herbal Technicians. I asked her to bring some salves for Caleb's head until the HydroHealer gets here. Though it does appear that you took care of most of the damage, I would like him to be treated with whatever else possible while he is in our village. Do you mind if she attends to him?" Maya smiled at me through her leathery wrinkles and I nodded graciously.

"Thank you, Maya. He's right back there with Morgan." And Joseph led her back to the sleeping area.

This left me alone with Gabriel and Thomas. I began pacing the room, while I waited for Amelia and Kevin to arrive. I just had a bad feeling in my stomach.

"What exactly happened with Caleb?" I directed my question at Thomas.

"He and Eden were the last ones left on their team, and then he tried to form a shield and it did not work. The coconut hit him straight on the head and he fell to the ground. He did not move after that, and the game was halted. We brought him straight here, but ..." He looked at me with an incredulous face. "I did not think I could help him. But you ... you healed him right before my very eyes. Are you sure you have never been here before? Never knew anything about us until a few days ago?" I nodded as I paced. "How did you do it?" he asked simply.

"I really don't know or understand why I have these abilities, Thomas. And I don't blame you for feeling the way you do about me. Even I am not sure that I am who they say—"

"No, I was wrong, Whitnee," Thomas interrupted me. "If I had not seen what you did with my own eyes—something that only very experienced people in my tribe have ever done—well, I would not have believed if I had not seen. And now I do believe that you are the Pilgrim." I stopped pacing to stare at him. There was complete sincerity in his face.

"I really thought that all Hydros could heal ..." I said.

"We can heal ourselves, and sometimes others, of small things. But only specific people go into training to learn the more difficult healing techniques. And it takes a long time to master it. So, no, not all Hydros choose that line of work. What you did was very complicated. You must be special if it can come that naturally to you."

"I don't know … maybe taking biology courses was worth it, after all." I gave a humorless laugh. "It seems like I have to visualize what the Water is doing for the body, and it works."

"Biology? Hmmm …" Thomas grew quiet, thinking about this and I picked up my pacing again.

"There is still much I do not know or understand about using the Water life force," I told him. "I will need you to show me. I could not figure out how to multiply the Water and shoot it like you did today."

"I can teach you that," he promised, and it felt like whatever animosity he might have had toward me had vanished completely.

"Whitnee." Gabriel spoke after listening quietly to our conversation. "Perhaps you should go wash your hands. They are still bloody. And you have some on your face too."

"Oh! Right …" I had forgotten. I darted back to the bedroom.

"How are we doing?" I asked when I found Caleb lying down again. Maya was preparing a very sharp-smelling mixture in a clay bowl.

"He's feeling nauseous and his head hurts, but that seems to be the only sign of anything wrong," Morgan explained. "He's completely alert and remembers everything up to the point of getting hit, which makes me think you really did heal the concussion part too. He needs rest and Maya is going to give him a compress to help with the remaining symptoms. Did you find Kevin and Amelia?" I shook my head and then started back toward the bathing room to wash myself up once again. Morgan followed me.

"They have to be around here somewhere," she said. "They were across the field while you were playing. After that … I just don't remember seeing them again. I know they weren't there when Caleb fell because I was the first one out on the field. Do you think they just wandered off?"

"During a game like that? What would possess them to do that? Especially after I *told* them to stay within sight? And both twins were in the game … *one* of them nailed me with that coconut," I reasoned out loud while I washed up. "I am going to kill Kevin and Amelia when I see them. Apparently I wasn't *harsh* enough." I gave her a pointed look and she had the good grace to look a bit sheepish.

When we moved back through the room, Caleb called out to us.

"Did you find them yet?"

"No," I told him with a sigh. "But don't worry about it. You just need to rest for now. We'll let you know when Eden brings them back." He reached out and squeezed my hand, giving me a reassuring smile as Maya began putting the salve on his injury. He didn't say anything, but that simple act gave me renewed strength.

Morgan and I moved back into the sitting area just as Eden was coming back with John, Jacob, and Elizabeth in tow. No Kevin or Amelia. Eden's face was flushed with anger as she spoke.

"They do not know where the two young Travelers are. Elizabeth tells me they left during the game and she has not seen them since!" We all turned to Elizabeth for more details.

"It was after Whitnee left the game." She looked like she was about to be in tears. "They told me they needed to talk to her about something, but they would not say what. They saw her leave with Gabriel, so they followed. I stayed and watched the game."

"Did they not ever find you?" Morgan turned to me, and I know she observed the terrified look Gabriel and I shared at that point. If they followed us … *Did they witness our argument? What about our kiss? What if they hid from us because of all they saw? It had to be a terrifying scene … oh, what had I done?*

I shook my head as these thoughts and what-ifs turned over and over in my head. "We never saw them," I choked.

THE NIGHTMARE BEGINS

"We must get search teams out looking immediately. They could just be somewhere in the village, but we need to find them now!" Gabriel was in his authoritative mode. He and Joseph set off outside the cabin, and I followed without thinking. Most of the villagers were wandering around the area, waiting for news of Caleb's injury. The people appeared shocked when Joseph announced the situation and encouraged anyone who had seen anything or had more information to come talk to him immediately. Meanwhile, Gabriel began rallying the people into search teams, and the loyal Geodorians willingly set off in different directions scouring the surrounding areas. I pulled Gabriel aside by the arm.

With fearful eyes, I looked up at him. "Gabriel, do you think they saw us—?"

"I do not know." He shook his head.

"What if we scared them and they ran off?"

"There are many theories about what could have happened, but I do not think they would be so scared as to run away from you, Whitnee."

I was full of guilt. I should have been at the game, keeping an eye on them, not running off and making out with Gabriel! This was all my fault.

"What should I do?"

"Stay here with Morgan and Caleb and do not leave this cabin," he instructed me.

"But I can help—"

"No! You stay here where it is safe. Do you understand me? Protect your friends. We will find the children," he insisted. "I must go." I couldn't reply and he was edging farther away from me. I didn't want him to go without me, and I guess he could read that emotion in my terrified expression. He paused and leaned down, placing his hands lightly on my shoulders and making me look directly into his eyes. "Keep your zephyra nearby so I can communicate with you. Now, go back inside!" I didn't like this idea at all, but what could I do except obey? He was backing away from me, and I watched him join Eden, Thomas, and Levi. The four of them ran out into the darkness, Gabriel's hands lighting the way. I turned to enter the cabin and found Morgan standing in the open doorway, surveying me with perceptive eyes. Had she seen a difference in my closeness with Gabriel? Heard my conversation with him? Thankfully, she did not question me. Now would not have been the time anyway.

"This is not good, Morgan," I told her as I rushed back to the sleeping quarters where my zephyra was tucked in my satchel. I didn't know how to make it work, so I hoped they were user-friendly.

"What's happening?" Caleb called from his bed-swing.

"The kids are missing ... nobody knows where they are. The villagers were just sent out in search teams," I told him robotically as I rifled through my bag.

"What?" he cried and sat up very quickly. "*Ughhh*," he groaned.

"Please lie back down, sir," Maya instructed gently. "The herbs need more time to work."

Reluctantly, Caleb lay back down while Morgan explained what we knew. I drew the zephyra out of the bag, and the silver metal felt warm in my hands. I flipped it open, but the little paddles inside did not come to life. I was sure I would never figure out how to make a call on this thing, so I closed it up and held it tightly in my hands.

"Well, we need to get out there and look for them!" Caleb pronounced.

"Gabriel said to stay here—" I started.

"Screw Gabriel and his commands! We can't just wait around and do nothing!" Caleb tried sitting up again.

"Yes, but somebody needs to stay here in case Amelia and Kevin show up at the cabin," Morgan swiftly reminded him. "Besides, we don't even know the layout of the village and you're hurt—"

Suddenly the zephyra in my hands began pulsing, and I jumped in surprise. The three of us stared at it as it started flashing. Not quite sure what was happening, I flipped it open and the little paddles whirred to life. An image began to form in the device; to my surprise, it was Abrianna.

"Um, hello?" I said tentatively.

"Ah, Whitnee! I am so delighted you answered." She spoke with a cautious smile as always. I never could sense what she was really thinking or feeling. "Are you with other people?"

"Uh, just Caleb and Morgan and … Maya," I answered her, shooting confused glances at my friends.

"Who is Maya?" she asked.

"A Geo nurse? Or, I think they called her …"

"An Herbal Technician," Morgan supplied.

"Why do you need an Herbal Technician?" She seemed perplexed by this.

"Well, Abrianna, it is kind of a long story and right now is kind of a bad time … Caleb got hurt and now we can't find Amelia and Kevin—"

"Wait a moment … where is Gabriel?" she questioned as her eyes darkened.

"He's out with the rest of the village looking for the kids."

"Whitnee, please have Maya leave the room," she commanded, all sense of congeniality gone. Maya could hear the conversation and immediately nodded graciously.

"I'm sorry, Maya. We will come get you in a little while," I apologized as she stood and left the room, closing the door behind her. "Okay, she's gone," I said into the zephyra.

"Now please tell me exactly what is transpiring there, because it sounds to me like my Attendant has lost control of his duties." She spoke harshly.

"This isn't Gabriel's fault. Caleb got knocked out by a coconut during a game." Never thought I'd be saying that phrase and it would actually make sense. "He's fine now, for the most part. But we think Amelia and Kevin got lost or ran off or something. It wouldn't be the first time they've done this," I told her, remembering the several occasions at camp that Kevin and Amelia had disobeyed rules and wandered off together. She watched me carefully through the device.

"Regardless of whether they willingly wandered away or were taken against their will, it does not matter. Has Gabriel not informed you of the kind of people we are trying to track down on the Island right now? They are extremely dangerous and will do anything to overthrow my authority. If they can get their hands on one of you, even if by *accident*, then they have power over me. Do you understand the implications of this situation?"

"Yes, Abrianna, I understand," I told her, trying to keep the tears from my eyes. She was not making me feel any better. "What should we do?"

"I will contact my Palladium guards, who just wrapped up their search of the Fire incident in the jungle. They can begin scouring the area and moving your direction. If somebody did take the children, they might run into them." She looked away from the zephyra and made gestures at what I could only assume was somebody else in the room with her. Then she turned her attention back to me. "You say Gabriel is out searching? Does that mean he left you three unattended?"

"Yes, but—"

"That is unacceptable. I will contact him immediately."

"Abrianna—"

"Perhaps you see now why I suggested Amelia and Kevin stay with me while you visit the villages? They are young and have no life force powers. They cannot defend themselves if the wrong people seize them."

"I know," I whispered.

"When we find them, we might need to discuss a change in plans. Contact me immediately if the situation changes." And the zephyra clicked off. I glanced over at Morgan and Caleb, thinking that I had no clue how to contact her even if I wanted to.

"Oh, please just let them be somewhere in the village goofing around..." I prayed out loud. "I should have sent them with her in the first place. This is all my fault."

"What are you talking about?" Caleb scoffed. "We are not letting *her* babysit for us. It's our responsibility to look out for them, and I'm not letting her separate us!"

"We already are separated, Caleb! We didn't exactly do a good job with our responsibility or we wouldn't be in this situation!" I could hear my voice rising in volume. "I told y'all we needed to be careful, and you didn't take me seriously!"

"Okay... we need to settle down," Morgan mediated before Caleb could respond. "Caleb and I are probably the most at blame here. You were right. But we can't determine what to do next until they're found." Though I wanted to be mad at both of them, I couldn't help feeling weighed down by my own guilt. They didn't know what I had been doing instead of... *ugh*. I was still responsible. And it didn't help my guilt that I could do nothing but sit here and wait.

"I hope Gabriel's not in trouble over this," I mumbled.

"Who cares if he is?" Caleb said grumpily. "He's supposed to be the one protecting us, isn't he? Or is he just here for you, Whitnee?"

"Caleb ... you're really not helping right now," I groaned.

"I just can't figure out why you're so worried about *him*," he said and then dropped his face into his hands. "*Ughhh ...* my head."

"Let's just drop it," Morgan suggested. "We don't know anything yet. Y'all are acting like they got kidnapped or something."

"I just have a bad feeling about this, don't y'all?" I confessed.

"I have a bad feeling, all right," Caleb groaned. "I think I'm gonna be sick ..." And he half-ran to the bathing rooms. Morgan followed him with a sigh, and I decided I just couldn't handle that right now. So I left the room and moved out to the sitting area, still clutching the zephyra. Maya was waiting patiently on a chair, and I suggested she go back and check on Caleb again.

I began pacing back and forth a couple of times, going over every scenario in my head of what could have happened. Was there somebody in this village who took them? Maybe they had snuck off to make out ... *oh, kill me.* I knew they were middle-schoolers and that's when the whole boy-girl thing really starts, but I just didn't want to imagine my campers doing *that* ... And if that was the case, boy, they were in trouble with me!

Come to think of it, though, Amelia really hadn't been acting so obsessed with boys since we'd left camp. She seemed to have put those tendencies aside since we'd gotten here, and I almost found myself wishing I had followed her example ... especially when it came to Gabriel. All these emotions and desires were new to me. I'd had the occasional crush here and there, but nothing like this ... and how could I have resisted him when he just grabbed me and kissed me like that? Nobody had ever been so bold as to treat me that way. And I'd never wanted it so badly, either.

Okay, I needed air. The cabin was getting too stuffy.

I took a step outside and peered into the darkness as I inhaled deeply and slowly to calm myself. A few villagers ran by in a group and I stepped further out into the road, calling out to them. "Have you heard or seen anything yet?"

"No, mistress—still looking!" they answered and kept moving. I surveyed the darkness for signs of anyone else. I could hear a few shouts off in the distance as people were probably communicating about the search, but there was nobody in sight of our cabin. And it was so dark here.

As I wandered a little down the road, remaining in view of the cabin door, I thought I saw movement in the dark line of trees.

"Hello?" I called out. There was no response, but somebody was definitely moving through there. I took a few steps closer to the edge of the road, clutching my zephyra in one hand and extending the other out in front of me defensively. "I can see you! Can you hear me?" I said again and decided that I needed some light. *Hmmm… how did Gabriel do that?* I tried imagining the glow of Fire and the shimmery light it cast. Immediately, the heat filled my body and my palm began to burn with light. But it was only bright enough to illuminate the immediate space in front of me. I pressed ahead and took one cautious step into the forest area in front of the cabin. I wasn't going to move in too far, just enough to find whomever was moving around in here.

A man appeared a few feet away in the faint glow of my hand. His back was to me as he was walking slowly away from me. I couldn't see him very well so I took a few more steps.

"Hey! Have you found anybody yet?" I asked him loudly. He didn't respond but kept walking away from me, his pace picking up speed. "Where are you going? I'm talking to you!" I started following him, because there was something familiar about him. But every time I thought I was moving closer, he moved further away. The forest grew darker and I could no longer see the light of the cabin behind me. What was this guy's deal? He wouldn't even turn around and look at me. "Will you please stop? I'm not going to hurt you. It's me, Whitnee … one of the Travelers? I'm just trying to find my friends!" I told him and finally he stopped mid-stride. But he didn't turn around—he just froze there. I took a few steps closer. "Sir, are you okay … ?" But my voice caught in my throat.

Something was very wrong here … this man's hair … it was too light. Maybe it was just a trick of the light, or he had silver hair and it just *looked* blond …

The man turned around and met my gaze—I couldn't even scream. My stomach dropped, and a chill ran down my back. We stood there staring at each other in the dim light.

"D-dad … ?"

EARTH-SHATTERING REALIZATION

He was older than I remembered him, and his face was sad. His hair had not been kept up and had grown unfashionably longer. He even had a beard to match. But it was him...it was him, because he had my face and my gray eyes and my hair. And he was close enough to reach out and touch.

He didn't answer me—just stared at me with somber eyes in the dim light. In my shock, I lost touch with the life force and felt the light from my palm extinguish. The forest grew dark around us, and a coldness invaded my body where the heat had previously been.

"Dad! Are you there?" I tried recalling the Firelight again, but I was unsuccessful. I heard movement in the wood around me and spun around, trying to figure out where he had gone. It was my *dad*...He was *here*, and I couldn't lose him again! What if he just didn't remember me? "Dad, it's me!" I called out in a panicked voice.

There was the sound of footsteps off to my right, so I started running that direction, fighting back the hysteria rising up in my chest. I kept calling out to him as I ran faster and faster, following the sound of whatever movement I could hear. I stopped when my chest felt like it would explode. It wasn't just the running but the ever-growing ball of tension that seemed to be choking off my air supply. Was this what a panic attack felt like? I could only gasp for breath while tears streamed down my face. I didn't even know when I had started sobbing.

I took as many ragged breaths as I could, trying not to give in to the fear at the edge of my thoughts. A cool breeze whipped through the trees then, and I used it to calm myself as best I could. The leaves rustled, and it almost felt like the forest was coming to life around me … like it was trying to speak to me.

But before I could give more attention to that thought, a twig snapped somewhere nearby and a dark shadow lunged at me—I was knocked down to the ground, cracking one side of my face into the forest floor. The stranger was feverishly hot as he grabbed at my hands and tried to pin them behind me. Acting on pure survival instinct, I kicked at my attacker. It was too dark to see who it was, but it was obviously a man. He smelled like burning sulfur as I tried clawing at his face. I made contact, and he growled in response to the pain. That was when I knew for sure it was not my father, because this man had no beard.

However, that was also the point when I knew I was going to lose this fight. He was much bigger than me, and the thought of some man having that kind of power over me sent a ripple of adrenaline through my body. I inhaled deeply and could feel the power of the Wind working itself into a hot, violent storm. Time didn't even slow down for this one, and when I exhaled, it was as if hell itself had unleashed its fury. I blasted a burning hot rush of Wind that sent him flying away, gasping as he hit the ground. The cracking of tree branches told me that something had been damaged in the dark.

"What … ?" His gravelly voice was startled. I could hear him trying to figure out what had just happened, and he was groaning in pain.

"Stay away from me!" I screamed and sent one more gust at him, not even sure if I had aimed correctly the second time. If

I had to conjure real Fire, I would. Every nerve in my body was on edge, and the thump of survival instinct pulsed through my entire being. But the thought ran through my head that there might be more of his type out here. And how could I fight off more of them? I began running away, but at this point I had no clue what direction I was running in. For all I knew I was retreating farther into the forest. I prayed I was heading toward the cabin, and too late I realized I had dropped the zephyra when I fell. No way I was going back to find it now. I was afraid to call out in case the person who heard me was not a friend, so I just kept hurtling over the rough terrain until I finally tripped and fell to the ground, tears leaking viciously from my bruised face onto the Earth below. I tried to remain very still and listen, but I could not stop the flow of tears. I was lost, and I had no stupid zephyra. I couldn't hear anyone out there anymore. Where were the searchers?

You're so stupid, Whitnee! Why did you leave the cabin? I berated myself. And then as the adrenaline died, I curled into a ball, with my cheek on the ground and moaned, "Daddy..." over and over again. If that had really been him, why hadn't he spoken to me? Why hadn't he helped me?

I stayed curled up in utter self-pity and loathing until a breeze rustled the trees, and I got the feeling again that somebody or some*thing* was trying to communicate with me. I paused in my helpless state and listened. Turning over on my stomach, I laid both hands palm-down on the ground and rested my ear and injured cheek there. My tears had mixed in with the dirt, coating my face with a cool clay, almost like a poultice. It was there in the darkness of the forest that I allowed the life force of the Earth to speak to me in my moment of desperation.

In its indefinable language, it instructed me simply to *stay*. And a peace and comfort began to steal over me as I lay there on the ground, listening and breathing. *Stay here.* The Earth could sense my needs, and it was reaching out to me. *Like a partnership* ... I remembered Joseph's words. I could hear life force speaking in every trembling leaf and creaking branch. The ground whispered in its deep, immovable voice, and I soaked up all the tranquility it offered.

Just stay here. My breathing began to even out, and my sobs lost their potency the longer I lay still on the ground. I didn't know how long I was supposed to stay, but I trusted the Earth. Even my thoughts became foggy as I rested under the coolness of night, waiting until I was told differently.

Eventually I began to hear voices in the distance, moving closer to me. My body became rigid as I listened desperately for signs of a friendly voice. I would run if it was ...

Wait, the voice of the Earth insisted.

"She must be over here ... ! Look around!" It was Eden. Was the Earth life force directing her to me? I jerked my head up and saw a glowing light moving my direction. That was when I felt the Earth bid me farewell, and I jumped up and ran ... right into the surprised and very tense arms of Gabriel.

"Whitnee!" he cried out in relief, enfolding me into those warm, strong arms.

"I'm sorry! I'm so sorry! I didn't mean to wander off ..." I sobbed and then pulled back in fear. "Somebody attacked me ... in the forest. I think it might have been a Pyra, but he could still be out there!"

"What? Which direction?" Gabriel asked, his face a mask of rage.

"I don't know ... I got lost. Somewhere not too far away from here, I think?" I told him, gesturing behind me. He kept a powerful grip on me as he used his zephyra to contact Joseph, who agreed to redirect some men out this way. Joseph sounded angry and upset by the news. When Gabriel closed the zephyra, I asked, "Did you find them yet?"

"Yes! Yes, they were found ... by Tamir, of all people!" Gabriel told me, and I probably would have dropped to the ground again in relief if he hadn't been holding me so tightly.

"Oh, thank God," I breathed.

"He is bringing them back to the village as we speak. I will explain once we get you safely back to the cabin. And you must tell me what happened to you." His voice hardened as he took in my appearance.

"Just get me out of the dark, please!" I begged. Tucked safely against his side, I willingly followed him and Eden back through the dark forest.

"After you spoke with Abrianna," Gabriel was explaining, "she contacted me in quite a fury. She had already alerted her guards to the situation and they contacted Tamir, who had begun his trek to the village. He was the one who came across a suspicious group of people in the forest who had both Kevin and Amelia with them."

I shuddered at this. We were all in the sitting room of the cabin, waiting on Tamir to arrive with the campers. Joseph, Joanna, and Eden were in our company, and Thomas had just arrived. Levi had already left to meet Tamir and the campers outside the village where the thunderfly would land.

I sat on the floor next to Gabriel, afraid to be away from him. With a damp towel, I cleaned my face and hands while we discussed recent developments in the situation. Just knowing Gabriel's warm body was an inch away from me gave me comfort. Caleb was resting on a chair nearby, and Morgan was standing protectively near him. I could tell they were torn about what to feel and could not understand what had possessed me to leave them there in the cabin. Morgan had been crying and visibly upset by the time I got back, but I hadn't had time yet to explain my story. And it wasn't a story I particularly wanted to share with the entire group, either.

"So how did Tamir free them?" Thomas questioned.

"Well, he remained in hiding while he observed the group and then contacted the Palladium guards for help. They were already heading that direction on Abrianna's orders, and they were able to force the group to surrender Amelia and Kevin. I am sure it was not quite as easy as it sounds, though."

"Was anyone hurt?" I asked.

"From my understanding, no. We shall see when they arrive," he answered.

"Did the children say how these people got a hold of them?" Joseph wanted to know. "I am appalled that this would happen in my own village. Missing Travelers ... and then Whitnee getting attacked right on our own land ... it is unacceptable! I will seek the most extreme punishment." His fat face was rippling with anger and burning bright red.

"Yes, this is very upsetting, Joseph," Gabriel agreed. "I appreciate all that you will do to provide security and aid to us as we investigate. I do not know the children's story yet, only that Tamir has them and is on his way here by thunderfly."

At that moment, Joseph's zephyra went off; it was Abrianna. He excused himself from the room.

"Can I get anything for you? Food? Drinks?" Joanna offered, and Gabriel requested more Water and a light snack for everyone. She left immediately to fulfill this request.

"Whitnee, please tell us what happened to you," Gabriel prompted, and all eyes were suddenly upon me. I shut my eyes and shook my head, dreading this moment. I just wanted to forget about what happened out there. I felt like a fool, and I already knew that Morgan and Caleb would think I was crazy if I told them about seeing my dad. Morgan came closer and sat on the floor in front of me. Caleb followed weakly.

"Whit, you're in a safe place now, and you can trust the people in this room," she soothed with tears still swimming in her blue eyes. "What happened out there? Your face is bruised, and you're covered in dirt."

"Did someone hit you?" Caleb growled, and I could feel Gabriel's body temperature shoot up at Caleb's question. He was watching me just as intensely for an answer. My face felt swollen, and I wasn't sure if it was from hitting the ground so hard or from crying so hard.

"He, uh ..." I swallowed with difficulty as I recalled those terrifying moments. "He came out of nowhere and knocked me to the ground. I only remember him trying to get a hold of my hands ... I fought with him, but he was bigger than me. And that's when I used the Wind and knocked him away. I couldn't see him in the dark, but I know he didn't have a beard. And he smelled funny. And he felt really hot ... like Gabriel. I assumed he was a Pyra, but he didn't use a life force on me." I squeezed my eyes shut as I finished everything in a rush. "And that's when I ran until I fell and I just ... stayed there until you found me."

"Why did you go into the forest, Whitnee? You knew better—" Gabriel started, and I shook my head vehemently, not wanting to talk about it yet.

"You wouldn't understand," I cried.

"Try us," Caleb spoke up, and I peered out at him through my blurry eyes. His face was full of concern. I hadn't told Gabriel or any of the Dorians the real story about my father. I doubted they would really understand my issue about this. And Morgan and Caleb would just think it was my imagination again.

"I just ... can't." I shrugged helplessly.

"Did you ... see something, Whit?" Morgan asked me, her eyes narrowing as she watched my expression. "You know what I mean ... something that wasn't supposed to be there? Is that what this is about?" Once again, I was struck by how well she knew me. I nodded and curled my knees up tight to my chest. I hid my face there and choked back panicked sobs. This was so unbelievably stupid, but seeing him had felt so real. I knew I hadn't imagined it. "She saw her dad," Morgan stated softly. I heard Caleb sigh.

"I do not understand ..." Gabriel mumbled.

"Whitnee's father went missing several years ago...they never found him or his body. He just vanished. Every once in awhile, she thinks she sees him in places—"

"No!" I cried. "I didn't imagine it! He looked different...older, with a beard...but it was him. He led me out further into the forest and I followed him, like an idiot!"

"Was it the same as when you saw him back at camp?" Morgan questioned.

"Sort of...yes," I told her, and Gabriel's face looked puzzled.

"You said your father had died, did you not?" Gabriel questioned.

"Well, if someone disappeared from your life for six years, wouldn't you assume he was dead too? I don't like talking about it," I told him.

"So you saw him tonight? Did he say anything to you?" Gabriel asked, and I couldn't tell if he thought I was a crazy idiot too.

"No." I shook my head, and I realized my dad's silence had been the worst part of seeing him. "He didn't even seem to recognize me. And then...I lost him." I choked on my tears.

"I am trying to understand...please. Tell me exactly what happened," Gabriel instructed, and so I went through all the details of how I found myself in the forest and how my father acted.

"But he never spoke to you, correct?" Gabriel clarified one more time. I nodded. "And this happened back on the Mainland as well?" I nodded again. "Tell me everything about this, please."

Morgan, sensing the emotional overload this was causing me, explained the story and finished with: "That's the whole reason we even crossed the river...she kept seeing him over there and wanted to investigate. Then we landed here."

Gabriel was definitely intrigued and seemed to be thinking deeply about something. "You say the man who attacked you might have been a Pyra because his body temperature was very warm?" I nodded again. "That is a defining trait of a Pyra ..." He stood up then very quickly and began pacing the room. "I believe that someone was trying to lure you out into the forest," he stated, and I could tell his mind was turning in many different directions.

"Well, isn't that kind of obvious?" Caleb muttered.

"Remember how I told you that Pyras can manipulate light and produce images? That is what it sounds like happened when you saw your father." He extended one hand, which began glowing. With a wiggle of his fingers, an exact image of Caleb appeared on the other side of the room. We all gasped.

"What the—?" Caleb began, but Gabriel interrupted.

"It is only an image of the real you, Caleb. It looks like you, but I cannot make it sound like you. I can only make it move." And the fake Caleb stood to his feet, but did not make a sound. It was the creepiest thing I think I had ever seen.

"So you think that someone cast an image of my father to lure me into the forest?" I asked incredulously.

"It makes sense, does it not? You said you thought the attacker was a Pyra, right? He would probably know how to do this," Gabriel explained.

"Okay, will you lose the image of me? It's freaking me out," Caleb said, and Gabriel dropped his hand. Fake Caleb disappeared.

"But how would a random Pyra know what my dad looks like?" This question caused everyone in the room to look at Gabriel for an explanation.

"That is the mystery here ... we can only cast images of what we have personally seen," he said—the implications of that statement hit me like a bag of bricks. Morgan still looked confused, but Caleb's face registered the same shock mine did.

"Somebody here has seen your dad ..." Caleb whispered.

"And since he disappeared ..." I breathed. "*Geez*! I can't even begin to think about what that means ... this changes everything, doesn't it?" I looked to Caleb and Morgan, who had finally caught on. They couldn't even respond. And I didn't even know how to feel about this. I had been through the full gamut of emotions once again in an exceedingly long day on this Island. What else was left to feel?

"Let us speak no more about this to anyone beyond these walls. Eden, can you remain quiet this time?" Gabriel looked to her, annoyance registering briefly in his eyes as he remembered her slip earlier.

"Yes, of course I can! I do not think I even understand enough of it to discuss anyway…" She looked perturbed.

"Why do we need more secrets?" Caleb demanded.

"*Why*, Caleb?" Gabriel spun on him in a flash of anger. "Have you forgotten that the explanation to this mystery lies with the man who attacked Whitnee? Whoever has seen her father is also willing to hurt others, perhaps to protect this very secret. I fear that this is more complicated than any of us realize. We cannot take any chances. Until I can research more fully, we should put it out of our minds." Gabriel came to my side then and knelt so he was on eye-level with me. "I have several theories, none of which I can share with you right now. And I need to know… can you… *will* you just trust me with this, Whitnee?" He was asking for my trust for the first time, and his eyes burned with a new intensity, like the Fire of purpose. I could sense Caleb holding his breath as he waited for my answer.

"Yes," I replied without hesitation.

After we had all taken baths and cleaned up from the evening's events, we were lounging in the sitting room with refreshments, waiting on Tamir's imminent arrival with Kevin and Amelia. There had been many zephyra conversations between Abrianna and the Council, but I had stayed out of it. I wanted no part in their politics at this point. I only wanted my friends safe and sound and together again. I could not eat or drink anything until this was accomplished.

The moment Tamir entered the cabin with Kevin and Amelia, we engulfed them with hugs and fresh tears and apologies. They both cried a little and looked so exhausted that we decided we would not question them yet. Ultimately, their youthful resilience kicked in once they had bathed and ingested more delicious Geo food and juice. Finally, we all gathered in the sleeping area, everyone taking a comfortable seat on a bed-swing where we could talk in a safe and warm environment. Amelia was sitting with me on my bed-swing, chugging down a glass of juice.

"Start with what happened at the game earlier," Caleb prompted. Kevin and Amelia exchanged hesitant glances before Amelia started speaking.

"We saw Whitnee leave and we decided we wanted to ask her ... *something*. But I'm not sure I'm allowed to say what." She looked to me with raised eyebrows.

"There are no secrets among the people in this room anymore. Did it have to do with my abilities?" I asked carefully, and she nodded.

"We wanted to see if you would gift us so we could try out some of the life force magic. You and Caleb were having so much fun, and I guess we felt left out that we couldn't participate," she explained. "So, we followed you back to the cabin, but then ..." She stopped again, and I could feel my whole body tense up.

"Then what happened?" Morgan pressed her gently.

"Well," Kevin began, and he and Amelia looked nervously at each other before turning back to me. "We saw you and Gabriel fighting ... and it looked really bad." I let out a sigh.

"What do you mean?" Caleb prodded and then all eyes turned toward Gabriel and me, sitting on opposite bed-swings. "Why were you fighting?"

"That is a private matter," Gabriel replied indifferently before I could say anything. "The more important point is that we did not hurt each other, and we are not fighting anymore."

"Yeah, we kind of figured that part out too ..." Kevin trailed off, and I began squirming. I could only assume they had seen the whole emotional blow-up *and* its dramatic resolution. Morgan did not look surprised, but Caleb was watching me with a strange look on his face.

"I am really sorry y'all had to see that," I told them sincerely. I still remembered the horror of watching Caleb and Claire kiss (which was precisely why I was avoiding making eye contact with Caleb at this point). It was ten times more awkward knowing Kevin and Amelia had observed me in a similar situation.

"Yeah, well, the fighting part was actually kind of cool," Kevin added. "Better than any movie I've ever seen ... especially when Whitnee shot the blue Fire at you, Gabe. Man, I thought you were a goner ..." he laughed nervously.

"Kevin!" Amelia scolded him. Then she turned to me, and I could tell she was trying to help me save face in front of everyone. "Listen, we knew we shouldn't have been spying on you, but we didn't know what to do when you were ... well, anyway, we hid in the trees until you went into the cabin. And we were about to go in and check on you because you looked really sick. That was when we were grabbed from behind. We didn't even hear anyone coming."

"Do you know who grabbed you?" Gabriel asked. I was glad he was in control of the conversation, because I was about to die of embarrassment.

"No. We never saw anyone because they blindfolded us," Kevin told us.

"They already gave me detailed descriptions of what they remember was said and done. All of that information has been passed on to the Palladium guards and the Guardian." Tamir spoke up from the corner.

"How many were there?" Gabriel asked Tamir.

"Only three from what we could tell," he answered, and Gabriel seemed perturbed by this information.

"Did they hurt you?" I asked, placing a gentle hand on Amelia's arm.

"Not really," she shrugged. "I didn't like being told what to do and being forced to do it. But nobody ever hit me or anything like that."

"Me neither," Kevin piped up. "And they didn't really talk a whole lot around us. We didn't even know how many there were. But don't worry. I told them that Whitnee and Gabriel would kick their—"

"Kevin!" Amelia shushed him again with an exasperated look. "Yeah, he kept shooting his mouth off about what would happen to them when everyone found out we were missing."

"Well, I wanted them to understand who they were messing with! They *should* be afraid ..." he defended himself.

"Did you say anything to them about Whitnee's abilities?" Gabriel asked him in an anxious voice.

"I don't remember ..." Kevin acted like he was thinking about it, but his face flushed red.

"Yes! He threatened them with all that Whitnee could do, and I told him he better shut up!" Amelia tattled. I heard Gabriel release an oath under his breath.

"What difference does it make?" Kevin responded. "Maybe they won't mess with her now!"

"Okay, we'll deal with that later. Was there anything else that we should know about?" Caleb asked.

"No ... the next thing we knew, Tamir and the guards showed up and they gave up pretty easily. We still never got to see them, though, because Tamir rushed us out of there really

fast in case it got ugly," Amelia told us, and I glanced appreciatively at Tamir.

"I don't know how to thank you, Tamir," I said with the
sting of tears in my eyes. "You have been a hero today, and I'm
sure you are exhausted and hungry..." I couldn't imagine all
that man had been through today on our account. He bowed to
me humbly.

Suddenly, there was a knock on the outer cabin door, and
Joseph stood up to answer it. Eden and Joanna took that opportunity to excuse themselves to go back home where the other
children were waiting, provided there was nothing more we
needed. Eden whispered in my ear as she hugged me, "I will see
you tomorrow for training."

Joseph entered again with the HydroHealer who had finally
arrived in the village. I sent Amelia to her first, and when Joseph
pulled Gabriel aside, I covertly listened in on their conversation.

"I have Geoguards posted all around the area for the
remainder of your time here. You and the Travelers should be
safe tonight. I am very sorry for what has happened," Joseph
told him in a hushed tone.

"Did your men find Whitnee's attacker?" Gabriel asked
him, and Joseph just shook his head in frustration.

"Nothing but her zephyra. It was obvious a scuffle had
taken place because the area exhibited Wind damage and several prints in the ground. As for where the attacker went... no
evidence."

"They will keep searching, though?"

"Yes."

"Joseph, do you find it strange that there were only three
men holding Amelia and Kevin? And that they gave them up
with hardly a fight?" Gabriel was whispering, and I had to strain
to hear him.

"Not exactly... I am just relieved we got them back so
quickly. Do *you* find it strange, Gabriel?" Joseph looked at him
with curiosity.

"It just does not seem to fit the pattern of behavior we have seen in the past … but there is really nothing I can do about it right now. If Palladium guards are handling it, I am sure the situation will be resolved." He paused and then added as an afterthought, "It just seemed too easy."

Joseph seemed to contemplate his words. "I shall keep that in mind as we investigate on our end."

"Yes, please keep me informed."

"Of course," Joseph agreed. "I hope you and the Travelers get as much sleep tonight as possible. I am sure they need it. We will meet again in the morning. Abrianna seems very concerned and wants to call off the rest of the travel plans. I do not think this is a good idea, but I do see the wisdom in sending the younger two to the Palladium where they will be completely protected. Five Travelers are difficult to protect all at once. Perhaps you should bring this up with the older ones in the morning?" Gabriel only grunted in response. Then they bade each other farewell and Joseph left. I turned away to hide my eavesdropping.

The HydroHealer was examining Caleb and suggested that she fix up his gash a little better. It had been healed, she said, but she believed she could completely rid him of a scar.

"No, leave it, please." And his green eyes found mine a few feet away. "I want to keep the scar," he said and then looked the other direction.

"You should allow her to heal your bruise instead of doing it on your own." A deep voice spoke to me, and I turned to see Gabriel standing over me. He perched himself next to me on the bed, careful to keep his distance. I found my fingers fluttering up to my swollen cheek, where I knew I was fostering a very lovely, purple bruise.

"I'm sorry I look so bad," I muttered to him. "Usually I take better care of myself—"

"Do not apologize." He silenced me as he moved a gentle hand to cradle my face. "You are beautiful to me. A bruise cannot change that. And when I find the man responsible for hurting you …" He dropped his hand, and it clenched involuntarily into a fist. "This whole evening turned out to be a disaster. I am not sure anymore if we are being responsible, taking you to each village." He was speaking mostly to himself, and I could tell he was struggling to do and say the right thing.

"Let's discuss it in the morning," I suggested with a yawn. "I don't think anybody is capable of making a wise decision at this late hour. Too many emotions. Besides …" I touched his fisted hand. Ever so tenderly, I uncurled his fingers and tucked mine into his sultry palm. "You need some rest." We both stared at our entwined fingers. The differences were profound. Everything about me—my pale skin, my petite frame, even my cool body temperature—was in direct contrast to him. We were light and dark, small and large, cold and hot. And nothing we did would ever change these differences. He was a Dorian, and I was not. We were meant for different worlds.

And yet, we were connected somehow—even if only by our choice to be together in this moment.

"Perhaps you are right," he said with a sigh. "I am sorry for all you and your friends have been through since you arrived. I had no idea it would become so … complicated." He would not meet my eyes then, so I gave his hand a comforting squeeze. I could hear the HydroHealer moving my direction so I looked away from Gabriel, only to find that Caleb was watching us from his bed. For the briefest of moments, he looked crestfallen, but then he turned his attention to Kevin and was all smiles—as if he'd never even looked over here. I sighed, releasing Gabriel's hand so the HydroHealer could do her work on me. He got up and prepared his bed-swing right next to mine.

The room began settling down for lights out. Caleb was reenacting the story of his coconut accident for Kevin and Amelia while the HydroHealer fixed my face. Her methods were much more professional and wholly effective than my attempts at healing. When she was finished, I felt more at peace in my body than ever before. Once she left, the lights were extinguished, and we all chatted quietly across the room in the dark. It almost felt like we were back at camp, and everything in life was as normal as possible. Caleb started to tell his infamous cow jokes as a bedtime story to entertain Amelia and Kevin, but I knew this was his way of keeping things lighthearted. He did it as much for himself as he did it for the kids after their experiences tonight.

"Knock, knock," he started.

"Who's there?" we all chanted in the dark (except for the Dorians in the room, who did not know this custom).

"Cow," he answered.

"Cow who?" we chorused.

"MOO!"

Nobody laughed.

"That's pretty lame, Caleb," Kevin told him honestly. I rolled my eyes because I knew exactly where these jokes were going. Caleb was so proud of his cow jokes and had recruited Morgan and me over the years to help him create new ones.

"Just wait," Caleb defended himself. "The cow jokes have to start with that one and they only get better. Stay with me. Knock, knock."

"Who's there?"

"Backwards Cow."

"Backwards Cow who?"

"OOM!" he exclaimed, eliciting a few giggles from the room.

"I still don't get it..." Amelia whined.

Unexpectedly, I felt Gabriel's hand stretch out across the space between our two beds in the dark. He rested it on the side of my bed-swing, palm up—an invitation to link our fingers together again. I didn't hesitate to lock my hand in with his and close my eyes as the comforting heat he provided traveled up my arm right into my very core. On the other side of the room, Caleb continued, "Okay, here's another one... Knock, knock."

"Who's there?" we chanted. The Dorians were catching on now.

"Dyslexic Cow."

"Dyslexic Cow who?"

"OMO!" This time we all laughed harder, except the Dorians didn't seem to understand the joke. Did they not have dyslexia here on the Island? Drowsily, I thought *that must be nice* ... I knew from experience that these jokes could go on a long time, and it didn't help that Gabriel's thumb was tracing a circular pattern on my hand, lulling me into sleep.

"Knock, knock."

"Who's there?"

"Rude, Impatient, Interrupting Cow."

"Rude, Impatient, Interrupt—"

"MOO!" he interrupted loudly and this one everybody seemed to get. I think I even heard a chuckle out of Gabriel.

"Go to sleep, Caleb ..." Morgan groaned. And that was the last thing I remembered as I fell asleep holding hands with Gabriel.

SEPARATION ISSUES

I woke up to cheerful sunlight streaming down on my face. I had slept so hard that I almost couldn't remember where I was. As I took my time to open my eyes and sit up, the events of the last few days slowly filtered back into my head. It wasn't until I looked over at Gabriel's empty bed that my heart began pulsing excitedly. The thought of him sent a ripple of warmth throughout my body, and I couldn't help the smile that broke out on my face. Even the precarious situation we were all in here on the Island didn't seem quite as bad in the light of morning—and with the promise of a new day with Gabriel.

Everybody was still fast asleep in the room. Quietly, with no idea what time it really was around there, I got up and moved to the bathing area to get ready for the day. My mind kept reliving every kiss, every touch, every look and word that Gabriel and I had shared. With last night's events happening the way they did, I hadn't been able to really consider the changes in our relationship. But now I found myself acting and thinking like a giddy girl in love … whoa, not *in love*. I didn't mean to think that.

I tried to make myself as cute as possible. In my satchel, I found a pair of loose, Capri-length drawstring pants and a sky blue sleeveless top that tied around my neck. I had seen many

Dorian girls with this style of clothing on, and it was actually kind of flattering. I definitely felt more feminine in it than the typical tunic top. Besides, if we would be training outside today, it would be hot. I needed to dress cool, and I could certainly use some sun on my bare shoulders ... I found my hair tie from home, and I pulled my golden hair up loosely off my neck. I even attempted to use some of the Island makeup, though finally achieving actual deep sleep had worked better on my face than anything else. I also wondered if the HydroHealer had given me a special glow or if it was just the radiance of my emotions showing on my face. For the first time, when I looked in the mirror, I did not absolutely hate my eye color. I was actually proud to be marked as an Aerodorian, a Daughter of the Wind. Briefly, I raised my hand to emit a cool breeze in the small bathing room, just so I could watch my eyes light up silver.

"Cool," I remarked to my reflection and then tiptoed back through the cabin and out the front door. The second I stepped outside, I was struck with the inviting smell of breakfast ... if I had to nickname the Geodora village, I would call it the Town of a Thousand Scents. You didn't go anywhere around there and not smell something new or different. I inhaled deeply as I trekked across the road to the banquet hall where the smell seemed to be originating.

There was nobody inside the kitchen area, but several plates of fresh food sat out for open serving. I wandered to the covered patio out back, where I found Joseph and his entire family. The adults were sitting leisurely around a table of used plates and cups, still sipping a hot drink that looked very close to coffee. The children were playing together in the garden. Gabriel reclined comfortably in his chair as he chatted animatedly with the group, including Thomas, Levi, and Tamir. For a moment, I was struck with how serene and normal the picture seemed. I watched them through the window, especially enjoying how relaxed Gabriel appeared in the midst of his fellow Dorians. Perhaps this journey we were on was giving him some common ground with them. I didn't think I had seen him look like that since I had arrived.

Finally, I stepped out through the door and was immediately greeted by the loud Geodorians. Elon ran to greet me with a hug and a fresh flower for my ponytail. Gabriel stood up immediately at my presence, and his hazel eyes lit up. He gazed appreciatively at my outfit but did not make any bold moves to touch or kiss me in front of the others. I gave him a shy smile as he pulled a chair up beside him at the table so I could eat.

I joined in on their light conversation, answering the expected questions about how I felt, how I slept, how hungry I must be. Joanna had shoved a full plate of food in front of me, and I picked a little at it but found that my appetite had disappeared. The little butterflies in my stomach had come to life the moment I had come into close proximity with Gabriel again. He kept stealing glances at me, and our eyes would make contact with each other even when we didn't mean to. I had to fight down the blush that kept rising to my cheeks every time I looked at him. He was wearing a casual white tunic with brown pants again, and I absolutely loved how the white made his dark skin gleam. I could even faintly see his Pyradorian birthmark through the thin material of his shirt, and my mind started wondering what that mark felt like on his bare skin ... I took a sip of juice to cool my thoughts down and nearly choked.

"Whitnee, now that you have had a full night of sleep, we should probably discuss some potential issues with the rest of your journey." Joseph addressed me, and the rest of the table turned serious at his change in subject. He dismissed the children to go play again, and I gave him my full attention. "I have been in contact with the Council and the Guardian several times. Naturally, last night's events have forced us to reconsider how we are approaching your presence here on the Island." I nodded.

Gabriel spoke up, "Everybody on the Council knows of your abilities in all four life forces now."

I raised my eyebrows at this. "Even the Guardian?" I clarified.
"Yes."

"And what do they think?" I asked, afraid to hear the answer
to this question.

"None seemed completely surprised, actually," Joseph said.
"But this news will spread rapidly throughout the Island, making you somewhat of a fascination. Your protection will become
quite a task. And I speak of protection against curiosity as much
as protection against danger. Does that make sense to you?"

"I think so …" I said, not sure I was really ready for that
kind of attention.

"We still think it best for you to visit each village while you
are here, but we are shortening it to one night in each place.
That means you will spend the day here—Eden tells me she
has some plans for you already—and then you will travel in
the afternoon to Hydrodora. Thomas and Eden have agreed to
continue to travel with you as extra protection."

"You say 'you' as if my friends won't be accompanying
me …?" I pointed out nervously. The Dorians glanced knowingly at each other then and my fears were confirmed. "You
don't think I should take my friends with me?"

"This goes against my better judgment, but there is concern
over protecting so many of you—"

"You cannot separate me from them! They could have gone
home, but they stayed here willingly with me! They will not
leave me here—"

Gabriel rested a gentle hand on my bare shoulder before I
could get too worked up. "I believe the suggestion is for them to
go on to the Palladium where they can be better protected and
taken care of while you travel. They will wait for you there and
then you can all go back to the Mainland together." He did not
look happy with that last part. "It is very difficult to keep track
of five of you, Whitnee. Last night proved that."

"So we bring more protection!" I argued. "We'll be better
about watching out for each other—"

"I am sorry, Whitnee, but you must consider our predicament as well," Joseph interrupted. "If any of you fall into the wrong hands, like what happened with the little ones last night, those people would have the power to overthrow our leadership. We could be forced to lose control of the Island in order to protect you. That is not a position any of us want to be put in. The best way to avoid that is to separate you."

"Caleb and Morgan will not go for that." I was sure of this, at least.

"What about the children? Amelia and Kevin?" Gabriel prompted.

I shook my head in exasperation. "How could you suggest—?"

"After what happened last night, Whitnee, they would be safer at the Palladium," he reminded me.

"I thought you caught all these bad people last night?"

"Not all of them," Joseph said darkly. "Abrianna is very adamant that if you are to continue traveling, then the group must split up. Unless you are ready to leave permanently."

I looked to Gabriel again to confirm what I was hearing.

"So, either we all go to the Palladium, and I leave this Island … forever, or we split up for two or three more days and then all go home together? Are those my choices?" He nodded at me, his eyebrows furrowed. "Wow," I breathed. Were they really telling me I could go home? And if so, was that really what I wanted? One look at Gabriel's face and I knew I wasn't ready to leave. As much as I knew it was a bad idea to get emotionally involved with him, it was too late. I already was. And though I had to leave eventually, there was still so much unresolved at this point. I was on the brink of discovering answers to the mysteries about my past and perhaps even my future if I stayed a bit longer. But we couldn't separate our group … could we? They did make a good point about Kevin and Amelia. I would never forgive myself if something bad happened to them. We got lucky last night, but who's to say that next time would turn out the same? I had to protect them … even if that meant doing something none of us particularly liked.

I turned back to Joseph, who was watching me very closely. "I need to talk to Caleb and Morgan first. I will give you an answer today." That seemed to pacify them temporarily.

"What? I don't want to go to the Palladium! I want to see the other villages!" Kevin said, and Amelia was storming around the room.

"Me too! This isn't fair!" she screamed. Morgan and Caleb and I glanced at each other. We had been expecting this kind of reaction. After we had discussed our options, we had finally concluded that sending Amelia and Kevin to the Palladium ahead of us was our best choice. Neither Caleb nor Morgan would hear of separating from me just because of potential danger. But when we had our little campers to consider, it became a harder choice. Caleb was the most resistant to the idea of sending the kids ahead because he still didn't trust Abrianna. Truthfully, he had felt that all of us should go and transport home before things got more out of control. However, there were no guarantees that they would even let us go home yet.

Morgan was in favor of sending Kevin and Amelia to a safe place—she was still terrorized by what had happened last night. I should have known that she would always pick the safe option over anything else because of what she had already been through in her life. Fear of losing someone close to her still ended up driving some of her choices. I wondered if that would always be a part of her personality. She was also more sympathetic to me than Caleb was about finding out this mystery of my father. So, together, she and I convinced Caleb to go this route.

"We're doing this to keep you two safe," I patiently reminded both of them.

"Sure you are! You guys just want us out of the way, so you can do whatever you want!" Amelia flung back.

"That is not true," I assured her.

"But we promised not to leave your side anymore! We'll be perfect and we won't bug you at all. Please don't send us away!" Kevin pleaded, and that was when I felt myself wavering on my decision. Fortunately, Morgan jumped in.

"This is nothing personal toward you guys. We love both of you, and that's the reason we have to do this. It is too dangerous and we have to get everybody home safely. Besides, it's just for a couple of days. And then we'll meet you there and we'll all go home." She made it sound so simple.

"You'll have fun at the Palladium... Abrianna says she has all kinds of surprises for you and she said they would gift you with life forces, if you could be responsible about it," I told them. Kevin seemed to calm down a little bit after this, but Amelia just looked more upset. She pointed at me.

"You're just trying to get rid of us!" she yelled. "You're even trying to make it sound like it's so great!"

"Amelia, it could be great if you—"

"Oh, please! You think I don't know when I'm not wanted? You're acting just like my dad, Whitnee!" she screamed and tears started running down her face. I stared at her in shock. "He used practically the same words before he dumped me at Camp Fusion this summer!"

"Nobody's dumping you anywhere, Amelia. We're trying to do the right thing here, and it's not easy on any of us," I told her.

"It's always about you, though, isn't it, Whitnee?" And she spun around to face me again. "*You* have all the powers, you're the special one, and everyone is fascinated by *you*! The rest of us don't even matter! And don't forget that all of you were busy last night having *fun* when we were kidnapped! You just don't want us ruining your fun again!"

"No, sweetie, you're understanding it wrong—" I was trying to be gentle because I had apparently hit on a soft spot without realizing it. And I truly was doing this for her safety...wasn't I? Her words seemed to have hit my soft spot too.

"No, I'm understanding perfectly! You want to be alone with Gabriel and enjoy your fantasy time on the Island and *we*"—she gestured to herself and Kevin—"don't fit in the picture! I can't believe I thought you were different." She had been violently throwing all of her stuff back into her satchel and now she flung the bag on her shoulder.

"Amelia, please don't be mad—" I was desperately trying to smooth things over because the wagon was ready outside to take them to the thunderfly landing. I couldn't let her leave like this.

"When we get back, I want a new mentor. I don't ever want to talk to you again!" she yelled on her way out the door.

"Amelia!" I called as I ran after her, but she ignored me and climbed aboard the wagon. She was crying, and I felt powerless to fix it. "Please be careful and know that I love you no matter what you think of me right now. I will see you in a couple of days."

The tears continued to pour down her face as she finally looked directly at me, her eyes full of loathing, and spat, "I hate you."

I pulled back as if I'd been slapped in the face. I couldn't remember anyone ever saying those words to me before, and they stung. Morgan had come up behind me. "Amelia! You don't mean that!" she reprimanded her, but Amelia ignored her too.

"I guess I'll see you when you get to the Palladium," Kevin remarked glumly as he boarded the wagon. Caleb gave him some words of encouragement and instructions to keep in touch by zephyra as much as possible. And then the wagon pulled away with Tamir and a few other Geo men as protection. Amelia never looked at me again, and then they were gone.

"Well, that went well." Morgan spoke sarcastically.

"I hope we're doing the right thing..." I whispered.

"Only time will tell, I guess," Caleb commented, which didn't make me feel better.

TRAINING DAY

Training was brutal that day, both physically and mentally. Eden had taken us to a private clearing out in the forest where nobody could witness what we were doing. It was there that Levi, Thomas, Eden, and Gabriel took turns instructing the three of us in the practical usage of each life force. Eden successfully gifted Caleb this time, and Thomas learned how to gift Morgan, so my friends were working just as hard as I was. I learned how to make objects fly with Wind power. Levi also taught me how to conjure breezes of different speeds and temperatures. Eden made Caleb and me listen to different plants and trees and interpret their varying messages. We began to grow and heal flowers, since she said flowers were the kindest and most flexible to work with in training.

Thomas taught Morgan and me how to multiply Water when it was in short supply. The Water lost some of its potency when this was done, but it was still effective for many different tasks. Since no one needed healing, we didn't really practice that. We did attempt to Water the ground, but when certain sprays went awry, we ended up drenching each other more than the ground. Eventually, we were splashing each other on purpose and ganged up on Thomas in a brief Water war.

Once we were all soaking wet, Gabriel took the opportunity to teach me how to use my inner body heat to dry quickly. I also learned how to radiate heat more controllably without casting flames. We worked on conjuring Firelight, and my field of light grew brighter the more I practiced. It was kind of fun to know my hands could become flashlights. Gabriel tried to teach me the art of creating holographic images, and this was much harder than I expected. I tried reproducing the image of a flower first and I succeeded after many attempts, but the image was a bit transparent. Any time I wasn't working with Gabriel, he took on the role of Mr. Miyagi, observing my progress, offering tidbits of wisdom, and forcing me to drink down Water like a camel.

When it came to these smaller, practical tasks in each life force, I struggled the most with Fire and Water. They didn't come as naturally to me, and I wasn't sure if that was because I had less experience with those two elements or if they were just natural weaknesses. Wind and Earth came very quickly and easily, and I found I used less and less energy and concentration when accessing them.

After we had practiced the simple, everyday conventions of each life force, we took a much-needed lunch break. Eden had packed us a delicious meal, and we plopped down right there on the grassy floor to devour every last morsel. I was weary by that point, but since I was learning how to pace myself when accessing life forces, I wasn't completely wiped out.

"This is intense work," Morgan commented between bites. "I can see why Whit has been exhausted since we got here. I just can't understand how the rest of you live with this kind of energy surging through you all the time."

"We are born with it, and we learn how to control it from a young age," Thomas told her. "I cannot imagine what it would feel like at my age to have to learn it all for the first time. What you are doing is difficult."

"Is the fighting part harder than this?" Caleb questioned.

"With Earth, I think it is. The defensive shield is the easiest part," Eden answered.

"Fighting with Water is only difficult when you don't have any to work with. That is probably the greatest weakness," Thomas pointed out.

"Wind and Fire are usually the fiercest when it comes to offensive fighting, as Whitnee has already discovered..." Gabriel commented and then gave me a knowing smile that had me blushing and losing my appetite again.

"It appears you two have already been working on that part," Eden needled us with a raise of her eyebrows.

"Apparently Whitnee can knock him flat to the ground," Morgan teased, and Eden became excited at the possibility of witnessing such an event.

"Yeah, what was all that about Whit shooting blue Fire at you, Gabe?" Caleb wanted to know, and I glanced nervously at Gabriel.

"All I will say is that she has quite a temper about her," Gabriel said with an easy laugh. "A temper which she must learn to control. She puts her emotions into her fighting, and that is why she nearly kills herself every time."

"Yeah, but I produce some pretty wicked moves every time," I reminded him.

"That will only last for so long. You have to learn to fight logically and without emotion or you will lose," he told me for the fifteenth time that day.

"I understand ... but I'm a girl. It's a little harder to separate those emotions out," I sighed.

"Well, I think you should both give us a demonstration before we start," Morgan suggested. I barely caught Caleb rolling his eyes, but he kept his mouth shut.

I raised my eyebrows at Gabriel. "I'm game, if you are. But I don't want to embarrass you in front of everyone."

"Oh, Little One ..." He shook his head as if he pitied me. "Your confidence is amusing as always."

I made a face. "Well, let's go." I stood up, brushing my hands off.

"Right now? Do you not need more rest?" He looked surprised.

"I'm fine...maybe *you* need more rest, though?" I smiled innocently and took a swig of Water. He smiled back and stood to his feet.

"Uh-oh. We should move," Morgan said.

Eden called out, "Try not to set the trees on Fire, Gabriel!" He gave her a dirty look as we moved into position several yards away from each other.

"You first." He took a defensive stance. I allowed myself to breathe evenly and feel the breeze within. Then, with a shout, I launched a mini-whirlwind at him. He burned it up the moment it came within reach. So I sent a mighty force of straight-line winds his direction. He emitted a wall of orange flame around himself that directed the winds away from his body and toward the onlookers. I heard Morgan squeal as the force blew away some of our picnic. I placed my hands on my hips and glared at him.

"Is that what you were doing last night? Using some kind of Fire barrier?"

"Yes," he grinned.

"*Geez*," I muttered. And I thought I had hurt him when he seemed to erupt into flames! I took a moment to catch my breath, and that was when I doubled over as if I was suddenly weak. I dropped to one knee on the ground, gasping.

"Whitnee?" Gabriel called, dropping his defenses and running toward me. I took a deep breath and threw the most powerful gust of Wind I could conjure right at him. His eyes widened in shock as he was launched backwards, realizing too late I had been faking. He landed on his rear and cursed out loud. Eden cheered while the others laughed uproariously. I skipped over to his sprawled position on the ground and leaned over on my knees.

"That is the second time I've knocked you on your butt. Now, where's the respect?" He shook his head, unsure if he should be mad or entertained by what happened.

"That was evil, Whitnee Terradora!" Morgan yelled.

"Beautiful tactic!" Caleb hollered. I was still laughing when Gabriel suddenly tackled me and we fell on the ground, his body taking the brunt of the force. He had me pinned between him and the ground and began mercilessly tickling me.

When I had screamed and laughed so hard that I thought I would die, he pulled me into his arms and mumbled in a breathless voice, "Be careful, or you will be the end of me someday." I couldn't tell if he was being serious or not. His eyes sparkled for the first time with something that looked like joy or happiness, and I was overwhelmed with the desire to kiss him again. His perfectly formed lips were right there, inches from my own. It would be so easy to lean in and taste some of that joy for myself. And if I wasn't completely off about reading him, he was thinking something among the same lines. But we had an audience—an audience which included the unamused Caleb. Instinctively, we pulled away from each other and straightened up our appearances as we rejoined the group. No matter what Caleb was thinking, I couldn't erase the silly smile on my face.

Gabriel addressed the other Dorians. "I would like each of you to teach Whitnee defensive strategies first. She can launch an attack easily enough, but her weakness is defense."

"And it is obvious that *your* weakness is *her*," Thomas remarked with a grin. I blushed at this, and Morgan giggled.

"Thank you for your observation, *friend*," Gabriel smirked, not showing any sign of embarrassment. "Are we ready to begin?"

And that was how the rest of the afternoon progressed. Again, each tribe member showed me the defensive techniques that worked best with each life force. I discovered that I had actually used the Wind defense last night in my argument with Gabriel and hadn't even realized it. It was a rapidly blowing circulation of air that spun around the body and deflected harmful blasts. Levi called it a Wind Blocker. I practiced this technique while the others took turns shooting at me with Fire, Water, and Wind. Eden said that the Earth life force would allow someone to shoot dirt and rocks at an attacker. But she did not want to do this since it could be damaging to the Earth itself, and we were only training.

Gabriel taught me how to create the "Wall of Fire" as I started calling it, and again, I had to work harder at controlling this one. No matter what most Dorians said about Pyras, I was starting to feel the most respect for them. No other life force seemed to take as much self-control and discipline as the element of Fire. And I could see why they were often perceived as passionate and emotional ... if I had a Fire raging inside me all the time, I'd be an emotional wreck too.

Eden worked with me more intensely on the Earth shield technique used in coconut launch. She instructed me on how to project it in different sizes and thickness. It could even be used to create what I thought of as a "greenhouse effect." It was like fostering a certain kind of climate for whatever lay beneath the shield.

Using Water defensively was a challenge since we were not near a fresh Water source. Basically, I learned that there were two ways a Hydro could defend himself with Water. The first worked best when a large amount of Water was available—it was similar to the Wall of Fire, but made of Water. The second technique was more difficult to accomplish, but could be used if the conjurer drank Water.

"It is similar to an Earth Shield and a Wind Blocker, but it attaches itself to your entire body. We call it the Mist because that is what you look like. Allow me to demonstrate." Thomas took a big chug of Water and then his eyes lit up sapphire blue. All of a sudden, we were looking at a wispy, watery version of him. His whole body had turned into liquid and was misting like the sprinklers in the vegetable section of a grocery store.

"Whoa," I responded when he released the Mist.

"That was so..." Caleb paused, searching for the word, "...so X-Men." The Dorians cocked their eyebrows at that, and Morgan jumped up and down, clapping excitedly. "Oh, show me! Show me how to do that!"

While he explained to Morgan and me how it worked, Gabriel also informed us that this particular technique was the most effective against Fire attacks, as Fire had more difficulty burning through Water. Neither of us was completely successful with it, but Morgan seemed to do better than me. Water just wasn't one of my stronger life forces. While we were in the middle of this frustrating exercise, Gabriel's zephyra went off. We decided to use that as an excuse to call it quits for the day. The intensity of our work was definitely taking its toll on all of us.

Hoping it would be Amelia calling for me, I watched anxiously as he answered. Unfortunately, it was Abrianna, and she asked to speak to me first.

"Hello, Abrianna," I greeted her while I sat on the grass away from the others, replenishing myself with Water. "How are Kevin and Amelia doing?"

"They are doing well!" she answered in a surprisingly bright voice. "We gave them a tour of the Palladium, and they played in the Dome where they could view the entire Island. I had them gifted in small amounts so they could learn a little about the life forces. I was correct... Amelia is a surprisingly sharp Pyra, while Kevin is certainly a Hydro. He is a very energetic child. And I must say, he has told me many... interesting stories of your abilities." She gave me a cool look then, and I returned her gaze in the zephyra, unflinching.

"Yes, well, Kevin does like to brag..." I said nonchalantly.

"Oh, do not be so modest, Whitnee. Rumors are already spreading across the Island. I do wish you would have told me immediately that you had access to all four life forces. That would have changed how we would have handled things."

"Would it? That's interesting..." I pretended to think about that and then looked right at her. "Surely you can understand why I would have a difficult time … trusting you with that information? After all, I didn't know anybody very well on this Island, and now that my friends and I have been under attack …" I trailed off and she was watching me with cold eyes.

"I can only imagine how traumatic it was for you to go through that. I am glad you made the right choice to send the little ones here. And as for your initial feelings of mistrust toward me … surely that is not still a problem for you? I cannot imagine that you would send two of your own group to me for *protection*, if that were the case?"

I felt my blood run cold at her words, and a sick feeling started swimming around in my stomach. She continued to look at me as if nothing was out of place, but why did I feel like she was really saying something else?

"How is Amelia?" I asked, changing the subject.

"Well, obviously, she was very angry about your decision—"

"Did you tell her I was forced to make that decision?" I couldn't control the slight annoyance that entered my tone.

"Nobody forced you to do anything," she replied innocently. "But do not worry, I explained to her the dangerous situation she had been in and promised that no harm would come to her here at the Palladium. We have spent most of the day together, and she really is a bright girl … just so hungry for *attention*." Something bothered me about the way she always spoke of Amelia. "You did the right thing by sending them here and, in time, they will see that. Kevin already seems to be adapting quite well. Amelia is more stubborn, but she will understand soon why this was best."

I didn't know what to say to her, and the sick feeling in my stomach kept growing. Perhaps I had done the wrong thing in sending them there. After all, did I really trust Abrianna? I guess I assumed she would protect us because it was in her best interest to do so. But what if she had another motive in mind? How could I be comfortable around this woman when I could not read her at all? "You look concerned, Whitnee. What is it?" she asked with mock kindness. Or so it seemed to me.

"I'm fine..." I swallowed with difficulty. "I guess I was missing them. Can I talk to Amelia?"

"Not right now. Eli took them on a walk through the gardens before dinner," she replied, and I couldn't help the face I made at the thought of them alone with Eli. Now *that* was definitely a man I did not trust.

"Will you have them call me when they return?"

"Of course!" she replied as if I had asked a stupid question. "Now, before you hand the zephyra back to my Attendant, I must ask if you have been following my advice... about certain matters?"

I pretended not to understand. "I don't remember what you are talking about..."

This seemed to frustrate her slightly as she replied, "I suppose the story Amelia told me was just an exaggeration then. She almost made it sound like you and Gabriel were... hmm, how did she word it exactly—?"

"You don't need to worry about that, Abrianna," I jumped in immediately. "Gabriel has done an excellent job of protecting us—"

"Really? Last night did not appear that way."

"Abrianna, surely you know that much of what happened was beyond his control."

"Of course... because I would hate to think that while these poor children were suffering at the hands of insurgents, he was distracted with... *other* issues." She had me where she wanted me then. The guilt was sitting in the pit of my stomach like a lead weight—I couldn't respond. "Remember to be careful with those emotions, Whitnee. You never know what kind of trouble you could be causing for yourself. I know you do not completely trust me. And I understand your reasons, since there is much I cannot tell you just yet. But do not forget that Gabriel works for me and is less than a year away from taking my position. He has his secrets, too, and you do not want to know all of them. Now, please put him on, as I have some issues I must discuss with him." And with that, she seemed to shut down our conversation. I did my best to keep my face expressionless while in view of the zephyra. I stood up from my place on the ground and marched over to Gabriel, handing him the zephyra without a word. Then I turned to Eden.

"I would really like to go back to the cabin now, if that's okay," I told her. She noticed my change in mood and agreed to walk us all back to the main part of the village.

"Will you take a walk with me? I must speak with you," Gabriel asked me later. We had already packed up our belongings and bathed again after our long day of training. Soon, the thunder-flies would take us to the Hydrodora village. Thomas informed us we would have yet another night of festive activities planned in our honor, and I just wasn't sure I was up for that.

Since we had returned to the cabin to get ready to leave, Gabriel had been using his zephyra off and on, leaving the room for various private conversations. He was growing more and more distant from the relaxed and friendly boy he had become today. And now his expression seemed burdened as he asked me to join him for a walk. As much as I was secretly hoping that "speaking with me" was an excuse to whisk me away where he could kiss me again, I could tell this was not the case.

We strolled in silence for a distance, heading in the direction of the spice fields. I waited patiently for him to talk first, and I was not expecting the first thing I heard come from his mouth.

"I have to leave you tonight," he said, a little indifferently.

"Why?" I blurted.

"It is too complicated to explain—"

"Is it Abrianna? Is she making you leave?" I could feel my own body heat start to rise at this idea.

"Nobody is making me do this. It is just something I must do."

"What do you mean? Does this have anything to do with ... us? I mean, with what happened last night ... between you and me?" He looked perplexed for a moment, trying to understand what I was referring to—and that had all my girl senses on red alert. Had he already forgotten the kisses and the "feelings" conversation? "I'm talking about our feelings for each other, Gabriel. Are you leaving because ... it's too much or you've changed your mind? I don't understand," I clarified. His face relaxed then as he realized what I meant.

"No. Nothing can change the way I feel about you," he told me with a small smile.

"So this has nothing to do with *us*?" I asked him again, gesturing between the two of us with my hand.

"It does, and it does not at the same time." He stopped walking altogether and took the opportunity to grab my hand and pull me closer to him. With his other hand, he traced his index finger in a line of Fire along my cheekbone to my lips. I could feel my heart stop beating as I watched the play of emotions on his beautiful face. "You are unlike anybody I have ever known. You are strong, and yet you open yourself up to be so vulnerable. I want nothing more than to stay by your side and watch you experience all these new places ..."

"Then why are you leaving?" I whispered, not understanding. He was leaning down closer to me, and I kept my eyes locked on his, wanting desperately to beg him to stay. His lips stopped about an inch away from mine.

"If I could not tell you where I was going or why, would you still trust me?" he asked in a surprisingly vulnerable voice. I closed my eyes and took a deep breath. However I answered this question would be an indicator of my true feelings for him. And we both knew it.

"I trust you," I answered back.

"Open your eyes, Whitnee Skye Terradora," he commanded me softly. And I did—just in time to see the open sincerity in his dark hazel eyes before one hand cupped my face protectively. As if it were the most natural thing in the world, he leaned down and gently pressed his lips to mine. My eyes closed again as I let him control the intensity. This kiss felt different than last night. It was delicate and searching, full of sweet possibility. There were no life forces battling this time, only a boy and a girl discovering a deeper meaning within each other's kiss. I sighed lightly as I leaned further into his embrace, but he kept the pressure of his kiss light. He traced a few tantalizing kisses across my cheek to just below my ear, and I had to stifle a giggle at the sensual tickle of his hot breath on my neck. Just when I was sure I would forever be lost in this moment, he pulled me into his arms for a sweet hug, pressing my face to his chest where his heartbeat hammered out a sharp rhythm.

"How long will you be gone?" I asked him as we held onto each other.

He rested his chin on the top of my head. "I will meet up with you again tomorrow before you leave Hydrodora."

"I don't know what it's like to be on this Island without you," I commented, not really sure what to say. I didn't want to tell him how nervous it made me to know I would be separated from him. He didn't need to know that I wouldn't feel safe again until I was with him. It was crazy to me how much could change in a few days.

"The safest village on the Island is Hydrodora. They have no enemies," he assured me. "But you will need to be wise about your choices. Trust no one except your friends, and contact me by zephyra if you feel that you are in trouble. It will be less than a day before I see you again. Will you be okay?" And he held me away at arm's length to search my face.

"Of course. I'll be fine." I tried to sound convincing and then, because an uneasy sensation was starting to wash over me, I asked, "Will you be okay?"

"You do not need to worry about me, Little One. Just take care of yourself," he smiled. But I wasn't so sure.

He held one hand out, palm facing toward me, as if inviting me to give him a high-five. I figured that wasn't exactly what he meant, so I stared at it uncertainly before reaching out and placing my own hand against his. His strong fingers folded down to lace with mine, and then I saw his palm glow orange and felt a tingling heat crawl up my arm toward my rapidly beating heart. His eyes were bright gold as he gazed intensely at our interlocked fingers. It seemed like he was trying to transfer some kind of comfort to me in the only other language he knew.

Without thinking, I conjured a cool breeze to tickle our palms in response. His face registered surprise, and his smile grew broader as he realized that I was returning the gesture. I smiled back, my own glowing eyes finding his while the orange and silver gleamed into a solid gold light between our hands.

Hello, again, Pilgrim. The scratchy voice echoed in my head as I prepared to board the thunderfly.

"Boomer?" I smiled in recognition.

Yes, it is I. The oversized insect tilted his large head my direction.

"I am so glad to see you again!" I told him, and I meant it.

Have you been training hard?

"Oh, yes. You have no idea … are your wings still sore or have you recuperated now?"

Something that sounded like nails raking a chalkboard echoed in my thoughts, and I concluded he was laughing. He replied, *All better now. Thank you for asking. Welcome onboard again, Pilgrim.*

"Thank you, Boomer. And, by the way, will you call me Whitnee, please?"

He chuckled again before agreeing to try.

After that, we said our last good-byes to our new Geo friends, who had loaded us up with snacks and specially mixed juices. Elon shed a few tears as she gave me a necklace of pink and white flowers. It was pretty difficult to leave, knowing I might not ever be back. The last person I hugged was Gabriel, who was also going his separate way then. He made me promise again to be careful, and then he helped me onto the carrier without any other physical contact. I was filled with an inexplicable sadness at knowing I wouldn't see him until tomorrow. And I scolded myself for being so weak as I climbed aboard Boomer's back.

We continued to wave good-bye as Boomer took off with his thunderous wings, and then we were above the treetops, looking out over the glorious Island sparkling in the late afternoon sun. Everything had a golden hue to it as we traveled through the sky. I was sitting next to Caleb, who had been uncharacteristically quiet since we returned from the meadow earlier. I had a feeling I knew why, but I did not want to discuss that with him just yet. Across from me, Morgan was asking Thomas more questions about Hydrodora.

"The village is settled on the Blue River," he was explaining, "which originates somewhere near the volcano as an underground spring and flows southward right between Pyradora and the Palladium hillside. Hydrodora is much further south, just before the river empties into the ocean. That is why, when we leave Hydrodora, we will travel by riverboat to the Pyradorian village. The Hydros and Pyras do much trading because of this easy access."

"So we're actually much closer to the Palladium there?" I wondered.

"If you travel by river, yes. The Palladium is further north and directly across the mountain from Pyradora. It is a very beautiful structure, with a silver dome that shines like a beacon in the sunlight. However, nothing compares to the beauty that is Hydrodora, in my opinion!"

We smiled at his enthusiasm and listened while he spoke proudly of his home. Well, I *tried* to listen. At his mention of the Palladium, I started worrying again about Amelia and Kevin. They hadn't checked in with us, and I vowed that as soon as we landed I would try contacting them again. Gabriel had finally shown me how to use the zephyra, including calling out and leaving a message.

It wasn't long before a huge winding river came into view ... and when I say huge, I am not exaggerating. The Blue River made the Frio River back in Texas look like a bubbling brook. True to its name, the water did indeed appear to be a glacier blue color, making me wonder if it was as cold as it looked. But the village itself was the real wonder. From up above, it looked like a Water park ... only people lived in it.

A series of clear tubes and long slides laced around the village. Boats of different shapes and sizes that were probably better described as floating buildings lined the broad river's edge for miles. Smaller canoe-sized boats raced in and around the village, reminding me of those water skater bugs back at Camp Fusion.

"Is the entire village on the river?" I asked Thomas as I noticed very few structures on land.

"Most of it." He told us this as if it were perfectly normal. "If you have the ability to manipulate the movement and flow of Water, then you are most at home around it. For this reason, most of our commerce takes place right on the Water, and we use the small wooden boats to get from place to place. There are land buildings too, just not as many."

"And what are all the slides for?" Morgan questioned, at which Thomas smiled boyishly.

"We like to have fun too."

"Do you swim a lot?" Caleb broke his silence to speak up, and his question evoked laughter from Thomas.

"Swimming is our greatest sport! I hope all of you are ready to get wet, because I am sure that will be a part of the activities tonight," he said, and I heard Levi sigh. Morgan traded glances with me, her face alight with excitement. I gave her a weak smile as I wondered what we would wear for such an activity. We touched down in the strange but beautiful Water-based settlement, and I surveyed the surroundings apprehensively. Nobody here knew about my crippling fish phobia. I wanted to keep it like that.

"Um, will there be ... fish anywhere?" I asked suddenly.

"Of course," Thomas answered, pointing to the village entrance. A great archway made of a unique white stone, much like the Watch Tower ruins, welcomed guests into the village. Two bright blue flags were flapping vivaciously along the sides of the arch while tall, majestic Water fountains, which seemed to come up straight from the ground of their own accord, created a welcoming pathway to the Water's edge. But what Thomas must have been pointing at was the Hydrodorian symbol carved into the great stone arch and stitched into the flags. It consisted of four wavy lines surrounding the silhouette of a fish.

Perfect.

The tribe dedicated its existence to a fish.

This was starting off well for me.

ALL ABOARD!

"Okay, does the constant rocking ever stop?" Caleb leaned over and whispered to me.

"What rocking? I don't feel anything." I gave him a confused look.

"Seriously? You don't feel that? If you sit really still, you can feel the whole place shift. I think I'm going to be sick." He did look rather pale.

"Well, do we need to get you to a bathing room or something?" He looked pretty miserable—and not just because of the seasickness. I knew there were other matters on his mind ... matters that I feared had to do with me.

"No, I think if I could just get some fresh air for a little bit, it would help ..." He was turning green now. We were surrounded by a small crowd of blue-eyed people on board a large boat with a restaurant, bedrooms, and recreational activities—much like a cruise ship, only smaller. Simeon had hosted a party aboard his entertainment ship for the entire evening. He was a humanist in the greatest way. Every question he asked was out of genuine interest and concern, and every story he told was of someone else's great accomplishments. He was a humble man with very little focus on himself—such a contrast to Ezekiel's extravagant nature.

By listening to him, I learned that the stone arch at the grand entrance was a gift from the Pyras, who were very gifted in creating and carving structures. Glass blowing and metal construction seemed to be specialties of the Pyras, and one look at Hydrodora spoke volumes about the relationship between the two tribes. The Pyras had helped construct many of the beautiful sights of the village. He explained that, in turn, the Pyras received much aid from the Hydros, who took care of their sickly and were quick to provide aid if Fire ever got out of control. With all that in mind, Simeon was disappointed to know that Gabriel could not join us for the evening. He did not say anything more on the topic, and I assumed if he did know what Gabriel was doing, he probably would not have said anything to me anyway.

Among the large and lively group aboard the ship were Simeon and his advisors. Thomas's parents and several of his blue-eyed friends added to the festive atmosphere. One girl in particular caught my attention early on. Her name was Lilley and she was the younger sister of Thomas's best friend, Mark. She was a couple of years younger than us, and it became obvious to me immediately that she was completely in love with Thomas. He talked to her and treated her like a little sister, but I was pretty sure he didn't notice the way her cheeks flushed when he threw a playful arm around her or bragged on her extraordinary abilities in healing. I wondered if someday he would figure out that she was no longer a little girl. By the look of things, it would be long after I was gone from here. Boys could be so dense.

I ended up listening and observing a lot through dinner, feeling like a piece of me was missing with my campers and now Gabriel gone. I picked at my plate, noting a lack of appetite that I knew had a lot to do with the fact that I still couldn't get a hold of Amelia or Kevin. When I had tried calling earlier,

Abrianna hadn't even answered. I knew this bugged Caleb just as much as it did me. Morgan, on the other hand, seemed to be in La-La Land the moment we got here—and I couldn't blame her. Hydrodora suited her in much the same way that Aerodora suited me. I still missed the constant airflow and the view of the ocean from my treetop balcony.

Everybody was mostly socializing by that point, so I turned to Simeon and rested a gentle hand on his wrinkled forearm.

"Simeon, would you mind if Caleb and I stepped out on the deck for a few minutes? I think he is feeling a bit nauseous, and I really need to try contacting Amelia and Kevin again at the Palladium."

He surveyed me with perceptive eyes as he nodded. "Not at all. There are guards posted all over the ship for your protection, so the entire ship is yours. We will all meet on the top deck soon anyway for some Water activities," he reminded me, and I nodded with appreciation.

"Thank you." But before I could move away, he reached out and touched my hand delicately. In a loud whisper, he said, "If you cannot reach the Palladium, I would encourage you not to worry. I cannot believe Abrianna would allow harm to visit your friends. Know that they are safe tonight and so are you."

He smiled, and I returned the smile weakly before grabbing a bottle of Water and standing to my feet. Several pairs of eyes followed my movements, and I motioned to Morgan that Caleb and I were going up to the deck. When she looked puzzled, I rubbed my belly and made a sick face. Understanding dawned on her face, and she waved before turning back to her crowd of admirers.

Caleb and I made our way upstairs, passing a few random people who were exploring the boat or engaged in private conversations. Once we reached the landing, he rushed to the side of the boat and leaned out into the night air, taking in deep breaths with his eyes closed. I offered him some Water. After he relaxed a little, we leaned against the railing, watching the boat move slowly and steadily along the River. I glanced sur-reptitiously at Caleb's miserable expression.

"Do you constantly feel the urge to pee in this village?" I blurted, hoping to lighten the mood. He puckered his eyebrows before letting out a mild laugh.

"You mean because everywhere you go there's the constant sound of moving water?"

"Yes! It's driving me mad!" I confessed dramatically. "I don't know how Morgan's dealing with it—she's the one with the small—"

"Yeah, yeah. I'm well aware of Morgan's bladder issues. More than I would like to be, actually. You know, sometimes I think you two forget that I'm a guy and don't need to hear all the personal stuff," he pointed out.

I sighed. "I would have thought with three older sisters, you'd heard it all."

"Ugh, don't remind me." He smiled and shook his head, then stared out over the water again. "I miss home."

"Me too." My mother's face flashed across my mind.

"Seriously?" He looked surprised.

"What does that mean? Of course I miss home!" I exclaimed like he was crazy—because he was. How could he doubt that?

"I guess you just seem so comfortable here. The people love you. You seem to understand every tribe and their customs without being taught … like you were born to be here. It's kind of weird, actually."

"Weird, as in I-can't-believe-my-best-friend-has-magical-powers kind of way? Because having the ability to create a tor-nado is definitely weird," I sighed.

"I didn't really understand the emotion and self-control it takes to use a life force until Joseph gifted me. It was scary to have access to such power, but it was the coolest thing I've ever experienced. Why do you think everyone is only able to use one, though? Present company excluded, of course."

"Well, who really knows why I can use more than one? I imagine everyone tends to relate to one more than the other three. It seems like it has to do with personality ... and eye color? Don't you think it's funny that our eye colors already matched the tribe we could relate to? I've always hated my gray eyes, but now they mean something. I wonder if the same rules apply to everybody back on the Mainland too?" We thought about this in silence for a moment, and I ran through the eye colors and personalities of the people back home. "You really are a Geo, you know. Even if your eyes weren't green, you'd still be a Geo."

"How's that?"

"You're honest and loyal even when it's probably not the easiest choice. You're usually as true and unchanging as the Earth itself. I know I can always depend on you ... and there are certain ways that you are absolutely predictable. You work hard at everything you do. That's why Steve always gives you extra responsibility at camp, because he knows you will do a quality job with it. Those seem to be defining traits of the Geodorians. They're just good, honest, hard-working people, you know? It would just be nice if you could learn to cook like them too ..." I gave a short laugh.

He seemed to ponder his response for a moment. When he spoke, he appeared a little frustrated. "It's hard to categorize you, though, Whit. I mean, you are so multi-faceted sometimes that you leave my head spinning. You definitely have the emotional and fiery side of a Pyra. But then, you can be loyal and honest just like the Geos too. You always like to have fun and laugh, which seems to be a Hydro's personality ... even if you don't like the whole fish thing. But then you're as dramatic and philosophical as an Aero, always wanting to try something new or go on some crazy adventure. It's hard to keep up with you."

"When you say it like that, it makes me feel like I should apologize or something. Is it a bad thing, what you're saying?"

"No, not a bad thing. Just more of a challenge, I guess." He smiled then. "Remember how theatrical Ezekiel was anytime he would tell us a story?" I nodded with a smile. "He reminded me of you. You do that, too, and it's highly entertaining ... and then the whole musical side of your personality fits. So, yeah, I guess I can see you primarily as an Aerodorian. I mean, you do look really cute when you use the Wind and your hair is flying all over the place ... And I suppose if I'm the unchanging Earth, then you *must* be the ever-changing Wind. Impossible to catch ..." And his face turned sullen again, and he wouldn't look at me.

"Caleb. Is there something on your mind?" I asked softly, knowing already what it was, but giving him permission to bring it up if he wanted to. He just stared unseeingly into the dark for a while, and I wasn't sure if I should press harder or wait.

"You know, I discovered something today, Whit," he finally responded in a low voice. I studied his face. I knew how his mind worked, and he was formulating exactly how he wanted to say whatever was coming next.

"What?"

"I thought I had seen all of your facial expressions and knew how to identify each one. But today—" He paused and took a deep breath. "Today I saw an expression on your face that I'd never seen before."

I was afraid to ask, but I did anyway. "Which one?"

"The one you use when you look at Gabriel," he answered. This time he did look directly at me, and it was my turn to shift my gaze away. I heard him sigh, as I was sure my face was already confirming whatever he was thinking.

"Caleb, I'm sorry ..." I didn't know what else to say. I truly was sorry that he was not the one I so desperately longed for out on this foreign boat in a foreign place.

"Don't apologize, Whit," he said quietly. "I just can't win ... on either side of the world," he added with a sardonic laugh. "But I think I'm okay with that ... or at least I don't seem to have a choice in it. I'm just meant to be your friend for now, right?"

"You'll always be my friend, Caleb," I replied pathetically.

"Of course. What every guy wants to hear from the girl he loves," he muttered, and I sucked in a breath at the impact of his words.

"Don't say that. You don't love me ... like that," I told him.

"How would you know, Whit?"

"Because if you truly did, you wouldn't have run off to Claire the night you tried to share your feelings with me!" I blurted. I know I had wanted to let go of all that, but it was the truth and he needed to hear it. "People just don't do that sort of thing when they know they've found the right person!"

"No, people don't do that sort of thing when they're thinking straight! I wasn't ... I just remember wondering why I should wait around for you anymore when Claire was obviously ready—"

"Ready to what? Make out with you? *Geez*, Caleb! That is such a selfish—"

"I'm not saying I don't regret it, because I do! And now we're here, and I really screwed up because I have to watch you and *Gabriel*—"

"Caleb!" I cut him off. "I know you ... so much better than you think I do. Someday, when you do find the right girl, you'll actually wait for her and work hard every day just to make her feel special and cherished. Because that's the kind of person you are. She will be so absolutely spoiled by you that I'm already jealous of her!" I exploded.

He held up his hands like he didn't want to hear anymore, so I stopped. We stood there in miserable silence, each trying to think of what to say to the other.

Finally, Caleb spoke again. "Maybe I just have some growing up to do."

"I think we both do," I agreed, focusing my gaze on the night sky filled with stars that someone somewhere on the Mainland had to be seeing too.

"You know, I don't hate him," Caleb mumbled.

"Who?"

"Gabriel. I really believe he wants what's best for you … if it weren't for that, I would have demanded we leave this Island much sooner. But I have a feeling he's the only one who can help you figure out this mystery about your dad."

"Maybe," I agreed, glad to hear him say something positive about Gabriel.

"But that doesn't mean I like seeing the way you two are together," he was quick to add. "It's worse knowing that he can actually help you with all this life force stuff and I can't. And he's obviously somebody important here on the Island—"

"He's the next Guardian, actually," I told him for the first time.

"Huh?"

"Yeah."

"Oh, even better! That's practically equivalent to being the president of the United States! How's a guy supposed to compete?" He threw up his hands, and his expression was so ridiculously frustrated that I almost choked trying to hold back my laughter. It was just so dang cute of him to react that way.

"Are my feelings that funny to you?" he growled at my expression, and I shook my head. But I couldn't help the amusement from escaping in short, muffled laughs. Eventually he cracked a smile too.

"That was just a *really* dramatic reaction … I'm sorry." I composed myself. "And if you only knew … he's completely jealous of you!"

"He is? Why?" He looked thirsty to hear more at that point.

"*Duh*, why do you think? You're my best friend and, unlike him, you actually have a right to be in my life. It frustrates him that there are things you know and understand about me that he can't figure out."

"Well, after putting up with you for the last five years, I should know more than a guy who's only known you for, what, four days?"

"Has it only been four days?" I gasped. "Feels like each day is worth one week here."

"Totally agree," he said, and his face seemed a bit lighter. Perhaps knowing that Gabriel was jealous of him boosted his confidence a bit.

"Listen, are we okay? Is *this* going to be okay between us?" I asked, and he shrugged.

"I'll survive ... at least until we get off the Island."

And I guess I was satisfied with that answer. "Can I ask you something?" I turned so I could face him.

"Of course. Unless it's a girl problem thing ... I don't really—"

"No, I'm being serious." I gave him a look.

"What is it?" He was giving me his full attention then, and I couldn't help reaching my hand out to his temple, lightly grazing the scar from his coconut accident.

"Why did you keep the scar? The HydroHealer could have fixed it for you."

"Are you kidding? My best friend heals me from a pretty serious head injury and you don't think I want to keep proof of that?" He raised his eyebrows and gave me a characteristic Caleb smile. "Every scar has a story, and this one is special."

I stared sadly at him for a moment and then pushed the feeling aside. And just in time ... our party crew was beginning to join us out on the deck and, apparently, the real fun was just beginning.

"That was the most fun ever!" Morgan gushed hours later when we were back in our shared bedroom aboard the boat. Caleb had a room across the hall, but he was currently sprawled out on our floor listening halfheartedly to our chatter. We had discovered that the beds were actually waterbeds! They didn't look the same as the waterbeds we were used to, but it was the same concept. Caleb had threatened to sleep on the floor instead of teetering back and forth on a bed made of Water. Simeon had given him a special drink to help with his seasickness, so I believed it was all in his head at this point. Eden and Levi had already retired to their own rooms on the hall. Thomas had gone home with his family for the night, but promised to meet up with us in the morning. "Have you ever seen people swim *that* fast? It was incredible."

"Well, it certainly helped that they could manipulate the Water into pushing them faster. I was like a turtle out there," Caleb griped, one half of his face smashed into the floor. There had been several organized games in the huge, interconnecting pools on the top deck, and Caleb had been the only one who couldn't use the Water life force. Levi and Eden had sat the games out, knowing immediately that they would never be able to compete with Hydros.

"Oh, please. With Thomas helping you cheat the whole time, you can't complain," Morgan chided him. "And speaking of Thomas,"—she threw herself down on one of the waterbeds and rocked back and forth—"is he not the cutest thing ever? I mean, he's no Gabriel, but he's definitely a hottie in his own right ... especially once he took off his shirt."

Caleb clapped his hands over his ears and groaned. "This is what I was talking about earlier ..." he muttered to me, and I couldn't help smiling sympathetically. While Morgan continued torturing him with her thoughts about Thomas's tribal birthmark and how it might make a cool tattoo when she turned eighteen, I flipped the zephyra over and over again in my hands, thinking.

I had successfully contacted Abrianna, but she had produced yet another excuse why Amelia and Kevin couldn't talk to me. She even said that Amelia was still refusing to communicate with me. It was starting to make me very uncomfortable. And I had received a message from Gabriel when I came back to the room. A miniature version of his handsome face had appeared in the device, setting my heart aflutter.

"Hello, Little One... I suppose you are out with the Hydros having fun right now. I tried contacting Simeon and did not receive an answer, but I have been assured that you arrived safely in Hydrodora. I will be traveling to Aerodora later tonight and then probably to the Palladium. I promise I will check on Kevin and Amelia for you. I will arrive in Hydrodora tomorrow morning so we can work on our training again before heading north to Pyradora. Contact me if you experience any troubles. I miss you... and I keep thinking about you. I can hear your laughter in my head sometimes and I... well, I look forward to seeing you tomorrow. Peaceful sleep, Whitnee." And I couldn't help curling my toes and smiling like an idiot every time I remembered the part where he said he missed me... it was so cute to watch him try to express himself. I knew it wasn't easy for him, but every attempt felt so good.

"What are you smiling about?" Morgan's voice interrupted my thoughts.

"Nothing," I replied. "Can we just go to bed, though? I'm exhausted." And that really was the truth.

"Do y'all care if I just stay in here? If you can spare a pillow and blanket, I'd prefer the floor anyway," Caleb mumbled from the floor space separating the beds.

"I don't care." I launched a pillow violently at him.

"Hey. That was unnecessary," he grumbled, pulling himself up on his elbows just in time for Morgan to throw a heavy blanket over his head.

"I am so abused..." His voice was muffled.

"Good night!" I called with a roll of my eyes.

"And no cow jokes," Morgan warned.

Once I had fallen asleep, I dreamed very vividly for the first time since being on the Island. In the dream, I was huddled in the corner of a dark concrete room that seemed to rock subtly back and forth. All was quiet except for a creaking sound somewhere deep below the foundation.

"Hello?" I called out.

"Whitnee, don't be afraid." A gruff but familiar voice spoke inside my head. I couldn't see him, but I could hear him as clearly as if he was right next to me.

"Dad?"

"Yes, Baby Doll, it's me. I don't have much time, so I need you to listen to me very carefully."

"Why can't I see you?" I asked, peering around the dim room.

"Whitnee, listen! I am so proud of you, but you need to get off this Island as soon as possible."

"Well, I'm trying ..."

"No, you're not. They're keeping you busy and separating you and your friends for a reason. You need to stay focused on getting home immediately!"

"How do I do that?"

"Get to the Palladium. There's an underground research facility where they experiment with portal development. There is an active portal there, but you have to find the entrance! Only an Aerodorian can access it—" He was speaking faster now.

"Whoa, whoa, wait. How do I know any of what you're saying is real? I don't understand—"

"I know you don't. But this is very real and you are in very *real* danger. There is so much I didn't tell you or your mother ... and I'm sorry for everything. I thought I was protecting both of you, and now if you don't get off the Island, it will all be for nothing!"

"Does that mean...Dad, are you here on the Island? Are you alive? Because if you are, I can come get you and take you back—!"

"No! You leave the Island, no matter what! That is your first priority, Whitnee Skye! Please, no matter what they tell you, use the portal and leave this place forever."

I was crying now. "Dad...my life has never been the same since you left. Mom still loves you, and in the back of her mind, I think she still expects you to come home. Please! If you're here...if there's some way...tell me!"

I could hear him sigh.

With intense emotion, like he was swallowing back his own tears, he choked, "You have no idea how much I love you. I never intended to leave you and Serena—" His voice cracked on her name. "Listen, Baby Doll, I need you to promise that you will do everything you can to get home to your mother! They will try to use you and your abilities if you stay any longer. You are on your own. Trust no one. Get your friends and go. Will you promise me that?"

"Okay..." I was openly sobbing now as I nodded reluctantly. "Okay, I'll try. I love you, Daddy. I love you so much, and I miss you every day of my life."

"I love you..." he replied in the faintest of voices.

"Dad? Don't leave me!" I called out to him. He was speaking, but it was no longer clear. He was fading from me. "Dad! I don't know how to use the portal! You didn't tell me what to do...Dad! Don't leave! Don't leave!" I screamed and clawed at the concrete walls. If only I could blast through them. The foundation beneath me rocked and creaked and I stood back, prepared to launch a Fireball of destruction at the room—

"*Whitnee! Wake up!*"

The concrete room faded, and I was jolted back into reality. A very frightening reality—I was standing atop my waterbed with my hands extended in front of me, each eliciting an orange glow as if prepared to unleash a fiery attack. Caleb and Morgan had cleared out from standing in front of me but were desperately trying to wake me up. I dropped my hands.

"Are you awake now? Whit, look at us!" Caleb demanded, and I obeyed by meeting his frightened eyes. "Oh, *geez*, Whit. I thought you were going to kill us all. What ... what happened?" He pulled me off the bed and into his trembling arms. Morgan exhaled loudly and placed a comforting hand on my back while I just sobbed and sobbed. It had been so real ...

I felt Caleb place a protective arm around my head as he traced circles along my back like he always did when comforting me. "*Shhh* ..." he soothed. "It was just a dream ... you were dreaming."

There was a sharp rap on the door then and Morgan moved to check it. Hydroguards had heard a commotion and needed to make sure everyone was safe. Morgan quickly assured them we were all okay and thanked them for checking on us. As soon as the door was shut again, she came and sat on the bed across from me.

"Do you want to talk about it?" Caleb prodded. I shook my head vehemently.

"Not now. Not yet. Maybe tomorrow." I sniffled and pulled away from both of them. "I'm sorry I woke you and nearly set Fire to the whole place." I attempted a fake smile, but they could see right through it. Besides, it just wasn't funny what had almost happened. I sighed and crawled back into the water-bed. "Go back to sleep. I'm fine now." They glanced at each other doubtfully, but I turned on my side where they couldn't see my face anymore. Eventually, I heard them settle back down and return to sleep.

But I didn't shut my eyes again. I stared unseeingly at the wall, running through every thought, every memory, every experience since being on this Island. I knew it was time to go home. I just didn't know how to make that happen yet.

TIME TO ROCK THE BOAT

I was floating in a wooden lounge chair, allowing my fingers to drift in the cold Blue River. And though I may have appeared relaxed to the onlookers (and there were several in the village), every nerve inside my body was on edge.

I'll be honest... a good portion of my anxiety was over the likely presence of fish in the blue Water around me. I found it pretty ridiculous that even on the White Island where I was supposedly all-powerful, I still cowered over a tiny, swimming, gilled creature. But the greater part of my anxiety originated from my disturbing dream—and from the fact that it was approaching lunchtime and Gabriel still hadn't shown up.

Halfheartedly, I watched Morgan playing in the Water like she was a native Hydrodorian. She even looked the part with her hair dyed dark and her blue eyes magically illuminated... the only difference was that her skin tone was not quite as dark as the others who surrounded her. Thomas and his friends were teaching her different tricks with the Water life force, and it seemed that everything they did ended up in a big splash fest. Naturally they had invited me to join in, but Morgan had bailed me out without letting everyone know of my fish phobia. However, watching her laugh and enjoy herself only made me feel more torn over our situation. I couldn't help but think guiltily that Kevin and Amelia should be here. With *us*, with people they *knew*. They should be playing out in the Water under my watchful eye. How had we convinced ourselves that sending them ahead to the Palladium had been the best choice?

My mind kept returning to my dream and the words I had been sure came directly from my dad. I was past questioning my own sanity. I mean, I would never have believed I could shoot flames from my own hands, and yet that was happening on this strange Island. Why *couldn't* my supposedly dead father speak to me while I slept? The contents of my dream hadn't faded from my vivid memory, as most dreams tend to do the longer you are awake. If anything, the details were becoming sharper to me. There were things that he mentioned that I wasn't sure my subconscious was capable of creating on its own. Like the existence of a portal in a research facility beneath the Palladium? Those were words I didn't typically use. And what about his reason for vanishing in the first place ... to protect me? In all these years, I had never dreamt of that being the reason. There was no logical explanation for why I would suddenly come up with that out of my own thoughts. I could only conclude that I had somehow, in some way, communicated with my father.

The only question was, *Where was he?* Somewhere on the Island? Or speaking from the afterlife? I shivered at that thought. That would've gone against everything I'd ever been taught about life and death ... dead people don't talk. But, if it was all real, then I had to assume several things.

Assumption Number One: My father is alive enough somewhere in order to be aware of my present predicament. And not only that, but he knows this Island and the people.

Assumption Number Two: Separating my group of friends is someone's master plan at manipulating me.

But for what purpose? That part I still couldn't figure out.

Assumption Number Three: I don't really know who I can trust outside of Morgan and Caleb.

And, yes, that meant Gabriel was suspect, too, as much as it pained me to admit that.

So here I was ... floating not just on the Blue River but also in a deep and dark sea of questions, suspicions, and fears. I desperately wanted to see Gabriel and talk these thoughts out. My trust in him wasn't completely wavering, but things had been slightly different yesterday when he had left me. Today, I needed answers. I needed to know his theories about my father. I needed to hear why he left. I refused to listen to that little nagging voice warning me that Gabriel might not be completely innocent. To give credibility to that stupid voice would be giving Abrianna power over me. I sensed that she wanted me to doubt Gabriel's character. She was the one who said he would use me to his own advantage, but so far he had only helped me understand and hone my abilities so that I could take better care of myself. She had warned me that his feelings might be out of wrong motivations, but I believed in his sincerity. No matter what she said, I still trusted Gabriel. He had been as honest with me as possible, and I knew that when the time was right, he would share everything else with me too.

But I couldn't get to that point until he arrived.

Suddenly, my thoughts were interrupted by a perfectly aimed splash right at my face.

"Wake up," Caleb called as he and Eden paddled over to me in a little wooden boat. I had seen these boats all over the village and they were powered by the Hydro life force. However, people who couldn't access that life force had to opt for traditional rowing with large paddles. Seeing the two of them return from their tour of the village made me wonder just how late it was getting.

"How was it? Did you see anything cool?" I asked, shielding my eyes from the sun as they pulled up right next to me.

"Uh, yeah! This place is amazing ... you should have come with us!"

"Sorry, I just didn't feel up to it. Tell me what you found."

"Well, we stopped at Marah, which is the place where they purify the Water and bottle it to send out to the entire Island. There are twelve springs that literally come right out of the ground... pretty sure I've never seen anything like that on the Mainland." Caleb chattered on, "Then we passed by the HydroHealing Center, which is actually a land building. That's where sick people from all the villages go. That was pretty cool, but then there was the recreation center and *wow*! It makes our water parks in Texas look like child's play."

"So... you're not wet. Did you not try it out?" I wanted to know.

"We thought we would wait and all go together later," Eden explained. "In fact, we were trying to figure out how we would train today without drawing the attention of others. It seems like everywhere we go, people are watching you. Any idea when Gabriel is supposed to arrive?"

"No. You mean he hasn't contacted any of you either?"

She shook her head. "No. Perhaps he got delayed somewhere. You did say he was going to the Palladium last night?"

"That was what his message said. But he's been so secretive about the whole thing. I don't even know what he's doing."

"That certainly sounds like Gabriel," she agreed. "He has always been so serious. Even when we were children, he would not play games with us. This is the first time I have been around him when he actually laughed and seemed to enjoy himself. I think you are the reason for that. He seems to want to make you happy and I think that in doing so, *he* is happy."

I blushed a little at her words, avoiding eye contact with Caleb. "He has definitely turned out different than my first impression of him. But sometimes, he acts like he has the burden of the whole world on his shoulders." I pictured his stoic features when he was contemplating something I couldn't understand. "Why do you think that is? Is it because he's the next Guardian or because of his parents?"

"Oh, you know about his parents?" Eden looked surprised. "We do not usually talk about that."

"Yes, I know he comes from an inter-tribal marriage or something like that. Is that really such a big deal on the Island?" Caleb and I waited curiously for an answer.

"It is slowly becoming more widely accepted by the younger generation, but yes, it typically is a big deal. It often confuses the children who result from such a relationship, because people look down on them for not having a defined tribe to belong to. It is sometimes believed that a child can be born with abilities in both life forces if the parents come from two different tribes, but there has never been proof of that theory. One life force will ultimately dominate the other. And as we always say, you are born into one tribe only."

"Well, it just seems silly that if two people from two different tribes love each other, they should be forbidden to be together. Isn't that a bit archaic?" I looked to Caleb for agreement.

"I do not know what you mean..." she confessed. "I only know how it has always been done here, and that has been the tradition."

"No wonder Gabriel doesn't have many friends... if people really look down on him because of his parents, I'm sure that changed everything growing up. And he wasn't even raised around his parents! Doesn't the future Guardian grow up at the Palladium away from their family?"

"Well, traditionally, yes, but—"

"Well, then it is unfair for people to judge him because of his parents' own choices! It wasn't like he could do anything about that. You don't choose your parents."

Eden was studying me then with a puzzled expression on her face. She seemed perturbed by something, and I started worrying I had said too much. After all, who was I to question their traditions? Just because we were different on the Mainland didn't mean that they were wrong...

"Whitnee, you must understand that people do not treat him differently because of *what* his parents are. It is usually the natural result of *who* they are."

"What do you mean?"

"Surely you can imagine the suspicions and mistrust surrounding his appointment as future Guardian? Especially since it was the first time in our history that the son of the current Guardian was chosen—"

"Say *what*?" I gasped. "Are you telling me his parents ... his mother is ... ?" I couldn't even finish my sentence as I met Caleb's shocked gaze.

I felt my stomach drop, and my heart started racing as Eden replied, "Well, yes, Abrianna is his mother. And Eli is his father. Did you not know that?"

I was shaking. I just needed to contact him. I needed to hear him tell me the truth. But I couldn't stop shaking enough to use the stupid zephyra. So I paced around my bedroom by myself, trying to calm down. A thousand emotions seemed to be running through my system, and it was taking all of my self-control to keep the powerful life forces from ripping out of my body and damaging something.

I was hurt that he had lied to me. Angry with him for being the son of the woman I least trusted on this Island. Angry at *myself* for trusting *him* so easily. And why? Just because he had a beautiful face and the lips of Adonis himself ... ? My *gosh*! Who *knew* what kind of lies I had swallowed? Did I really believe now that he hadn't known anything about how to transport me home? He was the one I had relied on for all my information about this forsaken place, and I didn't even know now how much of it was real and how much of it was his and Abrianna's manipulation of my situation. Was this what Abrianna meant when she told me he had his own secrets? *Family* secrets? *Ugh!* And the fact that Eli was his father … that intimidating, unnerving elder of the Pyradora tribe who stuck to Abrianna's side! What kind of a family was I dealing with here? This changed everything for me.

Except for a little voice in my head that told me to calm down and see what Gabriel had to say about this. He might have had a good reason for withholding this information from me. He might have a really good explanation for why he'd been gone, and maybe he would come out and tell me everything. I couldn't blame him until I had heard his side.

But I *could* blame him. That was a pretty major piece of information to withhold from me, and it made every other thing he refused to tell me even more important! With a violent snap, I opened the zephyra.

"Gabriel." I spoke forcefully into the little spinning paddles. Then I waited … and waited … and paced until a bright flash lit the device, which I knew was my cue to leave him a message.

"Hi … Gabriel." I didn't smile as I looked into the device, and my voice came out strained. "I don't know why you aren't picking up your zephyra … we've been waiting for you at Hydrodora, and I guess we're going to move ahead with our plans to travel to Pyradora later today, whether you're here or not …" But then I sighed and closed my eyes. "I really wish you could talk to me right now because … I found out something pretty important, and I guess I wanted to hear you tell me it's not a big deal. But it is a big deal … to me, at least. I don't know how to trust you anymore and … I guess I feel like my time here is coming to an end. I need to get Kevin and Amelia back, and we need to go home and … I'm sorry. Maybe you really were the only thing keeping me here and now … well, now that's changed. I guess I'll find you later … Bye." And I snapped it shut and took a deep breath. Not sure how wise it was to leave a message like that ... but if he wasn't going to answer my calls, then that's all he would get.

The next call I made was to Abrianna. And apparently, she and her *son* were more alike than I knew, because she didn't answer either. I didn't even bother leaving her a message, so I threw the zephyra across the room and stormed my way to the top deck of the boat. Morgan and Caleb and the others were still down in the restaurant area, and the deck was relatively deserted. I didn't even see any Hydroguards around. I found the place where Caleb and I had stood last night talking, and I sagged weakly against the railing. Though this would have been the perfect opportunity to cry, I couldn't. All I felt was a sense of anger and a new resolve to retrieve my campers and get off this Island. I was tired of feeling like I was being manipulated. I didn't care if I was their Pilgrim or not. I could not help an Island of people who could not be honest. And my father was very clear that "they" would try to use me and my abilities ...

"You look ill. Is there anything I can do to help you?" A kind voice interrupted my thoughts, and I straightened myself up to find Simeon surveying me quizzically. He was alone as far as I could tell, and his blue eyes watched me carefully.

"No, I am not sick. I was just ..." I trailed off, not able to come up with an excuse for my behavior. He nodded casually as he moved to stand beside me and look out over his Water-bound village.

"You were just feeling completely overwhelmed and confused. Am I right?" he said matter-of-factly. I just raised my eyebrows.

"Is it that obvious?"

"I just imagined how I would feel if it were me in your position right now. And those were the two primary emotions that came to mind." He smiled at me. "You found yourself in a place you had never heard of, and suddenly you were able to do great things you had never been able to do before. Then, you were told by a bunch of people who mean nothing to you that you are their 'chosen one,' their 'savior.' If anything would overwhelm and confuse a person, it would be that." This did invite a small smile from me, and it felt good to have somebody on this Island try to see things from my perspective.

"It is not that I don't care about the Island, Simeon...if anything, traveling to the different villages has shown me how much I could truly love this place and the people—"

"Ah!" he interrupted, and his blue eyes twinkled. "Then our primary goal for you was accomplished. After all, is love not the most important force of life? Just like the power of a life force, people are likely to achieve great things in the name of love. How could you really be the Pilgrim if you did not first love those you came to rescue?"

"But you assume that I am the Pilgrim!"

"Are you not?"

I sighed and realized that I truly didn't have an answer to that question yet. "I just don't know, Simeon. I hardly feel in touch with who I really am right now. There are too many complications...too many issues at hand. It's hard to figure myself out when nothing else seems to make sense."

"You cannot let circumstances dictate who you will be, Whitnee. Circumstances change, emotions change...but you *choose* your place in this world."

"And did you *choose* to be here on this Island?" I threw back at his lofty logic.

"In a way, yes. None of us can help where we are born and to whom. But I could have left and sought another life. There have been those who have done so in the past. But my role is here, as leader and protector of my tribe," he stated, and I shook my head slowly.

"I do not know what my role is... I'm very confused."

"Well, time reveals all things."

"Ezekiel said something kind of like that before I left Aerodora," I mumbled. "I think my time here is almost over, Simeon."

"You know, Whitnee, every beginning has its end. I remember when my wife became ill several years ago..." He gazed nostalgically out on the river, as if seeing his past before his very eyes. "I could not eat or sleep while she was in such pain. I did not even bathe or change my clothes, and then one day... she died. And I was just... finished. I realized there was nothing I could do to heal her. Someday I will go to her, but she will not return to me. And because I had much life left to live—responsibilities to maintain, people to take care of—I had to press on. She would not have wanted me to quit." I listened patiently to his story, surprised at how well I could relate. "But only *I* could decide that I was ready for change. And do you know the first thing I did?"

"What?"

"I bathed in the purest Water I had and put on fresh clothes."

I stared at him, waiting for more to his story, but he just smiled at me expectantly. "You took a bath and... you changed your clothes?"

"Exactly. And you, too, have a choice. If you feel that it is time for a change, then put your old clothes on"—he pulled gently at the sleeve of my Dorian tunic—"and do what you must. You have more control over your choices than you realize. Do not be fooled into believing you are powerless here."

I thought about what he was saying, briefly wondering if this was his subtle way of telling me I needed a bath. Did I stink? Or did he mean something else...?

He was smiling at me when he remarked, "We shall be leaving the village shortly and moving upriver to Pyradora. We will dock very close to the Palladium. Now, if you will excuse me, I have some matters to attend to. I wish you good fortune in your endeavors, and please know that no matter what you decide, you are always welcome in Hydrodora!" He gave my back a little pat and walked away before I could respond. And I was left contemplating what a strange conversation that had turned out to be.

GOOD-BYES

I was holed up in my little bedroom, staring out the small window, when Morgan and Caleb finally found me. I had intentionally avoided contact with anyone since my conversation with Simeon, and the only way I could successfully accomplish this was by staying in the room. The day was beautiful and the Water so clear and inviting, but I could not enjoy it. Somewhere in the distance a storm was brewing. All of my Aero instincts confirmed this. But, inside my mind, the storm was already raging as I tried to piece together everything I knew.

"Whitnee, what are you doing in here? You should've been outside enjoying the sights! And now we're leaving!" Morgan scolded me as she burst through the door. Caleb was right behind her.

"What is wrong with you?" he asked, probably noticing my posture and the way I clutched the zephyra to my chest. "Are you still upset about Gabriel? I bet he's probably already waiting for us at Pyradora."

"Then why wouldn't he call and tell me that?" I responded quietly. Neither of them had an answer to that question. "Nobody has been in contact with him. Listen ... what would you say if I told you we needed to leave this Island as soon as possible?"

"I would agree," Caleb said readily.

Morgan seemed more tortured over the concept. "You mean sooner than we planned?"

"Yes," I replied. "Much sooner. Like today."

"Okay … maybe you should tell us exactly what's going on," Morgan suggested. "You've been different since Gabriel left, and even more so since you had that dream about your dad last night."

"I never told you it was about my dad … how did you know that?"

Caleb and Morgan traded glances before Caleb said, "Whatever conversation you were having with him, we could hear your side of it."

"It was pretty creepy, Whit," Morgan admitted. "So, talk. We need to know everything."

And I agreed. I needed their help. So I told them everything about the dream, about my personal theories and questions. They listened carefully, becoming more upset about Amelia and Kevin as our discussion went on.

"We never should have let them go somewhere without us!" Caleb pounded his fist on the bed.

"But it sounded like the right thing to do!" Morgan said.

"It did. But now that none of us has talked to them, I have a very bad feeling. I can't even get Abrianna on her zephyra anymore. I am telling you that something is wrong—we need to get to the Palladium immediately, rescue Kevin and Amelia, and find that portal," I insisted.

"Okay, then. Let's tell Simeon that we changed our minds and we want to go—"

"No!" Caleb jumped in. "We don't know who we can trust."

"Fine, then we tell Thomas and Eden and Levi—" she started but stopped as I shook my head fiercely. "What? You don't trust them either?"

"Caleb has a point. We just don't know right now. We have to do this on our own, Morgie. Besides, we can't ask them to defy their leader when we don't even have proof that something shady is going on. They could end up in trouble. I mean, we are operating on suspicion and a dream ... I don't think anyone else should be involved."

"But what about Gabriel?" she asked, and I felt my facial expression harden.

"What about him?" I retorted.

"You don't think you should wait until you talk to him? I thought you believed he was trustworthy ..."

"I can't find him. And I just ... I just can't think about him right now, okay? It's time to get my head out of the clouds anyway. We've got bigger things to worry about, like finding our campers."

"And your dad? What about all of that?" Morgan pressed harder. I just crossed my arms and stared at her, unsure what to say.

"If that really was your dad, he would have a good reason for telling you to leave, right?" Caleb clarified, watching me carefully. I could only nod, because I realized then everything I was giving up by leaving quickly—and that included forfeiting the opportunity to figure out what happened to my dad. "Okay, then," he said. "If you're sure, then I'm ready. What do we do first?"

"We change clothes," I stated simply, thinking about Simeon. "After all, we can't go home in our Dorian clothes, right? Time to pull out the old Camp Fusion shirts ..."

They stared at me in confusion.

Once the khaki shorts and t-shirt slid over my skin, I felt like I was already halfway home. Even my green flip-flops greeted me with comforting familiarity as they slipped on my feet. Going home was the right thing—and all we had to do was figure out how to escape to the Palladium unnoticed.

Morgan had informed me that a smaller traveling boat would be picking us up soon, and we were now just waiting for an attendant to come get us. I could feel the bump of my little Swiss Army knife still in my back pocket, and I smiled ironically. To think I had brought that little thing for protection, only to discover I was capable of much greater powers than a little pink knife could offer.

Someone rapped sharply on the door, and I figured that was our cue to go. We picked up our bags and I pulled the door open only to run right into a towering figure with a devastatingly beautiful face. Sucking in my breath, I allowed myself a glorious few seconds just to appreciate once again how gorgeous he was, leaning on the doorway, his warm brown eyes focused only on me.

"Gabriel," I breathed, resisting the urge to throw my arms around him. All of the attraction I felt for him clashed with my anger toward him and launched me into one big pit of confusion. So I just stood there, frozen in place.

"I am sorry I am late." He spoke in muted tones, taking in my lack of emotional response. "I, uh … I received your message on the zephyra and traveled as quickly as I could." His eyes were tortured—they flicked to Morgan who was standing behind me, staring uncertainly at both of us. "Morgan, would you give me a few minutes alone with Whitnee?"

Before she could respond, I interrupted icily, "Anything you have to say to me can be said in front of her." I think I was terrified to be alone with him, especially since I couldn't make sense of how I wanted to feel about him.

"Actually," Morgan cut in, "I really need to check on Caleb … so, if you'll just let me get by—" She dropped her bag and moved determinedly past me and across the hall to Caleb's room. "Just come get us when you're … done," she called back, as I threw her an ugly look. That traitor! She frowned apologetically before disappearing behind Caleb's door.

"May I come in?" Gabriel asked hesitantly.

"Fine," was my frosty response as I moved back into the room. We turned to face each other once he had shut the door behind him. "Where have you been?" I demanded, deciding that once I was out of close proximity to his body, anger was the more dominant emotion within me.

"I will explain that in a moment. First, tell me what you meant in your message."

"What part?" I played dumb, and he gave me a withering look.

"You know what."

"It doesn't even matter anymore. Because we're going back to the Mainland ... tonight. And there's nothing you can do to stop us."

He let out a breath he must have been holding and then sank onto the edge of Morgan's bed wearily. Finally, he said, "That is probably for the best."

Confused by this, I took a step closer. "So you agree it is time for me to leave?"

"Yes. And I will help you," he answered, and for some stupid reason my feelings were hurt. "But please tell me ... what happened that caused you to change your mind so drastically?"

"First of all, I can't get in touch with Kevin or Amelia. Abrianna stopped answering her zephyra. And when she did answer, she made excuses about why the kids couldn't talk to me," I told him, and he raised his eyebrows.

"That is not quite so strange ... there is much to do at the Palladium. I am sure the children are being entertained—"

"Then why isn't she answering?"

"Zephyras are not always dependable, Whitnee. Surely you understand that?"

"No ..." I faltered a moment. "How would I understand that? In our world—"

"This is not your world."

"Okay, well..." I drifted off, folding my arms across my chest in frustration.

"Is that all? You said something about how you could not trust me anymore ...?" he prodded me.

"Exactly, which is why I'm saying nothing more on the subject. I just need to leave here, Gabriel. And it sounds like you are ready for me to go back too."

"I never said that." He glanced at me in surprise from his place on the bed. "I only agreed that it is time for you to return to your home. I have kept you here too long."

"*You* have kept me here?" I repeated, not understanding.

"Selfishly, yes. You were right—I could have demanded that you be sent home sooner. But I was not ready for you to leave."

This caused me to soften a little—only a little. "You mean, you weren't ready for me to leave because you wanted to make sure I really was the Pilgrim, right? Because you didn't want to disappoint your people again?" I wanted him to clarify.

"I *wish* I had been so noble and clear-minded as that," he said fiercely. "I did not *want* you to leave, Whitnee, because of who you are to *me*. I kept you here for my own selfish reasons. Even you said yourself that I might be the only reason you have stayed this long ... but that is the wrong reason. You should stay because you choose to do so, not because anybody is making you. However, it is obvious"—he gestured faintly at my wardrobe selection—"that once I was out of the picture, you made your choice."

"Actually, once you were out of the picture, I found out the truth!"

"About what?"

"Gabriel!" I sighed in frustration as I stood over him while he sat. "*Why* didn't you tell me who your parents really were?"

His face grew hard, and I detected that defensive wall rising up around him. "Why does it matter to you who my parents are?" he growled.

"Because it affects your motives! Just like finding out you were the next Guardian, it changes everything! How can I trust you, knowing that everything you do could have an ulterior motive behind it?"

"What exactly do you think my motives are, Whitnee?" He stood, and his large stature should have intimidated me—but I was done being a victim and a coward around these people.

"You tell *me*, Gabriel! How do I know all these feelings you profess for me are even real? How do I know they're not part of some plan between you and your *family* to use me? Who knows what y'all really have planned for my friends and me? For all I know, you guys have Kevin and Amelia locked up somewhere!" I was getting close to hysterical, and I swallowed with difficulty. As he listened to me, his face was a mask of disgust and hurt all at the same time.

In his dangerously calm voice, he said, "If that is what you think of me, then perhaps you did not come to know me as well as I had hoped." And he sat back down with a level of difficulty that I could not understand in my highly agitated state.

"Then prove me wrong and get me home! I have no desire whatsoever to be here any longer!" It wasn't the complete truth, but I was out of options. If I lost my hard resolve in the face of this attraction between us, I would never leave. And all the signs were pointing me to go home. I couldn't let anything stand in my way. It just seemed best to maintain a coldness to him, no matter how difficult it was.

"I will instruct Simeon of the change in plans," he said quietly and then winced. He was acting very strange. I had expected him to put up more of a fight. But I guess that just confirmed my theory.

"No. We don't tell anyone until we dock upriver. I don't want your *mother* receiving news of our change in plans. I would like to show up at the Palladium … unannounced," I told him firmly. He eyed me curiously before replying.

"They may not be as surprised as you think. After what is happening with the rebels—" He sighed and rubbed his forehead. Again, I was confused by his reaction and his lack of emotion.

"What is wrong with you?" I questioned harshly, and he just stared at me, almost in a daze. "Gabriel…?" And then it registered. The difficulty in moving, the weariness, the painful look in his eyes…"Oh my gosh, are you hurt?" I moved to him in a flash, studying him carefully. There was nothing visible to give any indication of an injury, but as I came closer, I noticed the dark circles around his eyes and the odd way he was holding one arm closer to his side.

"It is nothing." He held up one hand as if to wave me off. "I was planning to see a HydroHealer…but I wanted to see you first."

"Show me. Where are you hurt?" He did not obey me, so I instinctively moved my hands to the side he was holding. There was a greater concentration of heat there, and I gently pulled his arm away from his side. All thoughts of our current argument were replaced by concern for him. Slowly, I slid my cool hands under the hem of his tunic and lifted his shirt up to his chest. What I saw caused me to gasp out loud and my eyes to water in sympathetic pain.

"Who did this to you?" I whispered, staring in horror at the black and blue mesh of bruises slashed across his abdomen and chest. The discolored contusions even wrapped cruelly around his back. He winced as my cool fingers grazed his burning flesh, studying the markings.

"I had a situation with the rebels last night…"

"I thought they had been captured!" I exclaimed, while I peeled his tunic off in the gentlest way possible.

"Somehow they escaped the Palladium guards."

"Does Abrianna know?"

"At first I was unable to reach her or Eli. But, yes, they know now. I imagine that is why they have not been in touch with you." He inhaled sharply as his tunic came completely off.

"So, is that where you've been all this time?"

"I never even made it to Aerodora last night. They tried to force me to hand you over to them, and it was only because of a foolish mistake they made that I was able to escape this afternoon. You see now why I agree that you must return to your world immediately; they are looking for you not far from here. I already warned the Hydroguards on the boat, and I am sure Simeon is aware by now."

"Oh, Gabriel, I'm so sorry they did this...and because of me..." I choked out. I was aghast that the whole time I'd been in the village he'd been in captivity with a bunch of crazy people. How had they done this to him? It looked like he had been on the receiving end of violent kicks and punches all over his body—but I did not ask. Perhaps I did not want to know. While he had been talking, I had moved to retrieve a bottle of Water in my satchel.

"Can you lie down?" I asked when I returned to his side.

"No, I will just get a HydroHealer...I do not want you wasting energy on me—"

"Let me," I whispered as I searched his eyes for permission. Slowly, he relented and stretched himself out gingerly on the bed in such a way that I could work on the injuries. I wasn't even sure how extensive they were, but I would do the best I could to relieve his pain. As I was about to pour the Water into my hands, he reached one hand out to me, halting my progress.

"I am sorry I did not tell you about Abrianna and Eli." His eyes were on me, and it was one of the few times I thought I glimpsed true vulnerability in them. "My whole life I have been treated differently because of the position they hold and the scandal of their relationship. Some do not even believe that I deserve the position of Guardian...they believe that my selection at birth was a falsehood." He sighed and continued, "It was refreshing to meet someone who did not know any of that history. I suppose I wanted to know what it would feel like to be someone other than Abrianna and Eli's son and the next leader of our Island." His eyes were becoming glassy, even though his voice did not give into the emotion I knew he was feeling. "And it felt *good*...you made me feel like you truly saw *me* and not my authority or my parentage. Just me. I am only sorry that the very things I hid from you ended up hurting your trust in me."

I felt my resolve to remain emotionally distant from him wavering. Truthfully, I wanted to kiss him until the sadness in his eyes left. It ripped my heart up. I wanted to give in to everything inside me that said he was good, that he had just made a mistake. Nobody was perfect, right?

But I couldn't. He had lied—twice.

"What are we doing here, Gabriel?" I hid my face on the bed for a moment, trying to collect my emotions. I had to steel myself. "We're just playing a game that we can't win, and I'm *done*. I can't stay here any longer. I have to go home," I whispered sadly. "My real home is the Mainland. My family, my life, everything is *there*. Not here. Can't you understand that?"

"I understand that you have to look out for yourself and for your friends, Whitnee." He met my eyes. "The relationship you have with Morgan and Caleb is a life force in and of itself. There is a powerful connection there that I do not always understand. I wish for that kind of loyalty and friendship in my life …"

I could feel hot tears fighting their way to the surface at his words. "I am very blessed," I agreed with a nod. "And I wish I could stay and be that kind of friend for you …" But I couldn't, and knowing that *really* sucked. This was the emotion I was afraid of … As long as I didn't trust him, didn't care for him, I could more easily leave this place. I tried to focus on the seed of doubt I still had about his motives. But there was no arguing deep down that I would be leaving a piece of my heart behind forever with my guardian angel, Gabriel.

"I will take you to the Palladium immediately, and you will discover that you were wrong about your fears. My parents can be controlling, but it is usually for the greater good."

I was still skeptical. "I hope you're right. I won't feel better until I have Amelia and Kevin with me again."

"I am so sorry we did not figure out the mystery about your father, either. That was the reason I left you for Aerodora in the first place. I believe Ezekiel may know more about your father than he lets on. You see, I only know rumors of a man previously believed to be the Pilgrim—"

"You think that was my father?" I interrupted breathlessly.

"I wondered … but I cannot make the time work in my head. This person was on the Island long before you and I were born. I do not understand how your father could be that man when he only disappeared six years ago …" He trailed off, and I was equally as baffled by this news. "Ezekiel is the oldest Councilman and would have known of this situation. I had hoped to convince him to break his vow of silence to Abrianna and tell me what he knew … but I did not count on being held captive all night."

Once again, I was humbled to know that all along he had been trying to help me. And I probably should have told him then about the details of my dream last night, but I just couldn't. I wasn't sure how the rest of this day would play out and if it came down to it, I might need to protect how much even Gabriel knew. Besides, Gabriel made a good point … how could my father have been the one they spoke of when it had happened so long ago? The passage of time did not make sense.

So I just said, "My father would have wanted me to go home to my mother, instead of worrying about him." And I knew it was true, which was the final thought that pushed one teardrop over the edge of my eyelid. Before I could catch it, it had dropped to Gabriel's bruised chest, which filled me with incredible sadness. Carefully, I wiped it away, and then pulled away from him so I could start my healing work. I just hoped I would be able to heal my own heart when this was all said and done.

"Ah, I see you have changed your clothes," Simeon remarked as he helped us board the much smaller boat that would take us upriver. I met his bright blue eyes, and he winked at me.

"What exactly *are* you wearing?" Eden questioned, as she and Thomas looked skeptically at the three of us.

"This is what we wear back at home." I explained simply.

"But why did you change ... ?" she began and then her Geo instinct kicked in. "What are you not telling us?"

"I believe," Simeon spoke up, "this means there is a change in plans?" I glanced warily at Gabriel who, even after my healing attempts, did not seem up to his full energy.

"We will take no one up the river with us except Thomas, Eden, and Levi," Gabriel stated simply, releasing the other Hydros who were going to help transport us. "Thomas, you can operate the boat on your own, correct?"

"I believe so. Morgan can help me, if I need it."

"Are you absolutely sure of this, Gabriel? You might need the extra protection if—" Simeon was interrupted by Gabriel.

"We will be fine. Among the seven of us, there is plenty of protection. I trust that you will tell no one of our change in plans?" And Simeon nodded. I found it interesting that Gabriel did not want the extra protection, but he did not tell Simeon that we had been trained in fighting techniques already. I guessed that was the one secret we had all kept. Perhaps Gabriel had grown more confident in our ability to protect ourselves. And, true to his word, he was not letting anyone else know directly what we were doing.

"Well, then I bid you farewell and pray a safe journey for all of you," Simeon replied, once again looking directly at me. I stood up and moved off the boat again to hug him.

When I leaned in close, I whispered in his ear, "Thank you for the advice. I really do love the White Island, but I have to do what is best for my friends right now." He gave me an affirming pat on the back, and I left him quickly before I could start crying. This would be the last I would see of this village and of Simeon ever again. Morgan and Caleb followed suit and said good-bye to Simeon before Thomas directed the boat away from the dock. We moved slowly through the village, each of us lost in our own private thoughts. Once we had departed the heart of the village, Thomas increased the boat's speed until we were cruising briskly along, against the downriver flow of water. The river was choppy, and the Wind was picking up. I looked back once at the boats and buildings fading into the distance and discovered without surprise that dark storm clouds were blowing in from the west. Why that picture of the darkening sky filled me with a deep sense of dread, I did not know.

"So when are you going to admit we are actually going to the Palladium instead of Pyradora?" Eden questioned nonchalantly to no one in particular. Morgan's eyebrows lifted in surprise, and Caleb looked to me. I could tell that even Gabriel was waiting for me to respond. I kept my face emotionless and said nothing. We could not take them to the Palladium with us—that I knew for sure. All that remained at the end of this river was our next set of good-byes. And we would deal with that when we got there.

The storm was practically upon us by the time Thomas approached a large docking station near the base of the mountain. The towering volcano was more formidable up close, and I noticed a winding road to the east of the river that must have lead to the Pyradora village. From what I could see in the distance, there appeared to be houses all along the mountain and in the surrounding hills. If that was Pyradora, then it was nothing like what Hannah had described. It looked like a beautiful community set in a tropical mountainous region. I was instantly filled with regret that we were not going to visit there.

Stepping off the boat was a precarious task—the water had grown rough with the wind whipping across the hillside. Once we were all on the dock, Caleb, Morgan, and I faced our Dorian friends sadly.

"This is where we part ways," I told them over the wind and approaching rain. "We are going to the Palladium and transporting back to our home."

"Can we not go with you to the Palladium?" Thomas asked.

"No," Gabriel spoke up. "We need you to go into Pyradora and let Eli know we are not coming. Jezebel should be waiting for you, and she will provide a place for you to stay through the storm. Once it passes, you may go back to your villages."

Eden's face fell and Thomas shook his head in disappointment as Gabriel's words left no room for argument. Levi just stared at me, his eyebrows furrowed in concentration.

"Ezekiel will be grieved to hear this. With the storm, I am unable to contact him," he said, and he took a step toward me, bowing low. "But I was not sent with you to question your choices. It has been an honor to serve you, Whitnee."

"Levi, thank you for your protection and wisdom. I hope that now you will be able to go home to your family and get some real rest." I bowed to him in return, thinking how dependable he had been. "Please give Tamir my regards, and tell Ezekiel and Sarah ..." I paused, not sure why a ball formed in my throat as I imagined their reaction when they found out I left. "Tell them I am sorry ... but I will always remember them." He agreed with a short nod and took a step away. Morgan was bidding a tearful good-bye to Thomas while Caleb and Eden were hugging.

"You would have made an excellent addition to our tribe, Caleb! Just stay clear of coconuts when you return home," she grinned. I gave her a hug then, almost feeling like I was leaving behind a sister. So much had happened in so short a time that I felt like I had known her for years.

"Eden, thank you for all of your help! Please give your family my love ... especially Elon."

She nodded. "I will. She just adores you, you know. She keeps talking about her 'Whitnee Flower'—she is intent on creating it someday." She sighed then. "Be safe, Whitnee.

Remember that you always have friends here," she told me quickly, as if trying to hide any emotion she might be feeling. Then I turned to Thomas while the others said their good-byes. He had a perturbed look on his face.

"Good-bye, Thomas. You have been such a helpful companion." I said sincerely, and he shook his head in frustration.

"You are making a mistake, Whitnee." I stared at him in confusion. "You are the Pilgrim ... and if you leave ..."

"Thomas, I appreciate the confidence you have in me, but I am not—"

"Yes, you are. In time, you will see that. And when you do, you will find a way back here. I believe it with everything in me." His blue eyes burned with conviction as he spoke, and I was very humbled by his words. Eden gave him a firm pat on the back as they both watched me.

"Only time will tell ..." I said, thinking of how many times the same thing had been said to me. "Thank you again, Thomas. Please check on Gabriel when you can ... he needs friends like you," I whispered and gave him a hug whether he wanted one or not. Thomas and Eden insisted on gifting Morgan and Caleb with life force one last time in case they needed it—I suppose it was their farewell gift. Gabriel and I watched silently as they linked hands with one another and made the transfer. Once this was accomplished, Caleb and Morgan finished their good-byes, and we waved one last time before moving to the west. Our three friends walked hesitantly to the east. That was when the first drops of rain hit, sending us running in the direction of the Palladium. The stately silver structure peered down at us from its guard post atop the hill, making me wonder what exactly we would do once we got there.

THE SILVER DOME

As we ran, fat drops of rain speckled my green t-shirt and light-ning flashed across the sky. I felt alive in this storm—as if the electricity in the air was a part of me. All of my senses were keenly active. The smell of fresh rain pervaded the humid air. Each raindrop soaked into my skin and renewed my energy. Even the deep rumble of thunder vibrated within my very soul. I felt as if I could run forever and never grow weary. But once we reached the top of the first hill on the way to the Palladium, I was struck with the sensation that I was being watched. And I remembered those first few terrifying moments when I had woken up on the white sand beach. I had felt someone watching me then too. In fact, hadn't that been my motivation for mov-ing down shore and ultimately finding Gabriel...?

My pace began to slow as I contemplated this feeling. I threw glances in all directions around me before finally coming to a stop. Turning back over my shoulder, I squinted through the rain into the dark forest bordering the hill country in the distance.

"Why are you stopping? We're almost there!" Caleb cried when he noticed I wasn't keeping up. Gabriel spun around at this and the three of them halted.

"What is wrong?" Gabriel called out. I continued to survey the area as thunder crashed and echoed all around me. Someone was out there. I just knew it. Without realizing it, I was calling upon the Earth for clarification. One word registered in my mind. *Danger.*

"Run!" I yelled, catching up quickly to them. "They're here! The rebels! *Go!*" And we took off again. I couldn't see them yet, but I could sense them. Everything in nature cried out *enemy.*

"Where?" Gabriel yelled.

"The forest! They're watching us...hurry!" I screamed beside him, over the roar of the storm. We shot up the next hill which left us just one away from the heavy silver gates of the Palladium entrance. Gabriel and I kept throwing glances back over our shoulders, but still we could see no one in the ever-growing darkness of the storm.

We were completely soaked to the skin and had no more strength left to run when we mercifully reached the entrance. Gabriel shouted orders to the guards on the other side, and I half-expected him to just blast right through the gates at the pace we were going. The large iron-like gate swung open just far enough for us to run through.

"Close it! Immediately!" Gabriel commanded once we were safely on the other side. We slowed down to catch our breath, and while we stood there gasping for air in the pouring rain, I took in the sight before me.

It was like the first time I visited the state capitol building in Austin, Texas on a middle school field trip. It was dome-shaped and daunting in size and stature, leaving me feeling small just like I had as an eighth grader. But unlike the capitol, the Palladium dome was silver in color. I was not sure what material they had made it from, obviously something local to the Island, but it was breathtaking. Stretched out in a maze before the front door was a beautiful set of gardens currently being buffeted by the wind. Though we were desperate to move out of the pouring rain, we were so beat from our mad sprint over the hills that we trudged slowly through the garden to the massive front doors. Gabriel led the way, and Caleb clutched a stitch in his side. Morgan heaved deeply for air, and I just tried to control the shakiness spreading through my legs.

The moment we stepped inside the Palladium doors, Gabriel was barking out orders to surprised servants, and we followed him in a daze through the ornate interior.

"What is going on here?" A sharp female voice echoed in the high-ceilinged foyer. Abrianna was moving down the stairs, wearing a shimmering lavender dress, and I was struck again by her elegance.

"Does she ever dress down?" Morgan commented under her quick and gasping breaths.

"The rebels … are outside, surrounding the Palladium!" I called out to her desperately. She did not look completely surprised as she stepped off the last stair and moved deliberately in our direction.

"Well, what did you expect? They are here for you. If you come here, so do they." She spoke calmly, taking in our wet and windblown appearances. Without thinking, I began drying myself with the Wind life force.

"We must transport them home. Whitnee is no longer safe here." Gabriel walked to her side, and she sized up her son in one quick, cold glance.

"I understand that, Gabriel, but before we do anything of the sort, I must ask you to first handle the situation outside. This is your responsibility."

"Your guards failed to keep them in custody—" Gabriel retorted.

"And now you must fix that problem. This is your area of expertise. Go now and find out how many are out there and instruct the guards on how to approach the situation. Surely these people will not come too close to the Palladium. I daresay they will just wait for Whitnee to come out." She fluttered her hands as if this was not a big deal, and I couldn't help thinking how this rebel group's timing always messed everything up.

Gabriel looked torn between obeying her and wanting to stay with me. He reached for my hand and our glowing eyes connected. "Please do not leave until I return."

I felt him transfer that comforting heat through our palms like he had the first time we said good-bye, and I smiled weakly. Thunder rumbled over the Palladium as I watched him exit. Then I turned my attention on Abrianna, who was glaring at me after the apparent affection she had witnessed between her son and me. Still weird to think about her as Gabriel's mother...

"Where are Amelia and Kevin?" I demanded.

"They are watching the storm from the Dome. Would you like me to take you there?"

"Yes," I answered simply, meeting her surveying gaze. I would not let her intimidate me this time.

"Follow me," she instructed. Morgan, Caleb, and I cautiously followed her up the winding staircase. I was aware that several servants with different eye colors had joined our progress. They seemed to be posted everywhere, like guards, and we were flanked in the front and the back. I could feel my stomach growing nervous. What if she wasn't really taking us to the Dome? What if this was all a trap, and Amelia and Kevin weren't really up here? I couldn't rid myself of the sick feeling, even as she spoke again. "I apologize that we have not been in contact since last night. As I am sure Gabriel informed you, circumstances grew out of our control, and we have been working day and night to fix the problems. Did Jezebel give you Eli's instructions to come straight here instead of entering Pyradora?"

This threw me off. "No, we didn't even go to Pyradora. We came here by our own choice," I told her, as we arrived at the top of the stairs.

"Interesting..." she commented, and I had the same thought. She marched us down a long, dark corridor to another set of smaller, steeper stairs.

"How are Amelia and Kevin?" Morgan spoke up behind me.

"They are doing well. Today my attendants took them to the beach while we handled the situation with the rebels. They were very well protected, I assure you. See for yourself." And she opened a door at the top of the staircase. We entered into a majestic dome-ceilinged room with windows extending around the circular space. It was clearly designed to hold large groups of people. It made the Conclave look small and simple. Eli and Amelia were gazing through some kind of instrument on one side of the Dome, while Kevin played with another unknown object on the other. At least two servants were posted around the room silently. Kevin's blond head whipped around the moment we entered.

"Caleb! Whitnee!" he cried out in joy and ran to us. I could have sagged to the floor in relief at seeing his bright and happy face. I reached him first with a gigantic hug before Morgan and Caleb surrounded us.

"Kevin, we're so glad you're okay, man!" Caleb breathed, clapping the middle-schooler on the back. My eyes moved across the room, expecting a similar reaction from Amelia. No such luck. But at least I had been completely wrong about the situation. Neither camper looked as if they'd been terrorized during their stay here. In fact, they both had a healthy glow on their faces from being out in the sun all day.

"Amelia?" I walked over to her frigid position still at the window. She had turned to watch our exchange, but her face was pouting. I did not like the protective way Eli stood close to her, as if I was the enemy here. "Are you okay?" I asked.

"Of course I'm okay. What are you doing back so soon?" she questioned coldly.

"Well, we missed you guys," I started and then looked directly at her eyes, which had been layered again with dark kohl. She was trying to look older, just like she did back at camp. I was briefly irked to notice that the elegant dress she was wearing resembled Abrianna's unique look. "It's time to go home."

"We're going home?" Kevin repeated happily. "Is that why you have your Camp Fusion shirts on? I don't even know where my old clothes are ..."

"I'm not going with you," Amelia stated. I frowned, glancing uneasily at Eli who loomed over her silently.

"Are you still mad at me for sending you here?"

"No. Sending me here was the best thing you could have done. I totally belong here. I'm just not going back with you." She crossed her arms resolutely over her chest.

"Amelia, stop acting like that ... it's annoying!" Kevin scolded her from across the room. "She's letting her powers go to her head," he explained to us as if she wasn't standing right there.

"Whatever, Kevin. Just because I'm good at it and you're not—" she retorted.

"So what if you're good at it? This is not your home!" he reminded her. Apparently, they'd been having this argument already.

"Abrianna and Eli said it could be if that's what I wanted!" she yelled back. "And that's what I want! There's nothing any of you can do to change my mind."

I turned angrily to Abrianna who was stepping forward slowly. "Is that true?" I asked her, seething inside. "Did you really tell her she can *stay* here?"

"Of course she can!" Abrianna replied innocently. "There is nothing waiting for her back at home. Her parents sent her away and clearly do not care what she does. If she stays here, she can learn the art of Fire-making from Eli and become a great leader on the Island. Besides, I have always wanted a daughter ..."

"Stop it!" I screamed angrily at Abrianna. What game was she playing at here? Why would she try to manipulate Amelia into staying? "She is *not* your daughter! You have no right to promise her such things. She has a life back in our world ... and two parents who love her!" I heard Amelia snort, which caused me to whip back around and plead with her. "It's true, Amelia! Your parents *love* you. *I* love you ... you have to come back with us. There is no other option here."

"You don't love me. You got rid of me the first chance you could. Just like my parents," she spat.

"That is not true—" I groaned.

"She has options, Whitnee. And she is not the only one with choices to make here," Abrianna explained calmly.

"What is that supposed to mean?" I narrowed my eyes at her as she came and stood on Amelia's other side.

"It means that, just like Amelia, you also could choose to stay here. With your abilities, you could be a tremendous help to us."

"I have family back at home and responsibilities there."

"But it is your destiny to be here, Whitnee."

"I thought you said it was my *choice*. Where I come from, destiny is ruled by your choices. And I choose to get my friends and go home. *That* is my destiny." And then I reached out to Amelia and grabbed her arm. "Let's go," I said firmly but was surprised when Eli's burning hand shot out and gripped me tightly at the forearm.

"Do not touch her," he warned in his deep voice, so similar to Gabriel's. I yanked my hand away and then held it up defensively in front of me without a second thought. I was prepared to use life force on them, if necessary.

"She is coming with me. And you will not stop her," I told him fiercely.

"No one is stopping her from doing anything, except you," Abrianna stated smugly. And there we were in a standoff. Abrianna and Eli had positioned themselves on either side of Amelia as if she was already one of them. I never saw this coming. I never realized how they might use Amelia against me. There was no way I could leave the Island without her.

I was vaguely aware of the servants moving in closer to us as lightning flashed across the sky. A slow grin began to spread across Eli's face. "Step away from us!" I yelled, still holding my hands out. Caleb and Morgan had taken defensive stances, also, which only seemed to humor Eli more.

"Whitnee…" Kevin called, a hint of fear in his voice.

"What do you think you are accomplishing here, Whitnee?" Abrianna asked.

"What does it look like?" I replied. "Amelia, move away from them and come with me, okay? We have to go, honey. What they are telling you is wrong. Think of your real mom and how much she misses you back at home…" I tried appealing to her and, for a moment, she seemed to waver. "I'm sorry I sent you here. I made a huge mistake, and I need you to forgive me and trust me, okay? Just come with me willingly."

"Whitnee!" Morgan screamed, and I lost my focus on Amelia to spin around. The "servants" had come up behind Morgan and Caleb and somehow overpowered them, capturing their hands behind their back. Another one had grabbed Kevin. Morgan and Caleb struggled against them, but to no avail. I called on the Wind force and tried blasting them away… but nothing happened.

"What are you doing?" I heard Amelia gasp behind me, and when I turned back around, Eli had her by the throat with a dagger. I was horrified at what I was seeing. With terror in her eyes, she called, "Eli?" I could sense her disbelief and confusion. But his eyes were on me, and they were dark and dangerous. Once again, I tried calling on a life force, any life force, but nothing happened. I felt… empty. Eli just grinned sinisterly at me.

"The life forces don't work in the Dome!" Kevin called out to me.

"That would have been nice to know a few minutes ago!" I heard Caleb growl as he resisted the man holding him captive.

"Kevin is right." Abrianna nodded calmly, as if nothing remotely wrong had just happened. "And now you must make another choice, Whitnee. How important are your friends to you? If you do not want anyone hurt, then you must submit to armbands ... just in case you happen to be more powerful than my Dome."

"Armbands?" I hadn't lowered my hands, even though they were apparently useless here.

"A security measure ..." Abrianna explained. "They inject ocean water into your arm, thus preventing you from accessing a life force. The Dome is powerful, but I will not take any chances. I cannot have you getting out of control with your abilities when all I want to do is talk to you."

"Oh, yeah. Injecting poisonous water into my arm really makes me want to sit and chat!" I replied sarcastically. "Let them go!"

"You and I must discuss a few things first. It would be in your best interest, as well as in the interest of your *friends*, to give in and let us place the armbands on you. If you refuse, you are gambling with their well-being. Have you not already put poor Amelia through enough? Make this easy on everyone and do the right thing," she instructed me, with a nod toward my imprisoned companions. I hesitated. All eyes were on me, especially Amelia's very large and very scared brown eyes. If they hurt her ... *ugh.* Just the thought was enough for me to submit.

I lowered my hands.

"Whitnee, don't!" Kevin yelled, but it was too late. A guard had clapped bands over my wrists that were made of some strange material I did not recognize. That didn't seem to be a big deal, but then he tapped on the armband and the objects attached themselves immediately to my skin. In fact, it felt like tiny needles had suddenly and painfully injected themselves into my wrists. I gasped as a sensation of lethargy and weakness crept over me.

"It will hurt at first, but that will subside. If you feel weak, that means the ocean water is sapping your life force strength," Abrianna told me unemotionally. I heard my friends exclaim as the guards gave them armbands also.

"Let Amelia go," I said weakly.

"Eli…" Abrianna motioned to him, and he released her.

"How could you do that? You tricked me!" Amelia immediately mouthed off indignantly to Eli, who clapped armbands on her too. "Abrianna!" She looked betrayed.

"Amelia, dear, hush. This was never about you," Abrianna told her coldly, and I saw Amelia's eyes fill up with tears. But I was helpless to do anything about it. Eli grabbed me roughly and started yanking me to another door.

"Where are you taking her?" Caleb shouted as we passed him. But I could see the lethargy setting in for him and the others too. My body didn't feel like my own. It was heavy and unnatural, similar to that first day on the beach when I had swallowed too much ocean water. The fateful day I landed here and met Gabriel… *Oh, where was he?* Did he know what was happening to us? Was he part of this plan after all? My mistrust of him started gnawing at my insides again.

Eli pushed me through a doorway and down another lengthy corridor that smelled of dust. This time, the door that he opened did not lead into a large, airy dome-shaped room. Instead, I was shoved into a small, stuffy space with no windows. There was a single lamp hanging from the ceiling and the Firelight in the lamp dimly lit the small space.

"Wait in here *quietly* until we come back," he said gruffly.

"What are you going to do? Please don't hurt my friends! I'll do whatever you want, just don't hurt them!" I cried out, but the door slammed shut. I sank to the ground, fighting off the nausea that was creeping into my stomach. Fear had gripped every part of my body. Although the pain of the armbands had worn off significantly, I was left with only fatigue and a sense of dread. *How do we get out of this situation?*

I wracked my fuzzy brain, trying to come up with something brilliant—like people do in movies when they're tied up against their will. Surely there was a miraculous way to free myself, rescue my friends, find the portal, make it work, and get everyone home all in one piece?! *Yeah, if I was freaking Indiana Jones.*

I leaned against the wall and tried to curl my knees up to my chest because my stomach was rolling. My Swiss Army knife dug into my rear, though, rendering me even more uncomfortable. *Oh, hey!* My Swiss Army knife! If I could reach it, I might be able to free myself of the stupid armbands. My arms had been wound tightly behind my back, but I was still able to move my hands. With difficulty, I stood again and dug around in my back pocket. My fingers grasped the little knife but found something else stuffed deep into the pocket too—something I hadn't noticed or felt before … like paper. I grabbed both items and then dropped them to the floor. There actually was a small piece of paper there, thick like parchment. I bent back down with my hands still behind my back and picked up the knife again. While I worked to unfold it without cutting myself, I bent over on the ground to examine the paper there. I knew there hadn't been anything else in my pockets when I arrived here, so it must have been placed there while I was on the Island … Curiosity won over my survival instincts. I squinted in the dim light to read the handwriting on the note, ignoring my knife.

> *My Dearest Whitnee,*
>
> *I am writing this on the day that you are leaving Aerodora. I assume once you are ready to go back to your home, you will retrieve your native clothing; thus, I am placing this in your pocket.*
>
> *If you are truly planning to leave forever, then you must have decided you are not the Pilgrim. For this reason, I must beg you to stay long enough for me to explain the truth about your heritage. Perhaps in doing so, it will help you understand more about yourself and just how special you are. However, because I have been forbidden to speak of this matter, it would be too risky to write*

about it here. Every one of us is being monitored closely, and it is unclear who can be trusted these days.

If it is within your power, please come back to Aerodora before you decide to leave, and I will tell you all that I know. Destroy this letter as soon as possible and tell no one. I sincerely hope to see you again. Keep yourself safe.

Sarah

I got chills up and down my back at this point, and I leaned in closer to the paper—desperately trying to comprehend the cryptic messages in this letter. What truth did Sarah feel like I should know? And how was I supposed to find that out now? When she said *heritage*, was she referring to my father? And, if so, how could I leave the Island until I knew the truth?

Numbly, I scooted so that I could pick the paper up and stuff it back into my pocket. I stared helplessly at the blank wall in front of me, knowing I had no other options right now. I tried again to open my knife but found that I was growing weaker, and my fingers were not as deft as usual. My mind was even becoming foggy as pulses of dizziness swept over me. I pushed myself back up against the wall, temporarily giving up on the knife. I just wanted to close my eyes and sleep.

I don't know how long I rested in this position, feeling the vibrations of the storm raging somewhere outside. I had to fight off the urge to drift into dreary sleep. The armbands were having quite a dramatic effect on me. It felt like not only was the life force drained out of me but my own strength and will along with it.

Just when I wanted to give up, the heavy door clanked open and Abrianna in all her glory was silhouetted there. My eyes barely mustered the energy to squint up at her as my head lolled back. I was conscious enough to note that she carried a small satchel with her. I wildly wondered if it contained torture devices.

The door slammed shut behind her, and the two of us were alone in the tiny room. I watched her sluggishly as she set her satchel down and knelt in front of me. One cold hand reached out to peel back my eyelid and examine my eye. It was an uncomfortable feeling, and I wanted to complain but didn't have the energy.

"Interesting…if I do not remove the armbands from you soon, you will die." She was speaking quietly, as if my impending death was not a big issue. *Crazy psychopath.* "Already the pigment in your eyes is diminishing. Gabriel was not exaggerating. I have never seen someone react so strongly to ocean water. But before I remove them, I must have your word that you will behave yourself."

I could feel a maniacal carelessness rise up within me at her words. I knew a lazy grin was spreading across my face. "I make no promises," I told her defiantly, even though my voice came out scratchy and slurred.

"Now, Whitnee, be the smart girl that I know you are. As long as you behave yourself and do not attempt to use a life force, I will take these off. The alternative results in your death. Besides, you might be interested in hearing what I have to say."

I laughed bitterly. "There's nothing you could say to make me trust you." And I laid my head back against the wall and closed my eyes. I could not think clearly, and I just wanted to give up.

"Would you feel differently if I told you that your father, Nathan, is still alive here on the Island, and I can help you find him?"

THE COMBINATION OF LIFE FORCES

The grin left my face, and I felt my heart lurch at her words. Slowly, I forced my eyes open again and found Abrianna's face in my blurred vision.

"Ahh ... now I have your attention." She nodded with a condescending smile. "I thought that might interest you. Now be a good girl and let me take these armbands off." She pulled me forward and reached around. Immediately I felt the pressure release. Leaning back against the wall, I had the good sense to drop my little knife back into my pocket before pulling my hands to my lap and rubbing them. Already there were ugly bruises blackening my wrists. I said nothing as I embraced the slow relief working its way through my body. When I appeared lucid again, she said, "Your father is not dead. In fact, he is not far from here."

Again I didn't know what to say, so I stared at her, trying to read her motives in telling me this. "How do you even know who my father is?" I finally rasped.

"I have known your father a long time, Whitnee," she said with a sigh, and that unreadable emotion flickered across her face. It almost looked like sadness, but I was pretty sure Abrianna was not able to feel such a thing. "I know he calls himself Nathan Terradora and that he settled in a place called Texas. I know that he met a woman there named Serena and that, together, they had a daughter named Whitnee."

"You could have learned all of that from my friends just now. Why should I believe that you really know him?" I peered suspiciously at her. What exactly did she want from me, and what did my father have to do with any of it?

"I know that when you were five years old, you were fishing with your father and he caught a creature which he called 'catfish.' While holding the fish in his hands for you to see, its long whiskers sliced his palm and he began to bleed. Ever since then, you have feared fish."

My mouth dropped open as I realized nobody outside of my immediate family could have told her that, because I had not even remembered that experience until then. The memory came back to me very vividly. Was that really why I was afraid of fish? Could it be that I had repressed that memory all these years?

"How would you know that? Even I had forgotten..." I gawked at her.

"I know that your father's nickname for you is 'Baby Doll' because you reminded him of a little porcelain doll when you were born. I know that you look exactly like him, down to the same gray eyes. Now, how could I know these things, Whitnee, if I did not know your father?"

"How... *how* do you know him?"

"I already told you. He is on the Island as we speak. Do not pretend like that is impossible to believe. I know he contacted you... is that not why you chose to come here instead of traveling to Pyradora as planned?" This woman had to be the most mysterious and cunning person I had ever met. I stared at her incredulously.

"You know about... the dream?" I wondered aloud.

"Nathan is often predictable... I knew he would try to warn you about leaving the Island the moment he was given freedom to do so. In fact, I was hoping he would. Did he not also warn you on the Mainland about crossing the river to the portal?" I suppose the look on my face gave away my shock, so she continued with a grim smile. "I thought so. You see, men will do exactly what we expect them to do with a little prodding."

"Okay, hold up a minute. *How* was my father able to contact me like that?"

"It is a rare Aerodorian gift of communication to project your thoughts into another's mind. He was simply placing his thoughts in your consciousness by means of the portal... you are more sensitive to hearing it when you are asleep and your mind is free from constraints. I imagine he told you not to cross the river because as long as you did not, you would never stumble on to the portal, and this really is the last place he wanted you to end up."

Something about the way she said that made me think she was trying to hurt my feelings. It wasn't working. "What Nathan failed to understand about people your age is that instructing them *not* to do something usually produces the opposite effect. Curiosity is a powerful motivator. But can we really blame Nathan? I mean, after all, in his mind, you are still the little girl he left behind. The little girl that probably never would have defied Daddy's orders, am I right? You are not that little girl anymore." Now I knew she was trying to hurt me. And I hated the way she talked about him so informally... like she really *knew* him.

"So, when I saw my dad ... on the other side of the river ... that was really him?" I pictured his face staring down at me from the cliff.

"Oh, come now, Whitnee. I thought you were a smart girl..." She laughed as if what I had said was ludicrous. "Of course that was not really him. Some things have to be ... *falsified* in order to achieve a greater goal. I daresay that much of what you have experienced on this Island has been under some false pretense ... but always for the common good, of course."

This was news to me. "Like what?!" I was annoyed now with her condescending attitude.

"Whitnee, your innocence is so endearing. Do you really believe that you were able to gain the complete loyalty of your little circle of friends on the Island in such a short time?" I just stared at her, that feeling of dread stirring in the pit of my stomach. Was this another manipulation or was she trying to tell me that someone had betrayed me? It would explain how she always knew what was going on ... like the secrets Gabriel and I were keeping about my abilities and the emotional connection we had established. And when Kevin and Amelia had been kidnapped, Abrianna called on the zephyra almost immediately after it had happened, as if she knew—hadn't she been the one to warn us they might not be safe—?

"Oh my *gosh*," I breathed. "Did you ... I mean, *you* didn't have anything to do with Kevin and Amelia ..." *Oh, please don't let it be true.* I could feel the nausea returning, and it had nothing to do with ocean water.

"Now you are thinking in the right direction." She confirmed my fears without really admitting anything. "Nobody would have been hurt, Whitnee. Do not look so appalled."

"So the rebels are—"

"A real problem, but none of your concern. What you should be worrying about right now is your father. You want him back, and I will help you locate him."

"In exchange for what?"

She smiled coolly, apparently satisfied that I had asked. "I will help you, if you agree to release your abilities in all four life forces."

"What does that even mean?"

"It means that you permanently transfer your powers in the four elements to me."

"And how exactly does that work?"

"We have been developing a way to gift others with more than one life force. But I can explain that later. The point is that you and Nathan can go back home, never to return to this Island again, if you just release your access to the life forces."

I searched her face suspiciously. She made it sound so easy. "If all you want is my power, why not just take it from me?"

She gave a mirthless laugh. "Do you believe me to be a monster, Whitnee? Contrary to what you may believe about me, I am not heartless. Besides, it is not possible to just 'take' an individual's abilities. They must be freely given for the transfer to work. So you see, we both have something of importance to offer each other."

I blinked at her in doubt. "I just don't know why I should believe anything that you are telling me, Abrianna. You are very good at manipulating people. I need more than just your word as proof that my father is alive." Again she gave me an approving nod and smile.

"If you still want proof..." She reached into her satchel, rummaging around for something. When she removed her hand, she pulled out a tiny, shiny object. "Perhaps this will aid your decision." She held her hand out expectantly, and I laid my palm open.

What she dropped into my hand sent waves of emotion crashing through me. It was a simple gold wedding band. Just like my father's. Trying to clear my vision of the tears that had sprung there, I raised the ring higher to scrutinize the inside. If it had the inscription, I would know it really was his...

N + S. I found the one my heart loves, the inscription read, and I squeezed the ring into my ever-strengthening fist.

"*Why* do you have this?" I whispered, barely able to contain the rage I felt over this woman producing my father's wedding ring.

"Take it. It means nothing to me. I only kept it as proof to you that he is alive," she declared and watched me expectantly.

"What exactly will you do with all of those powers, Abrianna?" I hissed.

"I will be able to rule this Island in complete wisdom." She stood up and spoke passionately. "If I could know each life force as thoroughly as you do, I could unite these four tribes under one purpose. I could help them understand each other better, and the Island could prosper in new ways. Having access to all four elements means that I can communicate with each tribe in ways that nobody in our history ever could!"

"Your time is almost up, though, isn't it? I mean, Gabriel will be stepping in soon as Guardian … you would not have the time to accomplish what you say. Don't you think if I'm going to release my powers to anyone, it should be to him?" I pointed out. Everything she was saying sounded good in theory … but I couldn't shake the feeling that so much power within one person could be a bad thing.

"Gabriel is not ready for that kind of power."

"Yes, he is! Gabriel will make an excellent Guardian. He *knows* this Island and cares about the people."

"I will agree that Gabriel has been well-groomed for a position of authority. And he will continue to be a valuable asset to the government of this Island. But with your arrival here, the old order of things is changing. It may be time to do away with Guardians and prophecies and the like and set up a new kind of governor."

"That sounds like dictatorship," I commented ominously. "And what do you mean about doing away with prophecies? What about all that talk of the Pilgrim—?"

"Do you really believe you are the Pilgrim, Whitnee?" She gazed at me mockingly. "Could it be that people only see what they want to see in us? You fit the description of the supposed Pilgrim. So they believe in you, blind to the truth that you are just a simple young woman from another place who has no real understanding of their needs," she stated philosophically.

"I take it that you don't believe in the prophecy after all, then?" I was trying to understand her point.

"I am saying that prophecies and other such 'divine ordinations' should not rule the reality that we live in. If it makes the people feel better to know their prophecy has come true, then fine. Play that role for them, Whitnee. By releasing your abilities to me, you will, in fact, end up bringing peace to the Island, because I intend to use the life forces for the common good. It will make everyone happy. You will go down in history as our Pilgrim who helped bring about peace and prosperity by sacrificing your powers. In turn, you get your father back and you return to your world with no responsibility to us."

Even though I had a bad feeling about the ultimate outcome of giving her so much power, she *seemed* to want to use it for good ... I remembered how it had felt to combine life forces. It had been particularly helpful in healing Caleb and using the Earth to communicate healing with the Water life force. How much more could be done if everyone could access more than one life force?

"If you're experimenting with gifting others, is that something you will share with the people?" I wanted to know.

"Eventually. It is still such a new development for us and has been kept confidential, even from Gabriel. But, yes, the vision would include extending it to all people in the future. Imagine every Dorian having abilities in the four elements ..." Her eyes were alight with excitement, but it just didn't feel right. It seemed risky to me to upset the balance of this Island. Was there not an ultimate purpose for everyone being gifted in only one life force?

But I couldn't ignore the ring clutched in my hand. How tempting it would be if everything could work out exactly as she said. Besides, why should I feel any sense of responsibility to these people? Six days ago, I did not even know they existed.

And if she really knew where my dad was, I could end the years Mom and I had spent agonizing and wondering over what really happened to him. We could start our lives over again as a family. Perhaps the whole reason I came to this Island was ultimately just to rescue my father and not to be some "promised one" for a forgotten people group.

"If I chose to accept your offer, how would all of this work?" I asked Abrianna, standing weakly to my feet so I could face her more directly.

"If you are going to do this, *you* stay on the Island just a little while longer, but send your friends back to your world immediately."

"They will never agree to that."

"Then you find a way to convince them. I will only reveal what I know to you, not to your friends or even to Gabriel," she told me adamantly.

"He's your son!" I cried, indignant about the idea of her keeping more secrets from him.

"Those are my requirements. Gabriel cannot be brought into this."

I thought about it. I hated to lie to Gabriel. But if I did as she said and sent my friends back, I could find my father and make time for one stop in Aerodora at Sarah's secret request. It would be one of the hardest things I would ever do to send my friends away from me. But this could be my one and only chance to find Dad. I couldn't mess this up just because I was afraid. And I resolved that before I left this place permanently, I would find a way to tell Gabriel what Abrianna was doing. "Okay, so we send my friends back without me. Then what?"

"Then you make the life force transfer. After that, we will get Nathan—"

"Oh, no, no, *no*," I interrupted emphatically. "I am not making any such transfer until I have my father with me. And not some holographic image of him, either..." I warned, at which she appeared slightly confused. "I will agree to transport my friends back, and I will stay here only long enough to get my dad, visit Aerodora one last time, and then transfer whatever power you are wanting. Then my dad and I leave."

"Why Aerodora?" she questioned skeptically.

"I did not get to say good-bye to my friends there," I explained. "Does all of this sound agreeable to you?" She hesitated for a moment, then crossed her arms, reminding me ironically of Gabriel.

"Very well. And you agree to not speak to Gabriel about any of this? The less he knows on this topic, the better."

"I don't like that." I narrowed my eyes at her.

"How urgently do you want your father back, Whitnee? These are *my* terms."

"I just don't understand why you keep secrets from your own son. He's a good person."

"Of course you do not understand," she replied coldly. "Like a silly girl, you have convinced yourself that you love him. And love makes people blind." I could feel my heartbeat quicken and, though I wanted to correct her, I could not find the words. Whatever I said would be a lie anyway. "But you and I both know that there is no future for you with Gabriel. Once you leave the Island, he will matter no more to you and you will be nothing more than a strange memory to him. So do not ruin your opportunity to find your father simply because of some fleeting romance. I warned you that Pyras and Aeros can get caught up in unnecessary emotion. You fell right into the trap."

Her words made me feel ashamed and stupid. Because, ultimately, she was right. And I hated her for it.

"A trap you must know very well, huh, Abrianna?" I retorted. That fleeting sadness passed across her face again, taking me by surprise. She almost appeared vulnerable for a moment. But only for a moment.

"We all make our choices, Whitnee. And the time has come now for you to choose. Are you going to find your father or not?"

"Release them," Abrianna commanded as we joined the others still imprisoned in the Dome. Her guards obeyed, and I saw Eli's eyes connect with Abrianna's. Quickly, I placed my dad's wedding ring in my back pocket with Sarah's letter and my knife.

"What's going on?" Caleb called out as his armbands came off.

"We're going home now," I told him, helping Morgan to her feet.

"Just like that? You people threaten us one minute and now you're letting us go?" Caleb shouted at them.

"Caleb, just drop it. All that matters is that we're leaving now. Is everyone okay?" I moved to Amelia's side. Her dark eye makeup had run down her cheeks, and though her tears had dried, she appeared quietly despondent. "Amelia, will you please go back home with us?" She nodded forlornly, not meeting anybody's gaze. I could imagine how betrayed she felt and that made what I was about to do seem even worse. But I had to make them think I was leaving with them up until the last minute.

"Whitnee, what did they do to you?" Morgan asked fearfully.

"Nothing. We just talked."

"About what?" Caleb prodded.

"It doesn't matter! Let's go," I said firmly and looked to Abrianna expectantly.

"If you attempt to use life force against anybody once we leave this room, I promise you will regret it. Understood?" Abrianna commanded. I nodded in agreement, but noticed Caleb watching me skeptically. "Then follow us."

"We're going right now?" Caleb clarified.

"Yes," she answered.

"What's the rush? Is Gabriel even back yet?" He wouldn't budge even though the rest of us were starting toward the door. This caused everyone to pause.

"Caleb, it is important for you to go now. There are dangerous people waiting outside the Palladium for Whitnee—" Abrianna started, but Caleb interrupted her.

"Whit? Are you really going to leave without saying goodbye to Gabriel?" He was staring at me intensely—almost as if he knew something was wrong with this picture. I felt a moment of panic as I scavenged my mind for something to say.

"Gabriel would understand why we had to leave so quickly. Please don't ask any more questions," I told him, and my eyes burned with invisible tears. I turned and followed Abrianna without another word, acting as if the conversation was over. Rubbing my bruised wrists absentmindedly, I wondered if Caleb had any idea I was about to deceive him. He was probably reading my emotions as sadness at leaving Gabriel behind.

Escorted by guards, we followed Abrianna back down the stairs to the Palladium foyer. As if on cue, the front door flew open the moment we began to cross the wide area. Framed by wind and rain, his curly hair dripping, was Gabriel. He was accompanied by a few older men. I looked up to him in surprise before glancing warily at Abrianna. This was a complication I hadn't foreseen. Her face showed no emotion, though.

"What is the status?" she called out to him.

"They are making no advances. We moved out to reason with them, but they are neither surrendering nor coming closer. It is such strange behavior ... the next step is to forcefully remove them, but—" Then Gabriel stopped. "What is happening here?" In one sweeping glance, he had taken in Amelia's tearstained face and the cloud of tension surrounding our group. I wanted so badly to run to him, even in his completely drenched state, and let him hold me.

"We are taking them to the portal for transport. Perhaps you should say good-bye and then continue with your duties," Abrianna instructed him coldly.

"What?" Gabriel exclaimed and looked at me in confusion. "You are leaving right now?" I could see the panic in his eyes and my heart started thumping loudly at his reaction. He didn't want me to leave. I could see the raw emotion right there in his face. I could only nod slowly, wishing I could convey to him that I wasn't really leaving just yet ... that I only had to convince my friends that I was. "I am going with you to the portal then," Gabriel declared.

"No," Eli stated sharply. "You have responsibilities." Gabriel glared at his father.

"My responsibility is to see Whitnee and her friends home safely. The rebels can wait," he insisted fiercely.

"Gabriel!" Eli reprimanded him.

"It is just as well, Eli." Abrianna held up one hand. "Let him come with us, if he wishes. I suppose it is time to show him the portal anyway."

"Yes, I am very interested to see what you have been doing all these years." Gabriel scowled at his parents. Abrianna shot him a warning look before turning on her heel again and marching away. We all followed, a heavy silence hanging in the air. Gabriel fell into step beside me and took my cold hand in his. I could feel his warmth spread through me as we moved quickly and quietly down a long corridor and through a door that led us down a steep, suffocating stairwell.

"Would you have left without saying good-bye?" Gabriel whispered to me. The stairs were so narrow that our entire group was progressing single-file. Gabriel was right in front of me, his hand still firmly holding mine behind his back. When he glanced back to look at me, his features were tortured.

"No," I told him. "I had no other choice."

"What does that mean? What happened—?"

"*Shh,*" I warned him before he could get worked up. I leaned down as close to his ear as I could get while trekking down the darkened stairwell. "I will explain everything later."

"There is no later—!" He stopped on the stair and turned to face me.

"Just trust me!" I hissed and pushed him back around to keep going. Caleb, who had been in front of Gabriel, briefly glanced back at us with a suspicious look. Once we finally reached the bottom of the stairs, we were led down a low-ceilinged passageway that seemed endless. However, we were able to walk side-by-side at this point, and Gabriel tried again to understand what was wrong with me.

"You look sick, Whitnee."

"Wow, thanks." I rolled my eyes, trying to make light of the situation.

"Something has changed. I need to know what happened while I was gone." He had pulled me close to his side and ducked his head so only I could hear him.

"Nothing," I started, very aware that Caleb and Morgan were trying to listen to our conversation. "We had a discussion, and everyone agreed it was time for us to leave." I shrugged.

"What is wrong with Amelia?" he asked, and I avoided his eyes as the memory of Eli holding a knife to her throat had my stomach rolling again with disgust.

"She just didn't want to leave," I answered somewhat truthfully, waving my hand as if it was no big deal. With quick reflexes, his hand shot out and grabbed my forearm and he completely halted in the middle of the walkway. I saw the look of horror on his face as he took in my bruised wrist. That was when he pushed me against the wall, strategically positioning himself over me and nearly blocking my view of the rest of the group.

"What are you—" I was startled.

"Why do you have armband marks on your wrist? What did she do to you?" he hissed. The two guards who had been following close behind me took a defensive stance against Gabriel. Caleb and Morgan spun around to see what was happening. "Give me a moment!" he commanded the guards, who looked torn. Waves of furious heat rolled outward from his dark skin. I thought I even detected a bit of steam rising from his damp clothes, which would have been comical under different circumstances. The guards took a pensive step back. "Why did they hurt you, Whitnee? Tell me the truth! Those armbands could kill you—"

"Gabriel!" I whispered, placing a firm hand on his chest. "I am fine, but I need you to play along. Please!" I begged him, tears springing to my eyes.

"She is threatening you … I know it." He stared at me so intensely that I had to look away. When I refused to acknowledge his assumption, he let out a curse word before stating, "You absolutely must leave here now—"

"No!" I told him. "I can't leave yet, but I have to get my friends out. Please, just help me with this." He was livid, and I prayed silently that he would understand. Part of me was glad to know that he really hadn't been privy to how his parents had threatened us—and that my pain obviously upset him. But the bigger part of me was now worried he was about to blow my opportunity at finding Dad.

"Gabriel!" Eli shouted from up ahead. "Is there a problem?"

Gabriel gave me a tormented look. I could see the war within his expression over what to do.

"Don't," I whispered. "Act like you didn't notice. We'll talk about it later." And I gently pushed him back, so I could move away. "Everything is fine! I just felt kind of faint," I said to Eli before Gabriel could say anything. Moving forward, I caught up to Morgan and Caleb and gave them a *don't ask* look. I could sense Gabriel's watchful eye right behind me. We continued down the long passageway in silence after that. Guilt hung heavy within me over my deception. What would my friends do when they got back? How would they explain where I was? But I couldn't worry about that. When I showed up with my missing father in tow, all would be forgiven. *Wow … what a concept.* I had only dreamt of finding Dad. To think I was almost there … it was almost too much to hope for.

"You're hiding something from us," Caleb muttered under his breath. "It's all over your face." Darn Caleb's observant nature!

"I promise I will explain everything later," I told him, knowing there was no point in denying his wisdom. I really would tell him once I made it back on the other side. I felt Morgan's arm tuck into mine.

"I'm glad we're going home, Whit," she told me, and I nodded, forbidding the tears that currently blurred my vision to fall down my face.

Finally we reached the end of the passageway and yet another door with an array of silver bars of different lengths. We had seen one of these our first day in Aerodora, and I remembered Levi using the Wind to ping musical notes out of the bars. That had opened the doorway to the Aerodorian "elevator." Sure enough, Abrianna copied the process and the door slid open. Inside was a small circular room similar to the one in the tree at Aerodora. I suddenly understood why my father said that only an Aerodorian could access the portal. Abrianna must have designed it that way—so nobody could come down here without her.

We stepped uncertainly onto the platform, and I was sandwiched in between Morgan and Gabriel. We watched as Abrianna's exotic eyes illuminated, and the floor suddenly dropped down. I stumbled slightly and felt Gabriel's body brush up against mine. It was like electricity passing between us. I gazed up at him in the dark chamber, suddenly glad that at least I would have another day or two with him before leaving.

Gabriel put his arm around my waist protectively as he asked Abrianna and Eli, "Where exactly are we going?"

"We are no longer in the Palladium but below ground." Abrianna explained. "We have built a research facility deep into the heart of the Island. That seems to be where the fabric of our two worlds collide."

"How does *that* work?" I asked, slightly annoyed with her poetic way of explaining important things.

"It seems that there is a thin layer of separation between the Mainland and the Island down here. As for how you transport, well, I believe *you* will be able to help us with that part." She looked expectantly to me.

"Me?"

"Yes. You transported everyone here; you will have to send them back."

"But I don't know how to do that," I protested. "Transporting here was an accident."

"I imagine it will come easier to you than you think," she told me as the floor came to a stop. The chamber opened up again to a very large cavern, the roughly hewn interior carved out of a white stone that glittered in the faint light. Wide-eyed, we stepped out and gazed at our primitive surroundings. The earth beneath us vibrated slightly, like the hum of a machine. Gabriel released his hold on me as he wandered into the room, his eyes alight with curiosity.

The focal point of the room was a raised flat surface flanked by four colossal orbs, which rested at the corners like the points of a perfect square. They were made from the same white stone that lined the walls.

Abrianna approached the strange platform and turned back to me. "This is the portal," she said, and we could only stare in confusion. "Once the orbs are activated, it will open up and allow you to go back to the place you transported from." I took a step toward the one closest to me. The top of the orb came to my waist, and I noticed it had a marking on it. Upon closer inspection, I found that the marking was actually the Pyradorian sign, a triangle tip with four lines shooting out of its point. I reached out and lightly traced it with my finger. A hot well of liquid Fire came to life within me. The marking burned red, and the orb began to vibrate as if I had just thrown the power switch. Slowly, it began to rise from its resting point on the ground straight up into the air. I took a few steps back, and it paused and floated a few feet off the ground, rotating slowly in a circle.

"What is happening?" I asked, unable to remove my eyes from the suspended sphere. Morgan, Caleb, and Gabriel came to stand by my side, equally entranced. Only Kevin and Amelia stayed back.

"I told you it would be easier than you thought," Abrianna remarked. "You are opening the portal."

"How? By touching it?" I didn't understand.

"It is reacting to the life force within you. Try the others," she instructed, her eyes glittering as she watched me. So I moved to the one marked with the Geodorian symbol, and the symbol glowed green as the orb came to life with whispers that only I could hear. It also floated up a few feet before stopping to spin in mid-air. The Hydrodorian orb glowed blue, sending splashes of life throughout my weary body; and the last one, the one directly next to Abrianna, was the Aerodorian orb.

"Will you activate that one?" I asked her, and she gave me a curious look.

"You do it," she commanded and stepped away. I did not understand why I had to do it if she was capable of using the Wind to do it herself. With an inward shrug, I reached out and placed my palm on the last orb—it came to life in a bright flash of purple. A cool breeze issued from it, fluttering my limp hair away from my face. The buzzing in the ground grew louder, and the Earth below seemed to groan as the fourth orb joined the floating ranks of the other three. The orbs began to hum loudly, and a burst of light and Wind overtook us like the flash of a camera. Beams of light shot out of each spinning orb and met in the center of the square. A light mist trickled down like dry ice around the flat ground.

My mouth hung open as an image filtered downward like a curtain dropping in front of our eyes. Only this curtain contained a picture of a trickling river, much smaller than the Blue River. On the other side of the bank were a rock ledge and an old willow tree. Tucked in the shade of the tree was a dark green canoe shed ... we were looking at Camp Fusion from the other side of the Frio River.

"It's home!" Morgan cried.

"What are we supposed to do now?" Caleb asked loudly over the buzzing. He was surveying the unbelievable scene in front of him doubtfully.

"You have to walk through," Abrianna answered simply, gesturing with her hands.

"That's it?" Morgan clarified. "We just walk through and we're back in our world?"

Abrianna nodded. It just sounded too easy.

"What if we wanted to come back?" Caleb asked, and I found his question puzzling. "How long does the portal stay open?" Abrianna exchanged a meaningful glance with Eli that I did not miss.

"That is unclear. Either way, Whitnee is your only key through the portal. She is the one with the power," Abrianna told him, and we stared at the shimmering picture in front of us.

"So, once we walk through, there's no guarantee that we can ever come back or even that anyone from here can go there?" Caleb demanded, and I couldn't understand what he was getting at. Did he somehow guess what I was about to do? Abrianna hesitated a moment too long.

"Without Whitnee, no," she said. I guess that meant that I would not have a hard time transporting back later then. "The portal cannot stay open too long before it shuts down. You should say your good-byes quickly and go. Besides, we still have a situation above ground that must be dealt with." She gave Gabriel a pointed look.

"Okay..." Morgan turned and motioned for Kevin and Amelia to join us.

"Is this going to hurt like last time?" Amelia questioned. I could barely look at her—panic gripped every muscle in my body. I just froze as we moved into a circle, facing each other with fear on our faces.

"I guess we say good-bye now," Gabriel said, his face agonizingly sad.

"You should come with us, Gabe!" Kevin exclaimed. "I could teach you how to play basketball and we could go fishing and you could taste ice cream—"

"He can't come with us!" Amelia scolded him petulantly.

"She is right. I have responsibilities here. I am sorry, Kevin," Gabriel said, patting Kevin's shoulder affectionately. My heart was starting to race, and I could feel my hands becoming shaky the closer we came to the moment of departure. Was I really going to do this? Was I really going to separate myself completely from my friends because some random woman I barely knew promised to take me to my father? What if this was all an illusion? A well-constructed lie? Could I really stay here and risk never actually making it back?

I was vaguely aware of Morgan and Amelia saying their good-byes, and then it was time. I opened my mouth to tell them they had to go, but before I could say anything, Gabriel took me by the arms and made me look him straight in the eyes.

"Whitnee, good-bye has finally come..." He gazed at me intensely, his eyes a warm shade of brown. "You asked me to prove my motivations by helping you get home ... and now I will eagerly await the day that you find your way back here." What was he doing? Was he saying good-bye like this just to fool my friends? He pulled me in tightly to his chest, cradling my head, and I could sense him trembling. *Gabriel* ... trembling! When he pulled away, he gave me one last tortured look that had me on red alert. Something wasn't right ... he surprised me by turning abruptly to Caleb. "You will take care of her?" Caleb nodded with intensity as if some signal had just passed between them.

"You must go now!" Abrianna yelled, and I noticed that the vibrations in the ground had rapidly turned into tremors.

"Go!" I ushered my friends ahead of me, but did not step forward. A brisk Wind was picking up in the large cavern, somehow generated by the massive amount of energy it took to open the portal.

Morgan grabbed Amelia and Kevin and started toward the portal when she realized I was not right with her. She turned back around and shouted over the din echoing off the walls. "What are you doing? Let's go!"

I shook my head fiercely, my eyes filling with tears. "I can't go with you yet!" Caleb had only moved one step away from me before pausing. "I'm sorry!" I hollered, glancing apologetically at them.

"What? Why?" Morgan yelled, her blue eyes looking alarmed. "Caleb—"

"No!" I took a step away as Caleb moved back toward me. "I have to stay…just trust me! I'll be right behind you!" I told both of them.

"Whitnee, they have to walk through *now*!" Abrianna urged, panic distorting her beautiful features. She was glancing up at the orbs, which were spinning faster now.

"I'm not leaving you, Whitnee…come on!" Morgan insisted, and Caleb moved closer to me, his face terrified. I was visibly crying now. How could I make them go?

"Gabriel, help me!" I called out to him. With a fierceness in his eyes, he scooped me up into his arms, and it sounded like he mumbled, "Forgive me," before he called out, "Caleb! Take her!" Caleb was already by his side, and I felt myself being transferred out of Gabriel's warm arms and into Caleb's.

"What—? No! *No!*" I shrieked, trying to fight my way out of Caleb's firm grasp. He was dragging me toward the portal. "Abrianna!" I called out to her. Her eyes were narrowed into slits of anger.

"Gabriel! What have you *done*?!" she screamed and raised her hand as if to launch an attack—but Gabriel was faster. A wall of Fire rose up, its massive size unlike anything I'd seen him create, and blocked her view of the portal.

"Go now!" Gabriel commanded Caleb, who was in a wrestling match with me. I kicked and tried to pull away.

"No, Gabriel ... ! Please!" I cried, reaching out to him. "You don't understand! I can't leave—"

"You cannot stay here! Good-bye, Whitnee." He was losing strength, and I could see him struggling to maintain the defensive shield he had put up. I could faintly hear the shouts and calls of everyone on the other side of his wall. I had one fleeting look at his tormented face before Caleb pulled me through the shimmering curtain.

"*NOOOOOOOOOO!*" I screamed in agony as the ground dropped out beneath us again, and we fell through the darkness. Time and space seemed to fold around us in a thick blanket that I could not see in or breathe in ... and then I blacked out.

THE MAINLAND BEYOND

HISTORY LESSON

I woke up when my body slammed into the ground. Caleb's arms and body were still locked around mine, and we both opened our eyes at the same time. Once I caught my breath, I tried to pull away from him.

"What have you *done*!" I screeched hysterically, my voice a solid octave higher than normal. "You idiot! How could you? How *could* you!" I knew I sounded like a raving lunatic as I stood to my feet. Caleb stood, and I could hear Morgan and Kevin and Amelia moaning somewhere close by.

"We had to leave, Whit—"

"No, no, no! You have no idea what you just did, Caleb! We have to go back! I have to go back! *Now!*" And I held my arms out, trying to conjure the Wind or ... any kind of life force. But nothing happened. It was like there was a short in my connection with the Island. I could feel the power so close to me, but it wasn't transmitting right. How did this happen? I was supposed to be there, finding my father ... this had all gone wrong. I marched over to Caleb and pointed a sharp finger to his chest. "You find a way to take me back *right now*, Caleb! This is all your fault! It's all your fault!" I screamed, my voice distorting in my rage. He tried to calm me down by placing a hand on my shoulder. *"Don't touch me!"*

"Whitnee, I don't understand why—"

"Of course you don't understand why I had to stay! You never trust me! You think you know everything, Caleb, and you don't!"

"Everybody needs to calm down..." Morgan walked painfully to where we stood facing each other.

"There is no way I am calming down until I get back to the Island!" I yelled at her, still trying desperately to connect with a life force.

"You're not going back, Whitnee! It's gone! The Island is gone. *Gabriel* is gone! We're back in reality now. It's what you wanted, what your *dad* said to do—" Caleb yelled back and tried to grab me again by the arms, which only made me angrier.

I began beating his chest with my fists, screaming incoherent sentences. "You ruined it! I was going to find my dad! She was going to help me! And you ruined everything, Caleb! Why did you pull me through? *Why?*" And he captured my bruised wrists and forced me to stop hitting him. I had no choice but to give up. I sank to the ground, sobbing hopelessly at the opportunity I had just lost. And all because of Caleb. He knelt down with me, still holding my wrists too tightly. His eyes were a misty combination of anger and confusion. *"Why did you do that...?"* was all I could moan over and over. Morgan's comforting arms were around me then, and Caleb released his grip.

"Shh. It's going to be okay, Whit. At least we are all home safe." Amelia and Kevin had walked over to us, and I glimpsed silent tears in Amelia's eyes. I didn't care if I was acting immaturely in front of them. In that moment, I could only feel loss. The Island was gone. Gabriel was gone. My father... and the hope of finding him again...

Gone.

"You don't understand..." I sobbed. And it was true. They totally didn't get it.

I glanced up with wet eyes to take in my surroundings. We were still on the wrong side of the river. And it must have been dusk, because the daytime humidity still clung to the air. I wondered how many days had passed here since we'd left?

"Oh, no," I heard Morgan whisper. "We're in trouble now." She sighed—and that was when I caught sight of Ben, the camp maintenance manager, pulling himself up over the rope ladder.

"No, we're not," I told her and struggled to my feet. "Ben!" I cried, fresh tears forming. Morgan and Caleb watched in alarm as I ran straight into his large and powerful arms. "You have to get me back to the Island! Please help me! They know where my dad is! He's alive! I need you to transport me back!" I begged him, feeling him pat my back comfortingly. Ben could fix anything.

"Uh, sorry, Ben … Whitnee hit her head and she's not making any sense …" Caleb started, trying to cover for my obvious moment of insanity. But Caleb still didn't get it.

"Shut up, Caleb!" I spat at him. "Can't you see? Ben is an Aerodorian!" I pulled back to look up into Ben's familiar face. The tan skin, dark hair turning silver, the gray eyes so similar to mine … he was definitely a Dorian.

"Whitnee, you're imagining things …" Caleb began but stopped as he peered closely at Ben's face. Even Morgan moved in closer with Kevin and Amelia close behind.

Ben nodded reluctantly while they stared at him in fascination. "I am a native Aerodorian. And so was Whitnee's father, thus making her half-Dorian too."

Silence. The calm before the storm.

Then we all erupted into loud questions.

"*What*?!"

"You *knew* about this?"

"How is that *possible*?"

"*Why* didn't you warn us?"

"My *father* was a Dorian?"

Ben held up both hands to silence us again.

"There is much to explain, but this is not the right place," he told us.

"I am *dying* to know what the heck is going on here," Caleb muttered. "We've just spent five days on a magical Island and come home to find that both of you are *Dorians*? I don't get it!" He ran his hands through his hair in frustration.

"I can only imagine how confused you all are. Let's go to my house down the river, and I promise I will tell you what I know."

I allowed myself one last look around the "forbidden territory." There was nothing there, no orange mist, no unexplainable wind … the Island really was gone.

And a huge piece of me was gone with it.

"I'm so hungry!" Morgan exclaimed as Ben laid out some snacks. We sat around the table in his modest cabin overlooking the river. I intentionally sat as far away from Caleb as I could, anger still my dominant emotion.

The arrangement of snacks was so familiar and yet foreign at the same time. Ben had grabbed sodas for us, and I realized I hadn't had a Coke in several days. Instead, my body was craving the pure Water of the Island now. Even the modern electricity in the cabin didn't seem to cast light in the right way. Colors and light on the Island had seemed so much richer, more vivid. I found myself thinking longingly of Gabriel and the exquisite Fire he had created for us that first confusing night. Thoughts of Gabriel made my heart physically ache, so I shoved his beautiful face out of my head for now.

As soon as Ben settled into a chair, we did away with small talk.

"How long have we been missing?" Caleb asked.

"You transported last night," Ben informed him, which caused all of us to gasp.

"No, we were there for five days!" Kevin corrected him.

"Five days? Really?" Ben didn't look concerned.

"That means that either time does pass differently on the Island or we transported back in time," I mused.

Ben shrugged as if we were talking about nothing more than the weather. "It's always been an unstable way to travel from either place," he told us, taking a long swig of his soda. "I'm very thankful you made it back when you did. Tomorrow I was going to have to take desperate measures to explain your absence."

"Does Steve know we were missing?" Morgan fretted.

"He didn't even know you were gone until this morning, and I covered for you ... I made up a story about how Whitnee had to meet her mother to pick up some medicine, so Morgan and Caleb went with her. I even had to move your car. Once I figured out Kevin and Amelia had somehow gone with you, I forged some signatures and told Steve they had actually been signed out late ... but beyond that, I was out of ideas."

"My parents never even knew I was gone. Guess there aren't any search parties to call off..." Amelia muttered and gazed down at her snack in disappointment.

"How exactly did you two get tangled up in all of this?" Ben raised one curious eyebrow at the two campers, who sank a little further in their seats.

"We sort of snuck down to the river ..." Kevin stopped.

"They threatened to tell the others that we were break-ing the rules! I still can't believe I was blackmailed by middle-schoolers," I grumbled.

"Interesting..." Ben remarked. "I suppose they were in good company, though. When you three were campers—"

"Ben!" I rolled my eyes. "Not now! We want an explanation for everything we've just been through."

"Yeah, but I definitely want to hear camper stories about them later," Kevin cut in. Amelia had been awfully quiet and thoughtful since the Palladium, and I knew we would have to talk about all that had happened to her at some point.

"Okay, where should I start?" Ben asked, more to himself than to us. He took another long sip of his soda.

"Well, I want to know how it is that you and my father are both Dorians? Who exactly are you, Ben? There's apparently a whole other life of yours I know nothing about. How did you end up here?" The fact that Ben was actually a Dorian explained so much about him. I never knew where he was from, or if he had family, or where he got his weird accent ... it was all making sense now. But, again, everything I knew about my father didn't seem to fit. He didn't look like a Dorian, and he and my mother had met at Camp Fusion when they were younger.

"In order to explain your father, I must first explain my history. As I told you before, I am an Aerodorian, born on the White Island. I grew up at the Palladium because the night that my mother gave birth to me, the Aero sign appeared in the sky—"

"So you were the Guardian?" I exclaimed.

"Yes, I was. I governed the Island for twenty-eight years—"

"I thought Guardians governed for thirty years?" I interrupted.

"Stop interrupting him," Caleb growled, and I shot him a nasty look across the table.

"It's okay for you to interrupt ... especially if I say things that don't make sense," Ben returned graciously, and I gave him a short smile, ignoring Caleb completely. "So, yes, I became the Guardian, and in my tenth year of governing, another Aero sign appeared in the sky. A baby girl had been born to a poorer family in the tribe, and she was ordained the next Guardian—"

"Let me guess ... Abrianna?" I jumped in again. Ben raised his eyebrows.

"So you met her, then."

"Oh, we met her, all right." I shook my head. "Something is wrong with that woman ..."

"Abrianna is a force to reckon with, that is for sure. Unfortunately, I did not realize how far she would go to achieve her own glory until it was too late," Ben told us ominously.

"What happened?" Morgan questioned, her face full of suspense. I watched as Ben became thoughtful.

"Abrianna came to the Palladium as a baby, and she was raised there. Her birth parents died when she was still very small. Though I had female attendants who cared for her needs, I became attached very quickly. She was beautiful, smart, and a very quick learner. It took almost no time for me to think of her as my own daughter. Even my wife was extremely fond of her—"

"You had a wife?" Caleb spoke up.

"Now who's interrupting?" I muttered, rolling my eyes. Caleb didn't even look at me.

"I had a wonderfully loving wife, and she passed on when Abrianna was about two years old."

"That's so sad, Ben. I'm sorry," Morgan sympathized.

"It was a long time ago, Morgan, but thank you. We all experience loss at some point in our lives. And, unfortunately, I did not handle my loss very well. In fact, I blame myself for a lot of the reason Abrianna became the person she probably is today. After all, I am the only father she has ever really known." I noticed Amelia leaning in closer to give him her full attention at this point. "Strangely enough, around the time my wife died and Abrianna was two years old, a baby boy was born under extraordinary circumstances to an older couple in the Aerodora Tribe. This couple had previously been unable to have children, but it wasn't just the birth of the baby that came as a surprise." He paused for dramatic effect, and we had all stopped chewing to hear what would happen next. "This boy was born with fair skin, unlike the dark hue of the natives. His hair was equally as pale, and he bore no tribal birthmark. Only his vibrant gray eyes marked him as an Aerodorian."

I got chills up and down my spine as everyone looked to me for my reaction.

"My dad," I whispered.

"Yes," Ben nodded, his eyes full of emotion. "He was given the name of Nathan. Now, his coloring was a big deal because of a prophecy made—"

"Oh, we know all about the prophecy. You mean the one about the Pilgrim and all that?" Kevin interrupted this time. We paused to tell Ben about our meetings with the Council and how they believed me to be the Pilgrim.

"Well, the Council knew about Nathan, but it does not surprise me that Abrianna would forbid discussion about him. I am sure they knew the moment they saw you that you were Nathan's daughter. You look exactly alike," Ben mused. "And if you told them Nathan was dead, then of course they would assume you were the true Pilgrim..."

"I still don't understand what happened and how you and Dad ended up here..." I directed the conversation back to Ben's story.

"Well, Nathan's birth, at first, was quite confusing. People were doubtful that he could be the Pilgrim, because nobody expected that the Pilgrim would start as a baby born on our own land. They expected a rescuer from across the sea. So the boy was taken to the Palladium to be educated and trained as a potential ruler until a decision could be made about how to handle the prophecy. Abrianna, as a young child, did not understand how his coming to the Palladium would ultimately affect her own right to Guardianship. She had been told that she was my successor, so she looked at Nathan like he was just a little brother for her—a playmate to grow up at the Palladium with her. As for me, Nathan was my family as much as Abrianna was, and I treated them both as such.

"But as they grew older, there were obvious differences there. Nathan was pure in heart in a way that Abrianna was lacking. He genuinely loved the people and enjoyed visiting each tribe. The entire Island was his livelihood, and he found much comfort in traveling the far edges of the land. It was as if he and the Island had some kind of communication with one another. And the older he grew, a new hope stirred among the tribes. He was praised as the Pilgrim, but he never liked the attention he received—he always remained humble about it. Where he liked to be out among the people, Abrianna liked to stick by my side and soak up all that she could about the position of Guardian and the secrets of governing the people. But despite their differences, Nathan and Abrianna adored each other."

"Well, something must have happened to change that ..." I remarked.

"When my wife died, I plunged wholeheartedly into studying and experimenting with the unbalanced and unpredictable portal between our two worlds. Abrianna was watching and learning everything she could too. I allowed Abrianna and Nathan to have access to all the knowledge I was gaining, and it became something we worked on together. We built a facility deep underground that few people knew about. Eventually, Abrianna discovered a thread connecting the two worlds that would allow someone to pass between them. But it was too unstable, and I was uncomfortable trying it out until we developed it further."

"Yeah, we used that underground portal to get back here," I told him quietly.

"I knew she would continue developing it ... you will have to describe that to me later," Ben said thoughtfully. "Anyway, I was still dealing with the pain of losing my wife, and I suppose the fear of losing Abrianna or Nathan made me forget that all people need boundaries for their own good. I gave Abrianna everything she ever wanted—she did not know the word 'no,' and it became a problem the older she got. She became more and more greedy with her power and wanted more control over certain areas of the land. Nathan, on the other hand, became more and more repulsed at the idea of ruling and governing. He believed that it was too much power for one person. But what he failed to realize was that his understanding of how that power could be abused would make him the perfect governor.

"So when Abrianna was eighteen and Nathan was sixteen, the Council agreed it was time to start discussion over what to do with the two of them. Abrianna was the rightful successor to the Guardianship. But Nathan was believed to fulfill the prophecies. It created the problem of who would rule after me and how. Both of them were questioned in depth by the Council, and finally, it was determined that Nathan would become the next Guardian. Of course, Abrianna did not take well to this decision and, surprisingly, neither did Nathan. He did not want to rule; he only wanted to be a part of the Island and the people. A huge argument broke out at the Palladium over this news. It was that horrible night when Abrianna tricked me into entering the portal, and that's how I came here. The amazing part was that the portal worked. The bad part was that she sealed it and would not allow me to come back. I believe she knew that I would influence Nathan to rule, and she had to get rid of me."

"Wow," I breathed. In my heart I hated her for doing that to the man who loved her like her own father. "So you've never been able to get back?"

"No, which is what ultimately brought your father here." He took another deep breath. "I eventually found out that Abrianna told him that I had left by my own choice. She said that since my Guardianship was almost over and I had been so disappointed in Nathan's 'lack of purpose,' I transported away from there. Nathan never really believed her, and, of course, she was lying. He ended up choosing to relinquish the government of the Island to her. After a few years of her ruling—years that he never really gave me much detail about—he followed me here in the hopes of bringing me back and setting things right on the Island. By that point, though, I had settled here as the maintenance manager and was learning how to survive without using a life force."

"I bet that wasn't easy," Caleb commented.

"Ben." I paused, thinking about how this all sounded like a distant story of someone other than my father. I was still having a hard time connecting the Nathan in Ben's story to the man I had always known as Daddy. "Why did my father lie all these years? Why didn't he ever tell me the truth about himself? I don't even understand why he ultimately stayed here. Could he never find a way back?"

"We don't really know for sure … at first, the portal closed behind him and we had no idea when Abrianna might open it back up again. I took him on as my apprentice that summer, and we kept a wary eye on the river from that point forward. We made up a story about how he grew up in foster care and had no family, so the current camp manager was willing to hire him on to work with me. And then the summer staff got here and that was when Nathan met Serena … he was completely in love after the first conversation he ever had with her." He smiled in memory. I could feel that tingle in the back of my eyes as tears started to form. "Serena was beautiful and smart and ambitious, much like Abrianna, but her heart was good. And Nathan knew that about her immediately. It certainly complicated his feelings about returning to his homeland. He couldn't imagine being separated from Serena, even though she was in another relationship at the time.

"Nathan and I figured that, with both of us gone, Abrianna finally had all the power and glory she had always been seeking. However, we were confident that the Tetrarch Council would keep her power in check—and then only a few months after Nathan got here, the portal reopened. The problem was that an already psychologically disturbed camper happened onto it and transported to the Island before Nathan or I could stop him."

"*Ohhhh* … that must be the camper your mom was talking about!" Morgan proclaimed, looking to me as if everything made sense now. "They found him a few weeks after that in California or something, right?"

"Well, sort of," Ben answered. "What really happened was Nathan transported to the Island to retrieve him, but for some unknown reason, they came back by boat."

"What? You mean he sailed back from the Island?" Caleb clarified, and we were all confused at this news. "I thought you lost your memory of the Island when you went across the ocean?"

"Exactly," Ben said seriously. "Neither Nathan nor the boy had any memory of the Island, and I was the only one who knew where they had actually been. I still, to this day, do not know exactly what happened while they were there. I do not know how they made it back to the Mainland, but their little boat landed on the California coastline. All they could remember was their life prior to transporting."

"Maybe the Island is somewhere off the coast of California..." Caleb wondered aloud.

"So... did Dad remember anything about the years he grew up on the Island?" I asked.

"At first, no. And I still am not sure if it was the right thing to do, but I chose not to tell him."

"Why would you do that?" I asked him curiously, and Ben heaved a great sigh.

"I wanted him to be free of his past. He didn't ever want the life he had been given. And he was so happy here on the Mainland. He was in love with Serena, and his opportunities to explore and learn were limitless here. I suppose I just wanted him to be free to live his life the way he wanted. But it's like I told you earlier in the summer—you cannot ignore the past. If you do not deal with it properly, it has a way of showing up when you least expect it. And that's what happened to your dad."

"What do you mean?" I narrowed my eyes.

"Are you really ready to know all of this?" Ben asked me, his face a mask of concern.

"Yes, of course! I need to know the truth, Ben!" I declared. It was *past* time the truth came out.

"Okay..." he relented, but spoke more slowly, as if choosing his words carefully. "Nathan eventually moved to the same college as Serena, and he became obsessed with geology and the Earth's elements. I don't know that he knew why this was such an interest to him at the time, but I certainly did. Deep down inside him, he was searching for answers and understanding about the Island. Years later, after he married your mother and they had you, he could never rid himself of dreams containing the sights and sounds of a delightful and terrifyingly familiar Island. In his sleep, he would call out to a people and a place he could not remember. When I started receiving letters from him regarding these dreams and how I was connected to them, I felt it was time to tell him the truth. So he came and visited, and I shared everything. His memory began to return, but no matter how much he missed the place he had come from, it was nothing compared to the love he had for his family here."

Ben's face turned dark then. "After a while, Nathan started having nightmares. Through her dabblings, Abrianna had found a way to contact him through the portal. She was not having success keeping and sustaining control. She needed him and his knowledge of the Island. The people had blamed her for my disappearance and then his, and rightfully so. I am sure the Dorians were in complete upheaval once their Pilgrim disappeared. At first, she appealed to him using his relationship with her. Then she reminded him of his duty to the people by making him feel guilty for leaving. When that failed to bring him back, she started threatening him with nightmares, warning that she would bring harm to his wife and child if he did not come to her immediately."

"Oh my gosh. I can't believe her! What a b—"

"Whit." Morgan elbowed me.

"I was going to say *beast*," I muttered defensively.

"Nathan came to me once again and told me that it was time to face his past and face Abrianna. He told me she had opened a portal on the island of Kauai and wanted him to go and meet her there."

"The other woman he was seen with ..." I whispered as the pieces fell into place. "Abrianna fits the description of the last woman seen with my dad before he disappeared!"

"Yes, I believe you are correct in your assumption, but whether she convinced him to transport back or something terrible happened, I don't know...Nathan's hope was to try to appeal to her to release her hold on him and his family. He asked me in that last visit that if something happened to him, and he did not return from his journey, to make sure you were brought here to this camp. He thought it would help you heal and understand who you really are."

"And I guess I can finish the story from there. He never came back. And somehow you got me here. And I've believed all these years that he ran away from us." I spoke quietly, but my voice quavered. The sudden rush of understanding hit me like a powerful gust of Wind, and I could feel a long-kept tightness in my chest trying to release. I lowered my face into my hands and the tears just bubbled up from some deep reservoir within. Ben's great hand rested gently on my back and my friends watched quietly. I cried for so many reasons. I cried out all the doubt and fears I'd carried with me for six years. It was a cathartic experience to finally have some answers. And yet, so many years had passed...so much time had been lost.

When the initial shock had subsided, I said in a choked voice, "He's still alive. Abrianna told me he's somewhere on the Island. And she was going to take me to find him after I transported them back home." I gestured to the rest of the table.

"What? Are you serious?" Caleb responded.

"I told you that you shouldn't have pulled me through the portal, Caleb! I had it under control. I would have been just a day behind you!" I grabbed for a napkin to help wipe my tears, even though they continued to flow.

"I'm sorry, but..." he said quietly. "How do you know Abrianna's telling you the truth?"

"She is very good at lying in order to achieve her own goals," Ben agreed. "Did she make you promise anything in return?"

I nodded. "She said there was a way I could release my abilities and gift her with them ... if I did that, she would help me find Dad."

"Release your abilities? That sounds dangerous. Did she tell you how she would accomplish that?" Ben wondered, and I shook my head. He looked confused then. "And why would she need the Wind life force when she's already an Aerodorian?"

"Whitnee can use all four life forces without being gifted," Morgan explained, and none of us missed how sharply Ben inhaled his breath then.

"That has never been done before ..." he murmured, seeming deeply concerned by this news.

"Yeah, well ... apparently we were all experiencing a lot of firsts on the Island. The point is, though, that she's not lying. Look." And I pulled out Dad's wedding ring from my pocket and displayed it in the center of the table for them to see. "My dad's ring ... the inscription is his. How would she have that if she hadn't been with him since he disappeared?" Ben picked up the ring and examined it.

"She could have gotten it when she saw him in Hawaii ..." he pointed out.

"He is not dead, Ben."

His stormy gray eyes met mine before he would reply. "Listen, I do not believe he would have willingly stayed separated from you and your mother all these years if he was alive, but I wouldn't completely trust what Abrianna says."

"Isn't it possible, though, that Abrianna could be keeping him there against his will?" I pressed.

"I suppose so ... that just seems extreme, even for her."

"And it seems like once she would have gotten whatever she wanted from him, she would have released him, right?" Morgan said.

"I don't know, Whit ..." Caleb started, and his hesitance to believe me just set me off again.

"You just don't want to admit that you *really* screwed up by bringing me back too early, Caleb," I shot at him, and Ben's eyebrows raised to new heights.

"Why are you just mad at *me*? *Gabriel* was the one who told me to do it!" Caleb spat. "Oh, perfect Gabriel can do no wrong, right, Whit? But he's not the one here right now. I am!"

"You are an insensitive jerk, Caleb!" I cried in anger.

"Stop it!" Morgan pounded her fist on the table. "We had no idea what was really going on, Whitnee! You chose to leave us out of it. And I'm sorry you don't like what Caleb did, but there was no way we were leaving without you."

"I just…" I couldn't speak because I was so overwhelmed with anger and grief. My whole world had been tipped upside down. Couldn't they understand that? "I need a break. Y'all can fill Ben in on all that happened. I just can't do this right now…" And with tears in my eyes, I grabbed Dad's ring, stalked out of Ben's cabin, and walked down to the river's edge. Plopping down on the uncomfortable rocks, I allowed myself time to grieve. I grieved for my father. I grieved leaving the Island.

The locusts chirped and the river gurgled and a summer night breeze stirred the trees. But I just sat there and stared ahead, contemplating all my mixed-up emotions. It wasn't too long before I heard the crunch of heavy footsteps approaching. It was Ben, and he sat on the ground with a grunt.

I wiped the lingering tears away from my face with a sniff. "Why didn't you tell me all of this five years ago, Ben?"

"When you came here as a child, you were not a complete person, Whitnee. You were vulnerable, hurting, and you were not ready to understand the past or your purpose in the future. Only time would tell. If you had any of the power that Nathan had, I knew something would draw you back here. Draw you to the Island. It is a magic that cannot be ignored if it lies within you. And the moment I saw you this summer, I knew you were ready. You had matured and had found confidence within yourself—a confidence that did not rely on your mother or your father or your friends."

I thought about this for a moment. "You sent me there with no warning. You knew I would transport the moment I set foot on the other side," I accused.

"I thought you might. But if you remember, I reminded you to take your friends with you. I know you are angry with them right now for a myriad of reasons I do not understand. But I think you will find that things might have turned out differently if you hadn't brought them with you."

"Yeah, things might have been *better*," I said bitterly. "After all, Abrianna just used them against me to get what she wanted. She manipulated *everything* we did on that Island. I don't even know who to trust anymore."

"Perhaps. But, ultimately, *did* she get what she wanted? She still doesn't have your abilities, and every one of you made it back home together."

"But not with my father."

"Whitnee, as difficult as it is to say this, I'm just not completely sure she is telling you the truth about your father being alive. And if that's the case, then your friends saved you from another manipulation by her."

"He is *alive*, Ben!" I insisted. "I've heard him talking to me in my dreams. He told me before we ever left not to cross the river. Then, when I was on the Island, I had a dream in which he described to me how to find the portal. In fact, that dream was the reason we cut our journey short. He told me I was being manipulated. And he was right. Did I tell you that I saw him on the other side of the river? That day in the water when everyone thought I freaked over a fish? It was my dad...or an image of him that somebody planted there," I added bitterly, reminding myself that I had played right into every trap Abrianna had set for me. This seemed to get Ben's attention.

"Well, now, that does change things...maybe." And we both became contemplative after that. I took a deep breath.

"So," I said. "I guess I never really was the Pilgrim after all. Assuming Dad really is alive, he's the true Pilgrim, right?"

"I don't know that we can say that for sure at this point. You both fit the description of the prophecy. Both of you have Dorian blood. Your coloring is the same. And neither of you has a tribal birthmark."

"You know Abrianna doesn't even believe in the Pilgrim prophecy?"

"Well, that is not surprising. Believing in a Pilgrim would mean she'd have to give up her power and control. And it doesn't sound like she is willing to do that. She has convinced herself that the prophecy is just a man-made attempt at fixing the Island. But truth has a way of coming out. And she will have to face the truth sooner than later, I believe."

"And what is the truth? Which one of us fulfills the prophecy?"

"I imagine your choices in the future will determine that."

"You know, that doesn't really help," I told him.

"I know." He sighed.

"Ben, do you miss the Island?"

"Yes … and no. I've grown to love living on the Mainland. I feel connected to something bigger than myself here, and I don't miss the loneliness of being the Guardian. But I do miss the people and the villages … more than you know. And I can't tell you how many times I've wished over the years that I could conjure a cool Wind in this heat! But I have a part to play here. Even if it's just to look out for you." He smiled and then I had to ask.

"How old are you, Ben? I mean, I'm trying to do the math … if Abrianna is forty-nine, you *must* be pushing *eighty*! But you don't look a day past fifty." He gave a short laugh then.

"I *feel* old. I think that the Dorian blood keeps me younger-looking. On the Island, we live much longer than here on the Mainland." This news surprised me. He continued thoughtfully, "The longer I am here, the fainter the life force becomes in me. Though I've never been able to use it here, I've always sensed its presence. Now that feeling is rare. Sometimes on a quiet day, when the wind is moving through the trees, I can sense it."

Strangely enough, I understood what he meant. I could sense it too. I sensed it not just in the breeze, but also in the lapping of the river Water and the groaning of the huge cedar tree and the heat that sizzled up through the hot Texas ground. It was all a part of me in a way it had never been before.

"Things on the Island—the people and Abrianna—it's different now," I started, thinking about all the problems still unsolved and Gabriel—*my gosh*, Gabriel. "Abrianna is married to Eli, the Council member from the Pyradora tribe—"

"*Eli*? That obsessive Pyra kid is a Councilman? I never liked him. He was always coming around the Palladium looking for her. And they're married now? What was she *thinking*? He was always as power-hungry as she was, even worse—"

"Well, there's your answer. They are a very powerful couple on the Island. And they have a son—"

"Any child raised by those two is destined to be trouble."

"Actually, he's different. He's going to be the next Guardian."

"Abrianna's own *son* is the next Guardian? I wonder how she manipulated that into happening ..." Ben mused bitterly.

"Gabriel is not like them! He has a good heart!" I stepped in defensively.

"Gabriel, huh?" Ben raised his eyebrows at me and smiled slightly. "Is this the same Gabriel that forced Caleb to take you through the portal?"

"Yes," I hissed. "He was trying to protect me."

"Sounds like a good man ..." Ben said, and I couldn't tell if he really believed that. "Sounds like Caleb was trying to protect you too ..."

I felt a stab of guilt. With another meaningful sigh, I tucked my knees up under my chin. "I have to go back, Ben. Nothing was resolved ... Gabriel doesn't even know half of the stuff his own mother is up to ... my dad is there ... I mean, what was the point of all this if nothing changed?"

"It may take time to see the point, honey. But, think about it. You know the truth now."

"Yeah, but what good is knowing the truth if I can't go back and make things right?"

"I understand how you feel ... but unfortunately, we are left to their mercy. If they open the portal again, then maybe you *should* go back. But there's no way to know when or if that will ever happen."

"I can't just sit around and wait!" I exclaimed furiously.

"Then don't sit around and wait. Live your life. Do what you came to do here this summer. Be a mentor to those who need you. Be a Pilgrim in your own life, and when the time is right, you'll find a way back."

"Do you really believe that?"

"Absolutely, I do," Ben replied. "But we can always talk about that another day. You have too much else to think about right now, Whitnee. You need rest."

And he was right. My mind was so full. I just wasn't sure I could shut my brain down long enough to get real sleep. We stayed at Ben's that night long enough to give him more details about our journey and all that had happened. But when Kevin's head started nodding, Ben decided it was time to call it a night.

After sneaking back to the cabins, Morgan, Amelia, and I finally parted ways from Caleb and Kevin. I did not say another word to Caleb that night, and I could tell this frustrated him. But I just didn't care.

When the three of us entered our dark and deserted cabin, we were so grateful to find our own clothes and toiletries. However, getting ready for bed was not the same. I particularly missed the special mouthwash on the Island. My teeth just didn't feel as clean after brushing. And my pajamas felt a little bit scratchier than the soft weave used for Island clothing.

Once we had turned the lights out and gotten into our separate bunks, Morgan said into the darkness, "I'm sad."

"Me too." Amelia and I responded simultaneously.

"I miss the clothes," Amelia admitted.

"I miss the food … and the beach. It was so beautiful," Morgan replied.

"I miss …" *Gabriel.* I missed Gabriel's warm arms and his intense eyes. "I miss … everything," I finished dejectedly.

"Yeah," Morgan agreed, and I heard Amelia sigh over in her corner. We were quiet then until Amelia asked me to put my Sleepy Playlist on the speaker. I readily agreed, hoping it would make me fall asleep faster so I wouldn't have to lie there in utter depression.

RETURN TO CAMP FUSION, TAKE TWO

"Oh, you're all back?" Steve looked surprised at lunch on Sunday when he saw the five of us sitting in the cafeteria together— apart from the other random group of campers and mentors who had stayed all weekend. We had all slept through break- fast, so we were still rubbing the sleepies from our eyes.

"Oh, um, yes. We returned this morning," Caleb lied, look- ing cautiously at Morgan and me.

"Next time you have to leave like that, make sure you find me, okay? I mean, Ben told me you had to go, but I would feel better hearing it directly from you," Steve gently corrected.

"Yes, sir," we chorused.

"And Amelia and Kevin, right? Did your parents bring you back this morning?" He checked the clipboard that seemed to be a permanent fixture on his body.

"Yes," they replied.

"They forgot to sign you back in ... did they come by the office on the way out?" He was flipping pages on his clipboard. Kevin and Amelia looked to us in panic.

"If they didn't, I'd be happy to place a call to them and remind them of the policy next time," I offered.

"Yes, maybe …" Steve muttered to himself. "Well, I'm glad you made it back. Did you have a good time over the weekend?"

"Oh, yes!" Kevin exclaimed with a knowing look at the rest of us. "*Traveling* was a lot of *fun*."

"It was unlike any other weekend I've ever experienced," Amelia told him with a smirk. I kicked her under the table.

"Okay, well, good." Steve smiled, seeming unsure if he was missing something. "I will see you at the meeting later tonight?" he asked us mentors.

"Yes, sir," we told him again and then he was off. We exhaled collectively.

"I thought we were in trouble," Morgan breathed.

"We just got really lucky," Caleb commented.

"Hey, you guys know that we have to keep all of this a secret, right?" I pointed out, looking meaningfully at Kevin and Amelia. "As cool as it all sounds, we can't tell people what really happened. They would send us to the loony bin. Can you handle that?"

"I can. Besides, who would I tell? My grandparents would never believe me anyway," Kevin said sadly.

"Same with me. My parents wouldn't even listen long enough to decide they didn't believe me …" Amelia replied, equally depressed.

"You know what? None of us can tell our parents," Morgan said, and Caleb and I nodded. "But that doesn't mean it never happened. We will always know the truth between the five of us."

"Exactly. And we can always talk to each other about it. And Ben too," I reminded them.

"Whitnee?" Kevin looked at me wide-eyed. "Will you ever get to go back and find your dad?"

I poked at my plate before replying, "I don't know, Kevin."

"I hope you do. And if you want help, I would go back with you like that." And he snapped his fingers.

"Me too," Morgan said.

"And me!" Amelia stated.

I smiled at them. "Thank you. That means a lot, y'all."

Only Caleb remained silent, and I didn't even acknowledge him. Eventually, we would have to deal with the distance between us. But I would save that conversation for another time.

"Hey, Amelia," I called as she sat on her top bunk staring at the ceiling. "Want to go get an ice pop and take a walk before the other girls get here?"

She shrugged. "Sure."

We strolled to the snack shack and ordered our favorite ice pop flavors before heading down the winding trail to the river's edge. I knew the things I really needed to say, but was unsure how to start. And I still felt the guilt of being the world's worst mentor. So I just jumped in.

"Amelia, I'm really sorry about what happened on the Island. I should never have sent you to Abrianna, especially if I had known what was really going on—"

"Yeah, well, I didn't know what she was really like, either," she murmured.

"She's a very good liar, but I think she genuinely saw talent in you. Even Kevin said you were really good with Fire."

"You're just saying that to make me feel better. The whole time Abrianna just wanted to use me to get to you. And that sucked."

"I'm sorry," I told her, tasting my ice pop thoughtfully. "She was wrong ... and so was I. Will you forgive me?"

"*Me* forgive *you?*" Amelia looked surprised. "I think I'm the one who needs forgiveness. You know, I didn't mean it when I said I hated you. I was just mad at you for making me leave."

"Well, I don't blame you."

"Yeah, but I said a lot of mean things, Whitnee. It's just that..." She paused on the steep pathway and turned to look at me directly. So I stopped and gave her my attention. "I want to matter, you know? I want to be somebody important, and I think I was really jealous of all the attention you were getting. And then it was like Abrianna told me all these things about how powerful and special I could be... but she just lied. And after hearing everything that Ben said about her... well, I was just another person she manipulated, and I hate myself for that."

"Don't hate yourself. We were all manipulated by her, especially me. She's the one who made me believe I had to send you to the Palladium. She even got me to agree to send y'all back through the portal without me," I told her. "So, yeah, I know how you feel, and it does suck."

We started walking again.

"You know, I'm glad you're my mentor," Amelia confessed, not looking me in the eye.

"Really?"

She flashed me a genuine smile. "Yeah, I mean, I get annoyed sometimes, but it's mostly because you're the first person to actually make me follow the rules." Then her face turned mischievous. "But for every rule you make me obey, you teach me how to break another one... like sneaking to the other side of the river, leaving camp without permission, sleeping in the same room with a boy—"

"Oh, *geez*." I sighed.

"Lying about where we've been—"

"Okay, enough!" I blushed and gave a short laugh. "When you put it like that, I'm a terrible mentor!"

She laughed heartily. "No, you're the best. Nobody else could have taken me on such an adventure. And I don't want to get you worked up or anything, but I think I learned a lot about myself." She suddenly gave her ice pop special attention.

"Oh, really? And what's that?"

Her face turned solemn, and she took a deep breath. "I learned that if I don't make some changes, I could turn out like Abrianna. I mean, it sounds like she was spoiled a lot like me and all she wants is to be important to everyone. That's kind of like me, but I don't want to end up like her. Because she only hurts the people she's supposed to love."

I gave her a warm look. "That is the most mature thing I think I've ever heard anyone say, Amelia."

"Really? Good! 'Cause I've been thinking about it a lot since we got back!" she confessed. "No, seriously, I think I can find better role models ... like you. And Morgan." She got kind of shy at that, and I bumped her with my hip.

"Just be you, Amelia. Not who you think the world wants you to be," I told her.

"I'm going to try."

"Well, I'm proud of you. And I'm glad we still have a whole summer together." And I meant it. She felt more like a little sister to me than a camper after all we had been through. "Now tell me about the good parts I missed. What did you learn to do with Fire?"

Amelia and I were perched on the rock ledge still discussing life forces that Sunday afternoon when Morgan approached us.

"Hey, Amelia ... Bailey just arrived, and she's looking for you."

"Really?" Amelia perked up. "Let's go back to the cabin!"

"Actually," Morgan jumped in, "why don't you go up there first? I need to talk to Whitnee for a second. We'll be right behind you."

Amelia looked hesitant at first, but I nodded at her, so she jumped up and took off. Morgan took a seat next to me, and I prepared myself for what was to come.

"How long are you going to be mad at Caleb and me for bringing you back?"

I took a deep breath as I organized my thoughts. "I'm not mad at *you* ... and I'm only mad at Caleb because he took my choice away, you know? It's not that he brought me back here. He did what he thought was right, and I probably would have done the same thing. I guess I'm more upset about how close I was to fixing things ... I could have found my dad, given her my powers, and been done with the whole Island experience."

"Aside from finding your dad, is 'being done with the Island' really what you want? I mean, especially now that we know you're half-Dorian," she pointed out.

"I don't know ..."

"I don't believe for a second that you are done with the Island, Whitnee. Don't forget that I still think you are the true Pilgrim. Hearing about your dad didn't change my mind about that. But, for some reason, we can't get back to the Island yet. And since that's the case, we need to make right what we can here. You need to forgive Caleb for what he did. That boy is all tied up in knots, especially after he heard what Abrianna was telling you. He may not admit it to you, but he is beating himself up over the whole thing."

"I'm just not ready to deal with him yet, Morgie. Things just feel too complicated between us right now." I shook my head, pushing away the cloud of emotions. I reached up to rub my temples—I could feel a headache coming on. "I really think I'm just shell-shocked from everything. And I miss ..." I couldn't say it.

"Gabriel," she finished for me.

"*Ughh.*" I sighed. "Morgan, what was I thinking allowing myself to have such strong feelings for him? I mean, he *lied*—"

"Sometimes you can't control those feelings. And he was totally into you too, Whit. What girl wouldn't find that kind of attention attractive? Not to mention his hot physique ... you'd have to be a wet sock to ignore it."

"That doesn't make me feel better, Morgie! He lives on the Island … we can't ever have a real relationship. Pining for him is like pining for a fairy tale prince. It's never gonna happen."

"You don't know that," she objected. "After all, you're half-Dorian. The Island is as much your home as Texas is, right?" I remained silent, battling the pain of talking about Gabriel. "Listen, I know you have some complicated feelings for both Gabriel *and* Caleb. And nobody's making you choose one or the other right now. I mean, it's not like you're getting married tomorrow or something. You have time to figure out who you really want."

"But that's the thing. I broke our pinky promise to not get serious about a guy this summer. And I fell hard for Gabriel, Morgie. With Caleb, it's more complicated than just falling."

"I think you found your first love."

I assumed she meant Gabriel … "Is this what love feels like? The achy heart and the fist in your stomach and the darkness that takes over at the thought of his name?" I moaned, clutching my stomach.

"No, that's what a broken heart feels like," she responded gently, watching me with empathy on her face. "And I'm sorry that's what you're dealing with right now on top of everything else."

"I hate this," I told her, leaning my head on her shoulder. There was nobody else who could understand how I felt, except Morgan. Every girl needed at least one best girlfriend for these moments.

"That part will get better," she promised, resting her head on top of mine. "But the stuff with your dad … I just don't know, Whit."

"Me neither."

"I guess our only choice is to find a way back to the Island," she declared forcefully. "And when we do, we'll make things right. We'll find your dad, and you can see Gabriel again and figure out what's really there …"

"*If* we get back to the Island," I corrected.

"*When* we get back to the Island," she said stubbornly. "Have some faith!"

And even though my faith was lacking at the moment, hers was enough to carry me through for a while.

"Whitnee!" Emily cried when Morgan and I made our way back to the cabin. She was waving good-bye to her mom who was pulling away in the car.

"Hey, Em!" I was genuinely happy to see her. "How was the weekend?"

"It was good to be home, but, well, it was kind of boring after being here at camp," she admitted with a grin. Together we carried her stuff back inside, and Morgan got distracted by one of her own arriving campers.

"Did I miss anything exciting?" Emily asked as we entered the cabin.

With a secretive grin, I replied, "No, not really."

"Did things get better with Amelia?" she wanted to know, but we were interrupted by Amelia herself.

"Emily! You're back!" Amelia shouted and ran to give her a hug. Emily froze right there in the entrance to the room.

"Hi, Amelia…" She looked shocked, and I had to repress my laughter. "Are you feeling better?"

"Oh, yeah!" Amelia nodded quickly. "Put your stuff down and come sit on Bailey's bed with us. She was just telling me about her weekend." And Amelia gave me a wink before she joined Bailey again. I could only smile as I moved to straighten up my own bunk, listening in to the three girls' conversation.

"So, my cousin, Cole, came over and we were playing basketball—" Bailey was continuing her story when Amelia interrupted.

"Your cousin … is he cute? How old is he?" she questioned in typical Amelia fashion.

"He's fifteen," Bailey told her.

"Perfect age," Amelia acknowledged.

"Too old for you!" Emily disagreed. "Wait, is he blond or brunette? That makes a difference."

"He's really blond," Bailey informed them.

"Never mind then. I think I'm done with blonds for a while," Amelia responded, and I rolled my eyes. They were acting like such little teenagers.

"What about Kevin?" Bailey pressed. "He's blond and you didn't seem to mind … hey, didn't you guys stay here this weekend? Anything happen?"

"Ew, no," Amelia told them. "I'm so over Kevin … I mean, he's more like a brother to me. I think I prefer dark hair now, tan skin … you know, that exotic Island guy look?"

I shook my head in amusement, but was really proud when I heard her say, "But you know what? I'm not here this summer to meet boys. I've got things to work on, you know?"

Emily and Bailey's mouths dropped open.

"What *happened* this weekend?" Emily asked. "You're so … different."

Amelia shot me a look but before she could respond, Madison walked in with all her bags.

"Madi! You're back!" Amelia exclaimed and ran to give her a hug. Madison stood there in confusion at Amelia's excitement.

"Hey …" Madison replied, shooting perplexed glances at Bailey and Emily and me. I just shrugged.

"Meet the new Amelia," Bailey said, and everyone laughed good-naturedly. Okay, so maybe the whole experience on the Island hadn't been completely pointless …

Sunday night the mentors gathered in the lodge for a meeting. Morgan, Caleb, and I were still exhausted and feeling a bit of culture shock having to get back into the real world of our lives. So we were a bit flustered when we entered the lodge and the first people we ran into were Jaxson, Drew, and Claire. They had saved chairs for us near the back. Naturally, Drew approached Morgan first, and Claire ran up to hug Caleb. I turned my eyes away from their embrace. Jaxson moved hesitantly toward me, as if unsure how he should act. I had to think for a moment about our last conversation … it felt like a week had passed since then. Well, a week had passed, but to him, it had only been a couple of days.

"Hi, Jax. How was the weekend?"

"Good. I thought about you a lot … in fact, I tried calling, but I guess you didn't have any reception," he said nonchalantly.

"Oh. Yeah. Definitely didn't have cell phone coverage this weekend …" I attempted a friendly smile. "I'm sorry."

"So how were things around here? Boring without us?" he teased as we all sat down. I avoided making eye contact with Morgan and Caleb.

"Oh, very boring." I nodded seriously.

"I hope you got rest … hey, where are your bandages?" Jaxson asked as he placed his hand on my arm. Everyone looked expectantly at me.

"What bandages?" I asked, not understanding.

"Whit*nee*, remember how you fell and cut yourself up *three days ago*?" Caleb reminded me intensely.

"Oh, yeah!" I chuckled nervously, remembering. "Feels like that happened over a *week* ago! I guess I *heal* fast." And Morgan snorted beside me, which she then unsuccessfully tried to turn into a fake coughing fit.

"You okay?" Drew asked her.

"I'm great … sorry. Got something caught in my throat," she told him innocently.

"Need some Water, Morgan? Maybe that would *heal* your cough," I said with a wicked smile. Caleb rolled his eyes at me.

"You look different," Jaxson commented to me. "Did you hang out in the sun a lot this weekend?"

"Not really …" I told him, shooting a puzzled glance over at Morgan.

"Your hair … it seems lighter, maybe? Or you seem tanner?" Jaxson watched me closely, as if trying to figure something out.

"Yeah, your hair does look lighter," Claire spoke up. "Did you do something different?"

"Nope," I replied.

"You know, you do have kind of a *magical* look about you," Morgan agreed solemnly, but her eyes were twinkling at her double meaning.

"Really, Morgan. There's no such thing as *magic*," Caleb stated, jumping in on our fun but acting equally as serious. "I think she looks a bit *wind*ed, actually. Maybe she needs more rest."

"Well, if I hadn't stayed up so late reading *Pilgrim's Progress*, I might not feel so tired," I quipped, and that was the final straw. The three of us howled with laughter.

"I don't get what's so funny." Claire looked slightly annoyed, so we were forced to get control of ourselves. But then she gave her attention to Caleb and cooed, "By the way, I think you look really nice in earth tones, Caleb. Really brings out your eyes." She pulled at his dark green t-shirt flirtatiously, and that set Morgan and me off into raucous fits of laughter again. "What did I say?" she scowled, and we just laughed harder.

"Thank you, Claire," Caleb choked, as he suppressed his own amusement. "That's very nice of you. I really do like *Earth* tones." Morgan and I could only nod in agreement.

"I don't think y'all got nearly enough sleep this weekend," Claire commented, crossing her arms over her chest.

"If you only knew..." I mumbled, thinking that I needed more than one day to catch up on sleep. Drew and Jaxson were still clueless, and it felt good to see that everything was still normal around here. Steve chose that moment to call our meeting to attention, so we refocused on him. But not before I exchanged smiles with Morgan. It was good to laugh together. But when I saw Claire link her fingers with Caleb's, I could feel that distance once again between him and me. He avoided making eye contact with me after that, and though I knew I would have to find him later and work all of this out, I still didn't have the energy.

MAKING THINGS RIGHT

"Later" ended up taking longer than I had expected. Now that everyone was back from the weekend, Camp Fusion was up and running in full force, never the wiser about our five-day excursion to the White Island. And though we were all plunged back into our camp routines, I felt disconnected that entire week following our travels. I never found an appropriate moment to talk to Caleb, and Claire seemed to be attached to him during every free moment. I couldn't even raise enough energy to let their slowly imploding relationship bother me. I put off Jaxson's attentions as much as possible and even kept my distance from Morgan. There just wasn't much left to say. I couldn't put into words what I was feeling, so I just remained quiet.

A shroud of darkness pervaded my thoughts, and I couldn't shake off the despair in my heart. It was like I could only focus on the fact that my whole life had been a lie. I was able to perform my duties as a mentor without letting it affect me, but it was in my alone time that my mind drifted a million miles away. At night, I wished for a dream from my father so I could ask him questions. I needed reassurance, direction, some kind of guidance about how to get back to the Island.

But my dreams were nonexistent. And so the darkness continued to envelop my mind and emotions. I had received several voice-mails from my mother, but I just couldn't find the courage to call her back. What could I say? Anything I said about the weekend would be a lie, and I didn't want to live like that. I so desperately wanted to let her in on all of this, to tell her the truth about Dad, and to promise that I would bring him back home. But knowing that I had to remain silent just led me back into the vicious cycle of depression.

Finally, on Friday night, exactly one week in Mainland time since we had transported to the Island, I had wandered off on my own again. The camp staff was hosting another social, so the mentors were able to take a break. I hadn't meant to walk away from Morgan and Caleb without any warning. I only thought that sunset was my favorite time of day on the river. And then somehow, I was perched on my rock ledge before I even questioned when I had really decided to go down there.

I turned my dad's wedding ring over and over again in my hand. I had kept it on me at all times, pushing my fingers through it without thinking, even when it was in my pocket. It had just become a fidgeting distraction for me when I was lost inside my dark thoughts.

And so there I was that Friday night, staring hopelessly out at the Frio River without really seeing its beauty, when Caleb found me.

"Whit, I'm worried about you," he said softly, lowering himself beside me. For the briefest of moments, I was reminded of the conversation we had the last time we had sat together here on this rock ledge. He had given me butterflies in my stomach ... and it was the first time I had become aware that there might be something more between us. So much had changed since then.

"I'm sorry," I told him honestly. "I didn't mean to wander off ..."

"It's not just that," he insisted, and I could feel his watchful eyes on me. "You've not been yourself since we got back. You don't really eat, you drift off into your own thoughts ..."

"I do?" I questioned. I thought I had only been doing that when I was alone. I had tried really hard to stay energetic and positive around the campers.

"You're acting depressed, Whitnee."

"Maybe..." I said, thinking about this. "I'm sorry. I'm not trying to be a downer. There's just so much in my head that I don't know how to handle."

"Look at me," he commanded, and I tore my distant gaze away from the riverbank to look into his green eyes. "Whit, I remember when I first met you. You were this alien kid who had pulled deep into herself and wouldn't let anyone in ... you remember that, don't you?" I nodded. "I can't let you go back to being that person again."

"You have no idea how hard it is to wonder what might have been ... Just when I thought I had put the questions about my dad to rest, all of this happened. And leaving the Island like that ... it just felt kind of traumatic."

"I'm sorry I screwed up! I had no idea what was going on!" he cried, his green eyes burning with intensity. "I only knew that you were lying to me, and when I realized you were planning to stay without us, I couldn't even think straight. When Gabriel said to take you with me, I didn't even hesitate because *here* is where you belong, not *there*... or at least that's what I thought at the time. Now that I know you're half-Dorian, I don't even know *what* to think..."

"Well, that makes two of us," I whispered. We peered honestly at each other for what felt like the first time in a long time.

"I know your life has changed. I know that your ... emotions have changed about certain things. I mean, I'm no dummy ... you and Gabriel are ..." he trailed off, and I could sense the pain behind his words.

"And you and Claire—"

"Are nothing!" he interrupted and then sighed. "Don't get me wrong. She is a really awesome girl, and you have no idea how much I wish I could feel for her what I feel for you...but it's just not going to happen. And don't think that I'm expecting you to return my feelings anytime soon. I know how much you care about Gabriel—"

"Please don't talk about him, Caleb. He's not here and that whole thing, whatever it was, is over now," I said flatly.

"Whether he's here or not, you can't deny how you feel about him any more than I can pretend not to notice it." He said it so gently...and that's when I started crying. Because he was right. About the depression. About Gabriel. About us.

"I am so sorry, Caleb," I sobbed, my face falling into my hands. "I never intended for that to happen...with Gabriel. I never wanted to hurt you—"

"I know," he answered, and then I felt his arms around me, and I pressed my face to his shoulder and let the tears fall. I couldn't deny that it still felt good to be in Caleb's embrace, but in a different way than with Gabriel. It didn't rock my world. More specifically, he calmed my chaotic world in the way that only someone you absolutely love and trust can do. It wasn't attraction then; it was friendship.

"I'm sorry I blamed you for transporting me back," I blubbered, feeling the need to make at least something in my world right again. "It was easy to be mad at you because, like you said, you're here and he's not."

"I understand," he sighed. "I just don't want to lose you—"

"I don't want to lose you either!" I confessed, and it was the absolute truth.

"Then *don't*, Whit. I want whatever part of your life I can have. And if that's just friendship right now, then that's what I want. You keep me on my toes and challenge me to be a better person. I need that in my life. So, we're okay. It's all okay." He was rubbing my back in gentle circles, and my tears slowed at his words. We remained silent for a while, listening to the cicadas and soaking in the tenderness of the moment. Our friendship had turned a new corner...it felt deeper somehow. The peace that comes after a good cry began to settle over me when he finally broke our companionable silence.

"Whitnee, you can't let what happened on the Island affect who you are." He gave me a short squeeze, and I pulled away to look up at his face. "When you came to Camp Fusion the first time, you were alone. But you're not alone now. You still have me...and Morgan."

"I know you hate to admit it, Whit, but he's right!" a female voice exclaimed softly from behind us, and the next thing I knew Morgan had plopped down on the other side of me. Caleb still had an arm around me, and I felt Morgan do the same. And there I was, sandwiched in between my two best friends, a safe cocoon of love and friendship. Gabriel had said my friendship with them was a life force in and of itself. And now I knew what he meant. I felt a transfer of their strength and warmth fill my very soul in that moment, and I could not imagine how I could ever become the reclusive girl I had been after Dad first disappeared. Circumstances were different now. *I* was different now, and to fall back into old patterns would make everything I had worked so hard for in my life become meaningless.

"You know, Ben did make an interesting point," I said quietly through my sniffles. "He suggested that things might have turned out differently if you guys hadn't been there with me on the Island. And I think he's right. Gabriel would have taken me straight to the Palladium and who knows what Abrianna would have done with me then? But, because y'all were there, it changed everything." I paused, trying to put into words what was really on my heart. "I guess what I'm trying to say is...thank you." I just received an encouraging squeeze from both of them in return. I heaved a great, calming sigh as a single lightning bug floated past us, flitting its glowing tail. "I hope we can go back there someday soon. I feel like I had a chance to finally change the world, and I blew it."

"You can still change the world without all your superhero powers, you know," Caleb reminded me lightly, doing a dramatic imitation of me using a life force.

"How's that?" I wanted to know, giving a light laugh at his antics.

"One camper at a time, right? Isn't that why we're here this summer? To help change lives?"

"Yeah, and you can totally see a change in Amelia since we've been back, Whit. She looks up to you so much," Morgan reminded me.

"She *is* doing great, isn't she? But I had nothing to do with that. It's a choice *she* made," I admitted.

"*She* made the choice, but *you* pointed her in the right direction," Morgan said.

"It always comes down to our choices, doesn't it?" Caleb said thoughtfully. "People don't realize how much power that is."

"You're right," I agreed, thinking about that concept.

"When are you two going to realize I'm *always* right?" he teased.

We snorted in response and Morgan piped up, "So, can the three of us agree to move on? It's only June! We've still got the entire summer ahead of us. And there's still so much that can happen ..." And her words ignited a tiny spark of hope in the dark spaces of my heart.

Because, ultimately, she was right. Anything could happen.

Laundry Day. *Ick*. I had let my dirty clothes pile up all week, and it was finally time to lug the massive basket in the heat to the laundry room across from our cabin. Once I had trudged over there, I was pleasantly surprised to find Ben leaning over a washer and shuffling tools around.

"Hi, Ben!" I greeted him warmly, dropping my basket on the floor gratefully.

"Oh, hey, Whitnee!" He paused in his work to give me his full attention. "I was going to come find you today, actually after I finished fixing this washer ... how are you feeling?" He crossed his arms and surveyed me closely.

"Better," I answered honestly, then narrowed my eyes at him. "Did Morgan or Caleb come talk to you or something?"

His face broke into a smile. "Well, they were worried about you a couple of days ago."

"Yeah, we talked about everything, and it helped. I'm okay ... really!" I stated and began to separate my laundry out into a nearby washer. I checked all my pockets before tossing the clothes in.

"Maybe I shouldn't have told you everything."

"No!" I disagreed. "I mean, it was quite a surprise to hear all of that, but I'm glad I know the truth now."

He was still looking uncertain when I pulled out the khaki shorts I had worn to the Island. I plunged my hands into the pockets and was surprised to pull out a piece of paper with my Swiss Army knife ... it was Sarah's letter! I had forgotten about it.

"Hey, Ben. Do you know Ezekiel and Sarah?" I asked him, and a strange look passed across his face.

"I certainly do. Why?" He looked curious.

"I forgot about this, but Sarah left this letter in my pocket, and I didn't get it until I was already at the Palladium. Read it." And I handed it over to him. I continued to separate my laundry but frequently glanced at him for his reaction. I was surprised to find that his Aerodorian gray eyes became misty as he read to the bottom. "What's wrong, Ben?"

He took a moment to compose himself before he spoke softly. "Ezekiel is my brother."

"Seriously?" Now that I had met Ezekiel, and seen Ben for the true Aerodorian that he was, I could actually see a family resemblance there. Maybe that was why Ezekiel seemed so familiar to me. "So Ezekiel and Sarah knew my father? Is that what she wanted to tell me?"

Ben shook his head slowly. "I wasn't going to tell you this yet ... you seemed overwhelmed enough the other day, but ..."

"What, Ben?"

"Do you remember how I told you that Nathan was born to an older couple in the village who had never been able to have children?" I nodded. "Ezekiel and Sarah ..." he said, and I had never heard Ben's voice so quiet. "They are your grandparents." And he watched my face carefully for a reaction, but I didn't have one yet.

"My grandparents? Which would make you my ..."

"Great-uncle," he answered. "I can only imagine how difficult it was for them to see you ... and not be able to tell you the truth. From the sound of this letter, it is apparent that Abrianna has threatened them about saying anything. It seems like she's trying to wipe away Nathan's existence completely ..." He trailed off at my lack of response. I was still registering the fact that I had grandparents and an uncle from my dad's side of the family.

I started laughing.

Ben looked on in slight confusion, but I couldn't stop laughing. "This is great!" I exclaimed. "I mean, how cool is that? We're related! And Ezekiel ... even Caleb said that Ezekiel's dramatic personality was similar to mine, but I just thought all Aeros ... *wow*." I shook my head.

"So, you're okay?"

"Oh, yeah," I nodded, allowing my laughter to die down. "I don't think there's anything anybody could say to surprise me."

"I'm sorry for all the secrets," Ben said.

"Aren't you the one who said that everyone is entitled to their secrets?" I raised my eyebrows. "Besides, *this*"—and I gestured between the two of us—"feels good. I've always felt like you were family to me. I just never knew why."

He held out his arms to me then for a giant bear hug. "You're a good girl, Whitnee. Your father would be so proud."

And I hoped I could live up to my father's legacy. I realized that I *wanted* to make him proud. Instead of bringing tears to my eyes, Ben's words only sufficed to ignite a fire and purpose in my heart.

There was just one thing left to do... one person I still hadn't talked to since my return from the White Island. And it was the conversation I dreaded and needed the most.

Once I had started my laundry, I hustled back to my cabin and dug around for my cell phone. I had to call her before I could change my mind again. With my phone clutched in my hand, I practically ran to my special rock where I had cell phone service. I pushed away the memories of finding Caleb and Claire kissing there. I still felt the twinge of jealousy and protectiveness over Caleb, but I just couldn't get my feelings of friendship toward him tangled up in that again.

As soon as my reception bars went up, I dialed the familiar number and listened to my heart pound as it rang.

"Whitnee!" my mother answered excitedly.

"Mom!" I sighed and sank to the ground. It felt like it had been so long since I'd heard her voice.

"What's been going on—?" she asked at the same time I said, "I'm sorry I haven't called!"

"I've been worried, *mija*. Usually I hear from you every few days, and you haven't called in almost two weeks! I was about to call Morgan or Caleb or Ben..."

"Yeah, I'm really sorry. Things have just been busy. But I've thought about you a *lot*," I said honestly. "And I don't have long to talk because I have to get back and change out my laundry. I guess I just wanted to hear your voice..."

"I am so glad you called," she told me, and I could hear the joy in her voice. After all, she was by herself without me there. "Papi is planning a big fiesta for the Fourth of July! He already has your favorite chicken fajitas on the menu. We can't wait to see you." Mom's dad, whom I called Papi, was a very vibrant man who loved to host parties and dinners for any occasion. And, as his only granddaughter, I was very spoiled by him.

"I can't wait to come home for a weekend... I miss you so much." I sighed and dropped my face into my hand. I wanted to tell her the truth so badly. I wanted to tell her about everything I had been through. But it was a burden I could not share with the most important woman in my life.

"Are you feeling okay, Whitnee?" she asked lightly.

"Yeah, I'm fine. Just missing home, I guess..." I told her, because it was true. "Can I ask you a question?"

"Of course."

"Why did you name me Whitnee?" I wondered if her answer would give me any indication that my dad actually had told her about his past.

"Well, that's a random question."

"I guess I was just thinking about name meanings, and I was curious as to why you picked that name."

"I didn't pick it, actually. Your dad did," she said softly. "When you were born as blonde and fair-skinned as him, he insisted that we name you Whitnee Skye, and I guess I was too drugged to argue." She laughed. "I had a Spanish name picked out for you, but I couldn't give a Spanish name to a child who didn't even look Spanish." So I guess that answered my question. She didn't know the truth about Dad.

"What would my Spanish name have been?" My curiosity was piqued anyway.

"Viviana Rose..."

"Seriously? Viviana? Wow, I wish I could tell Dad thank you for saving me from that fate..." I smiled, thinking of what it would have been like to be called *Viviana*.

"Hey, be nice. It's a family name, meaning 'full of life'... which definitely would have suited you!" she reprimanded gently. "But you are right. Whitnee Skye fits you better. It's more American-sounding anyway." And I had to contain a laugh as I thought about how my name actually had more to do with Dad's distant Dorian memories.

"I love you, Mom," I proclaimed suddenly.

"I love you, too, *mija*," she said. "Are you sure you're okay?"

"I'm great. Really. I feel better than I have in a long time," I answered sincerely.

The truth was that I had purpose now. And for the first time, the heaviness lifted from me as I allowed myself to be excited about the future that stretched before me. There was something enthralling about knowing that anything could happen. And I felt deep down inside me that I hadn't seen the last of my Island ... or my father.

Check out a sneak peek from...

WaterCrossing

BOOK 3 of the PHANTOM ISLAND series

He slowly rolled his head in a circular motion, stretching the taut muscles in his neck. He was careful to keep any grimace of pain from showing on his bloody face—not that any form of expression felt possible through the swelling. His dark eyes flicked unceasingly around the sparkling cavern, observing their faces, their body language, and any possible weakness that might provide a route of escape.

With his wrists locked into the armbands, he had no access to his life force, and he was outnumbered by about seven to one. However, he knew the armbands and the beating had been a formality. After all, one does not defy the Guardian—not even if one is the future ruler and present son of the Guardian. In his culture—and in his family—orders were made to be followed.

He had apparently stepped into a situation he did not know nearly enough about, and perhaps that was why he made the choice to protect *her* instead. His mother and father had acted as if he had just brought about the destruction of the Island itself and, truthfully, he had gained some satisfaction in knowing he had thrown a kink into their carefully laid plans.

Not more than an hour ago, he had watched *her* disappear— a shimmering, hazy image moving out of his arms and into a foreign, otherworldly portrait. And it had been his seemingly brilliant idea to make her cross over ... only now he could not erase the image of her golden hair whipping around, her face contorted with confusion and panic, the horrifying sound of her screaming his name before she disappeared ...

He closed his eyes and allowed himself to feel the torture of the moment again before consciously pushing away the emotion that threatened his calm and cautious exterior. That was the problem with *her* ... she made him feel what he had been trained to ignore. And like the weakness of his Pyradorian nature, the emotion was almost uncontainable at this point.

He glanced again at his mother across the room and studied her cool manner as she was deep in conversation with his father. She was very adept at staying calm and in-control, no matter what the situation. Though Abrianna had been openly furious with him for what he had done, she was the one who had quickly put an end to Eli's beating. He knew his father was probably the only person on the Island who could overpower him physically—and that had definitely been proven true with the current state he was in. But as he observed his parents, he could see no love or tenderness between them—only a shared desire for power and importance, a desire that bordered on greed.

His mother turned sharply away from Eli then and made a quick motion with her hand to a servant across the room. She had a delicate, graceful way about her ... but that delicacy was an act he knew well. She carried the weight of authority and the cunning of intelligence in that one small flick of her hand. The servant jumped into action and met her halfway as she swept toward her son.

"You did not hold to the plan, Gabriel," she said coldly. He met her gaze without flinching.

"I was never aware of a plan to torture our Pilgrim and her friends," he replied haughtily, because even though he had collected his thoughts, his emotions were still very close to the surface.

"Torture? Is that what she told you?"

"She did not need to—I saw the armband marks. I know you threatened her. I just do not know why yet."

Abrianna stared at him in silence for a moment.

"I had no choice but to place her in armbands—"

"Do not try to justify your actions!" he snapped, ignoring the presence of the blue-eyed servant standing behind her. "I told you those could kill her!"

"I would not have allowed that, Gabriel, but you should understand better than anyone how powerful she is. I could not risk her using a life force against me," Abrianna tried reasoning with him.

"In the Dome?" he scoffed. "Impossible."

"The realm of possibility extends further for people like her."

"*People?* You mean there are others like her?" Gabriel narrowed his puffy eyes at her. Abrianna paused and watched him carefully, wondering just how much he had discovered since the Travelers had arrived.

"It is possible."

"You mean her father." He stated it boldly to force a reaction from her. She flinched—it was almost imperceptible, but it was there. And he knew then he had struck on some kind of buried emotion. It was in her eyes, even if it was not on her face.

"What did she tell you about him?"

"It hardly matters what she told me, *Mother*. She knows nothing of what happened to him, though I suspect you do know ... in fact, I believe he is here on the Island somewhere as a prisoner. As *your* prisoner."

"As a matter of fact, he is on the Island ... and has been for six years," Abrianna admitted offhandedly. He was surprised at her candidness.

"Well, that is an important detail you failed to share with me!" he growled. "Where exactly are you keeping him? And why? It is time you tell me the truth, or I will—"

"You will what, Gabriel? You already destroyed Whitnee's hope of retrieving her father ... not to mention the fact that you sent away one of the most gifted people to arrive on this Island."

"She was in danger here—"

"Oh, please ... do not act as if you were being noble." She waved him off with that delicate hand. "You allowed your Pyra emotions to control you. You were thinking with the affections of a lustful boy instead of with the rational mind of a ruler. It is disgusting, and you will have to correct this problem immediately."

He hid his emotions well at her words. If she only knew how small she could make him feel ... He gazed up at her with ferocity in his eyes. "I want the truth about her father."

Her eyes slid sideways toward the silent Hydro servant behind her. "That is a conversation for a more private setting. For now, Michael will clean you up. In light of present circumstances, your duties with the rebels have been reassigned." And she gave a slight nod to Michael who pulled a bright blue bottle of sparkling Water from his guard pouch. He knelt in front of Gabriel, but Gabriel pulled his face away.

"What is my new assignment?"

Abrianna gave a short look over her shoulder at Eli, who continued shooting dark glances their way. Then she lowered her voice, "I am sending you to the Mainland to bring her back. Eli does not wish for you to go. Needless to say, his trust in you has been broken. But I believe she will listen to *you*. I do not care how you get her here—use whatever force or *persuasion* you choose, but bring her only. We do not need her friends interfering this time." She gave him a piercing stare before adding, "Failure is not an option, Gabriel. She wants her father back, and I agreed to help her with that."

"And what did she agree to help *you* with?" Gabriel asked knowingly, trying to ignore the way his heart had quickened at his mother's words, the pathetic way hope flared in his chest at the thought of seeing *her* again.

"It does not matter. We need her. She is the key to everything. Do not fail me," she commanded, but it almost came across as pleading. She glanced back at Eli one more time and then turned to the servant. "Michael, fix his face and any other injuries he might have. I do not want one scratch or mark on his body."

"What if I am tired of blindly following your orders? What if I choose not to do this?" Gabriel asked defiantly.

She raised her voice in authority. "There is no choice here. Your loyalty is to this Island first—not to some girl who bats her eyes at you and makes you feel good about yourself. She does not truly *know* you, nor does she respect the position you hold." Her words were like knives cutting into his chest. She gave him a condescending look. "Did you even tell her about your... commitments? Or was that just one more thing you lied to her about?"

He gave her a grim look.

"I will take that as a no, then." Abrianna shook her head in pity. "What a shame... and she actually trusts you. The reality is, Gabriel, that we cannot afford to get close. The burdens we bear to our people are too much for others to understand. You cannot let yourself feel anything toward her, especially if she is the Pilgrim. That is not the Pilgrim's purpose, and you need to start treating this situation with a bit more reverence. You had your fun and your little romance, but you know that is as far as it can ever go. Quit torturing yourself by thinking there is more."

He bristled visibly at her words, amazed as always at how she was able to manipulate him. "When do I go?"

"Soon. There are some adjustments I must make to the portal. It will take some time. But soon…" She gave him a last piercing look. Then she walked purposefully away so Michael could erase the evidence of her husband's abuse … something Michael had done for them on several occasions. She was moving toward Eli when the slight, familiar ringing sounded in her head … a sound only she could hear, a sound she dreaded at that moment.

And then the voice she knew so well entered her mind, almost whispering … *I felt something.*

She sighed and paused in her stride across the cavern. *Yes, that was the portal*, she answered, but not aloud.

Is she gone then?

Yes, just as you asked.

She chose not to disclose that it hadn't happened *exactly* as he had asked. In fact, it had been quite the opposite. Her own plan had failed, thanks to Gabriel's intervention.

Then why are your guards moving me again? What is going on?

She tried to hide the weariness in her response. *I cannot discuss this right now. I will come visit you soon and explain.*

Explain now. *What have you done? If she is really gone—*

Then you would still sense her here … do you?

There was a pause.

No, I guess not, he replied slowly. *Please, Bri, stop these experiments. I have done all I can for you. Maybe it is time things change. Maybe I can go home—*

Stop calling it that. This *is your home!* Without guilt, she admitted, *Besides, you are the only reason that she will come back.*

There was panic in his voice. *You can't bring her back … You promised me you'd send her home!*

I never promised to let her stay there. You know we need her here.

No, we do not! I left everything behind in order to keep her away from here. She tried to steel herself against his words, but then he said, *Bri, you have no right to do this. You are out of control! If you don't stop—*